INFINITE SUMMER

ALSO BY EDOARDO NESI

Story of My People

INFINITE SUMMER

Edoardo Nesi

TRANSLATED FROM THE ITALIAN BY

Alice Kilgarriff

OTHER PRESS
NEW YORK

Copyright © 2015 Bompiani / RCS Libri S.p.A., Milan

First published in Italian as *L'estate infinita* in 2015 by Bompiani

English translation copyright © 2016 Other Press

Billy Joel "Scenes from an Italian Restaurant" lyrics on page 226
from the Columbia album *The Stranger* (1977).
Bob Dylan "Like a Rolling Stone" lyrics on page 264
from a 1965 Columbia single.

Production editor: Yvonne E. Cárdenas
Text designer: Julie Fry
This book was set in Perpetua with Didot by
Alpha Design & Composition of Pittsfield, NH.

2 4 6 8 10 9 7 5 3 1

Library of Congress Cataloging-in-Publication Data

Names: Nesi, Edoardo, 1964- author. | Kilgarriff, Alice, translator.
Title: Infinite summer / Edoardo Nesi ; translated by Alice Kilgarriff.
Other titles: Estate infinita. English
Description: New York : Other Press, 2017. | "First published in Italian as L'estate
infinita in 2015 by Bompiani" [Milano] —Verso title page.
Identifiers: LCCN 2016047145 (print) | LCCN 2017009327 (ebook) |
ISBN 9781590518229 (hardback) | ISBN 9781590518236 (e-book)
Subjects: LCSH: Young men—Italy—Fiction. | Entrepreneurship—Fiction. | Textile
factories—Fiction. | Businesspeople—Family relationships—Fiction. | Tuscany
(Italy)—Fiction. | Domestic fiction. | BISAC: FICTION / Coming of Age. |
FICTION / Family Life. | FICTION / Literary.
Classification: LCC PQ4874.E728 E7513 2017 (print) | LCC PQ4874.E728 (ebook) |
DDC 853/.914—dc23
LC record available at https://lccn.loc.gov/2016047145

To my family

How can we live without our lives?
How will we know it's us without our past?
—JOHN STEINBECK,
The Grapes of Wrath

After the miracle of the early 1960s,
the Italian economy continued to grow:
between 1970 and 1979, the GDP grew at 40%.
In the following decade the rapid growth
slowed, but still managed to reach 25%.
—ISTAT, *Italia in Cifre*, 2011

Contents

Saturday, 7 August 1982

INFINITE SUMMER

THE SKY IS PERFECT

IT IS THE SUMMER OF 1972, and an August day shines on Italy.

The sky is perfect, so miraculously clear as to seem painted. Not so much as a cloud swells innocently on the horizon, or stretches out, elongated by the high-altitude winds until it dissolves into the absolute blue. And the sea—lightly rippled by a breeze coming from Corsica, its blue only slightly more intense than that of the sky, as if trying to mimic its perfection—kisses a long stretch of fine white sand which extends as far as the eye can see, in an apparent attempt to protect the sea from the mountains, which are covered in impenetrable forest and split by deep veins of pure marble, so implausibly high that they appear to have only recently burst forth from the earth out of some mysterious movement of tectonic plates.

It is a mountain range, the smallest in the world, and its violent slope toward the shore is populated with ancient and mighty holm oaks which, upon meeting the ground, leave the way clear for the thousands of trunks of an immense pine grove, contorted by storms and chance. There is a village at the center of the pine grove, and the roofs of its houses are protected by the same terra-cotta tiles used by the Etruscans. The three or four hotels—ghost white, awkward, adorned with proudly modernist names—are only just visible among the tips of the pines lit up by the vivid green of the new needles. The soft curve of the bleached asphalt road accompanies the shoreline, almost touching a large beachside house that, on closer inspection, is actually a nightclub.

And beyond the pine grove hundreds of multicolored beach umbrellas, loungers, flagpoles, cabanas of every color—white, yellow, blue, orange, turquoise, and bottle green—punctuate the long beach and transform it into a carnival.

Listen to the concert of a thousand sounds: the flutter of air caught in bicycle spokes, the metallic fart of the Vespas, the never-ending hum of scooters, the growl of the few cars that vainly charge along the empty coast road as if it were a race-track, the distant rumble of the diesel engines of sporadic buses, the clattering of the slow trains running along the single track that follows the coast.

Listen to the omnipresent melodies of the songs: the elementary chord sequences, rhythms fast and slow; the wise, stupid, sweet lyrics that emanate from the omnipresent battery radios in brightly colored plastic and shake the passion-filled hearts of the men, women, and teenagers who silently listen and dance and at times sing in chorus without imagining or caring that once the tepid air had melted them away, those songs would rise into the sky and reach outer space, where they would continue to travel forever, and forever they would recount to the aliens the eternal glory of being *a-a-abbronzatissima.*

Good God, listen to that deafening beating of hearts, recognize the ardor of their hope and the incessant activity of their dreams, treasure their vain and highly important words and the cries and shrieks of children and all the lies and boasts and prayers and promises and whispers and sighs and declarations of love that provide the soundtrack to these intrepid Italian days.

And just as it seems nothing could interrupt the slow, empty decline of the morning, a faraway spot appears in the sky and slowly grows bigger, losing its roundness and taking on the bird-like form of a small propeller airplane that flies low and slow and heavy, ever closer to the sea, right in front of the beach, and suddenly emits dozens of tiny red and white parachutes that splatter the perfect sky, levitate for a while in the still air, and then begin to fall slowly, oscillating, shiny like toys.

From the beach, an army runs toward the water: men, women, teenagers, and children rise from their director's chairs and their sun loungers and the sand, and start running. The teenage boys are first. They look like a phalanx of equatorial natives pursuing an enormous fleeing beast, entirely naked except for their minuscule bathing trunks. They set off at speed, kicking up the sand with their feet, their backs taut from the contractions of the miraculous muscles of youth. Behind them, men with large backs slicked with sun cream and sweat are limping and laughing and snorting with embarrassment, risking the health of their ankles in the soft burning sand, egged on by their wives and children, who had started to run but, quickly overtaken, had decided to go back to the umbrellas and cheer them on instead.

A crowd is now invading the sea. With water up to their knees, even the fastest among them are forced to slow down or change their step: some march energetically as if trying to plow the seabed with their feet, some jump awkwardly, some are convinced they can run over the water like basilisks, but only the smartest decide to throw themselves in and start swimming in the shallow sea, sending water flying with their strokes and filling the sea with foam.

The swimmers arrive first; breathless and dripping they turn to the beach and hold up the colored plastic cards that had been attached to the parachutes. They scream with joy. If and when they visit a drugstore, they will win an inflatable rubber cow, a large blue-and-white-striped beach ball from Nivea, a one-liter bottle of Coca-Cola, or a jar of Nutella.

For a few minutes, the air fills with shouts of jubilation until even the slowest manage to grab their own little parachute with its gift card. Then everything becomes quiet, and in a big peaceful invasion of the naked, dozens of men and children in swimsuits slowly return to the beach, clutching their parachutes, panting and smiling, and do not even cast a glance at those who didn't move from their sun loungers—those who stayed put, incredulous and disdainful, watching that caravansary.

As they return to the shore, satisfied and dripping, they feel no shame at having suddenly thrown themselves into the sea: they know it is not an inflatable rubber cow that is being given them, but the raw and immensely human idea that life can be the stuff of dreams, and that dreams have nothing to do with ideals (ah, ideals!), but with *things*: the incessant shower of new, shiny products that the radio and newspapers and television shows constantly advertise and that these same people imagine, build, package, transport, sell, and, of course, consume. Why should they doubt these things were made for them, and are therefore already theirs, if they fall like manna from heaven?

An eight-year-old boy is lying on the fine sand next to a beach umbrella. His name is Vittorio Vezzosi. He is frowning with his arms crossed, ostentatiously turning his back on his mother, who, as always, wouldn't let him run into the water with the other kids, even though this time he had fallen on his knees to beg her, on the verge of tears, his hands clasped.

—There have been accidents, and children have been trampled by the crowd and drowned. His mother had said this as she watched the sea, protected by the screen of her tortoiseshell sunglasses.

—No, Mom, if you are trampled you die on the beach, not in the water, Vittorio had answered in vain, and upon hearing those words his mother turned to face him: he was quivering, almost trembling with anticipation of the run, like a young deer or an antelope.

4

—Mom! Come on, let me go! Please!

—No, Vittorio! No! That's enough! And Arianna had lain back on her lounger.

It had been a difficult morning. First her husband had called at the house they were renting from June to September (a newly renovated lemonary) to tell her that he would not be able to join her that evening, because he had to go with his friend to watch Juventus play in a prechampionship friendly, in a nearby seaside town.

At first Arianna thought it was a joke, so she didn't say anything, holding the receiver and watching Vittorio performing tricks on his bicycle and muttering the implausible names of famous cyclists, dangerously close to the vases of agave and the leaf-filled branches of the large magnolia from the villa next door that reached well into their tiny garden.

It was impossible that Cesare had forgotten that it was her birthday—her badly timed midsummer birthday that she had never been able to celebrate as she would have liked, not even when she was a child—and it wasn't just any birthday, but that terrible, fateful thirtieth birthday, and so she responded simply with a "yes," two sharp "okays," and a "bye" before hanging up.

It was a joke—one of his usual stupid jokes—and he was already dialing the number to welcome her with that raspy, vulgar laugh and tell her she had been had, because he actually held in his hands a wonderful present for her and he would come to the seaside to take her out for dinner and eat spaghetti with clams, no soccer and no Juventus. So she had waited by the phone for five minutes, and then another five, but Cesare never called back, and after five more interminable minutes Arianna got on her bike and went to the beach without saying a word, followed by the boy, who kept standing up on the pedals, muttering wildly about legendary Alpine climbs.

As soon as they had reached the beach, she had slipped into her cabana without greeting a single person, changed into her swimsuit and sarong—she who hated sarongs—and stepped down onto the beach in a slalom between the tight rows of beach umbrellas, barely acknowledging those families who occupied every square centimeter of the beach in military fashion the entire month of August. She carefully spread Nivea all over Vittorio's shoulders and left him to run toward the sea, then lay down on her lounger and realized she was alone. Abandoned. Forgotten.

Her summer was over. She didn't want it anymore. She didn't want the sun and the sky and the sea and the green mountains streaked with marble. She felt imprisoned by the thought that she would have to stay there until mid-September in that tiny town where she had arrived at the end of June with Vittorio because her husband wanted to tell his friends that he had sent his family to the seaside for the entire summer, and only went to visit them on weekends. Now she understood why.

Arianna bit her lower lip and gave in to one of her invisible crying fits behind the black lenses of her tortoiseshell sunglasses. She used a technique she had learned as a child: if she stayed perfectly still, if she didn't move, if she pretended she was just tanning, she would soon disappear from the attentions of those greasy matrons who surrounded her, pretending to do the crossword when in fact all they were doing was giving her hate-filled stares because their husbands had accidently paid her a compliment. Although she was turning thirty that day, she didn't look a day over twenty-five and didn't seem to take the slightest interest in her beauty, which was so simple and obvious as to be indisputable and, therefore, unforgivable.

She stayed there lying on her lounger for a long while, her face buried in the cushion, locked inside her sobbing, lost in a fog of thoughts that kept going at her while her mood swung wildly between repeating to herself that she was exaggerating—there certainly had to be an explanation for it all and her husband loved her and he really was going to see Juventus and not out to dinner in Portovenere with a younger thing—and feeling totally

6

empty, deprived of a future, washed up, old, certainly betrayed, consigned to the life of a separated wife, blameless and, as such, comforted in public but derided in private, nothing more than prey, soon to be on the receiving end of unctuous phone calls from her husband's friends.

Luckily, the miraculous arrival of the airplane broke that unbearable train of thought, and when she sat up to look for Vittorio, she was consoled to find him kneeling next to her, begging her to let him go and claim his first miniparachute—that skinny son of hers with his broad shoulders, long legs, bright white teeth, and jet-black hair which was inexplicably turning curly.

She had smiled and turned her mind back to when he was a kid and would always run away as soon as he realized no one was paying attention. Naked, silent, and unsteady, he would go off to patrol the beach, as proud as a king surveying his kingdom, and nothing would remain of him under the parasol but his bucket and spade. When Arianna noticed her child was no longer there, she would feel her throat closing, and would be assailed by fear, and would stand up and start running around madly, calling out to him and becoming increasingly desperate, her voice broken.

Search patrols would immediately be launched, with fathers and other children offering unconditional help and splitting up into two groups to go in opposite directions and comb the beach in search of the naked fugitive, while her husband, who never offered to help nor rose from his lounger, would sit there smiling, telling everyone proudly that they needed to tether their adventurous son to the parasol to keep him nearby, and growling at her under his breath that it was all her fault the child had run off, for God's sake, and she would agree—"Yes, it's true, it's my fault, I'm an idiot"—and she stayed there, pinned to the spot, shaking and crying in the middle of the beach, her thoughts filled with maniacs and kidnappers and child-snatchers, her glasses unable to hide the tears of fear and rage that streaked her face and fell onto the sand creating tiny round craters of a darker-colored beige: a twenty-five-year-old Madonna, wounded and suffering and, as such, irresistible to both the fathers of other children and the boys themselves, in whose dreams she often appeared.

When they eventually found him, Vittorio was often very, very far from her parents' umbrella, and always surrounded by women stroking his jet-black hair and cooing over him, complimenting his eternally good nature. It really was impossible to be angry with him: he was always smiling and in no way scared by finding himself alone. He never asked after his mother: he knew someone would come to collect him, and that it would all be fine in the end. For him, it was like traveling.

—No, Vittorio! No! That's enough! Arianna said before lying down on the lounger as she tried hard not to think that, just a few hours earlier, it was he who had woken her with a warm embrace and lots of kisses before singing her Happy Birthday and bringing her breakfast in bed—a glass of cold milk and three biscuits because, he had apologized, he didn't know how to make coffee yet.

Vittorio knelt on the sand for a few minutes more, clutching his hands, then shook his head, gave her one last defeated look, sighed melodramatically, and sat down cross-legged in front of the parasol with his back to her, watching the great race to the sea and grumbling that it wasn't right he couldn't take part because no child ever died of it and there was nothing to be scared of, and even if he wasn't one of the fastest, he would have definitely beaten all of his friends, and would have certainly got a miniparachute.

—It's not fair, he continues under his breath, scratching away at the scar left by a smallpox vaccination and beating the sand with his fist, more to get his mother's attention than out of real anger.

He closes his eyes out of irritation and is immediately distracted by the contemplation of the amoebas of light that appear on the screen of his closed eyelids. Suddenly his frustration disappears, his anger subsides, and in a moment everything is forgotten: all he is left with is the good fortune of being a child in summer, and he decides to run to the shore with his net and bucket to catch crabs and sea horses. He opens his eyes and is about to stand up and get going when a stray parachute — the last to be released by the airplane and the only one to get caught in an updraft that took it so high it almost became invisible before the whimsical wind suddenly dropped, leaving it to fall slowly onto the beach rather than into the sea, out of time and forgotten, ignored by all — reaches the end of its descent and falls silently onto the sand right in front of him, without anyone else noticing.

Vittorio looks at it, then at his mother. He raises his eyes to the perfect sky and smiles.

— Hey, thanks.

A NEW BUSINESS

THE BRONZE-COLORED ALFETTA I.8 slowly makes its way up a dirt track riddled with potholes, cutting through a rough field on the far outskirts of the desolate plain that surrounds the city. If it weren't for the light mist that had set in, we might be able to see the cathedral bell tower in the distance. It is the end of a cold, dry October. The sky seems made of steel.

The Alfetta stops with the stutter it makes when the handbrake is applied too fast, and two men get out. They stand in front of the car's hood, in silence. The one who had been driving has a great mane of white hair and a face carved with the marks and wrinkles of forty years of hard work. The other is much younger. It's not that they look alike: one is the younger version of the other—father and son, separated by thirty years of life. They have the same severe, angular features. They are dressed the same way. If they are handsome, it is that hard, worn-out beauty of sailors or soldiers. They are wearing suede jackets, flannel trousers of a very similar gray mélange—steely for the old man, graphite for the younger man—and black moccasins. Under their jackets they are wearing matching navy blue lambswool V-neck sweaters and sky-blue Oxford shirts that differ only in cut and size, sewn by their usual tailor.

The son realizes his father is waiting for him to speak first. He swallows hard, and begins.

—I'm sorry we've only managed to get here now, when it's nearly dark, because during the day, with the light, it would have been better. But anyway, you see all this empty land…No, well, it's not empty, I'm sorry…It's…that is, well, it's empty now, but it will…well, it will become…Wait, Dad, wait a moment. Let me start again, okay?

The father nods almost imperceptibly, and his son's heart skips a beat.

—So…this is ten thousand square meters of land, and it has just gone from being greenfield to being given building per-mission, okay? It means it can be built on. So, only yesterday, I think, or the day before that, not long ago at all, anyway…And you could buy it for next to nothing, Dad. It belongs to an old woman, no children, widowed…I spoke to her yesterday, we've already reached an agreement—

—What? What?—A snarl.—You've already reached an agreement?

—No. That is, Dad, wait, I'm sorry, I put it badly: I haven't already made a formal agreement, I spoke to her. Calm down, Dad. We've discussed it, that's all.

—Ah.

—I just spoke to her about it. I gathered information.

—Ah. And?

—And she would sell. Tomorrow, even.

The father remains silent and keeps his gaze on the horizon.

—Her husband bought it a long time ago, as an investment. And then he died. She doesn't know what to do with it. There's an old farmer who keeps an allotment, and every so often he brings her tomatoes, zucchini, peppers…

—It looks like poor Melchiorre's field...

—Pardon?

—No, nothing...I bet she'd sell. What could she do with it, besides grow radicchio? There aren't even any roads...

—But there will be, Dad. The council has already put plans forward. This will become an industrial park...It will be subdivided and sold...and this dirt track will become a kind of ring road...No, perhaps not a ring road, but certainly a very important road, okay?

—And what would you want to do with this field then?

—Come on Dad, you know. The new business!

The old man shook his head, closed his eyes, ran his hands through his thick hair, and snorted.

—Ivo, Ivo, I...you worry me. What will you do when I'm dead, huh? How are you going to maintain a business with these childish dreams? Can you tell me that?

—But Dad...

—Ten thousand square meters of land! Do you have any idea how big our warehouse is?

—One thousand nine hundred and ninety-two square meters, Dad.

—Exactly...And have you calculated how much this field would cost?

—Yes, Dad. I've calculated everything. Do you want to know how much it would cost?

—No, I don't. And do you know why? Because I don't want to spend that money, understand? Work is what it is.

—Dad, work is going well...

—Yes, but we aren't earning much.

—Of course not, Dad, you only want to sell blankets!

The father's gaze hardens as he turns to face his son, who looks right back at him. It is the first time.

—Blankets have given you everything you have, young man.

Don't despise them. If it wasn't for those blankets, we would still all be living in the apartment above the factory...

—Yes, Dad, but we've done everything we can with blankets...What kind of a future is there for brown blankets with Greek frets? Plus they only sell in Veneto and Naples...

—And do you think you are good enough to try your hand at something different?

—I want to make textiles, Dad! And sell them for export!

—Well, *I want* never *gets*!

—But so many people are doing it, and successfully!

—They aren't successful! There is no market here in Italy.

—Of course there is!

—That is not true. This is a poor country!

—But it's growing, Dad.

—Yes, it's growing. It's growing even too fast, but it will always be a poor country, and people will always need blankets. And we make them! And we export them!

—No, Dad, we make half-size, khaki-colored pieces with recycled wool and acrylic, and we sell them to that crook in Milan who sends them to Kenya to make army uniforms. I want to make real fabrics, for clothing. Textiles with a wool mix for overcoats, jackets, skirts, trousers, everything, that we can sell to Germany, France, Great Britain, even Holland...

—Ah, but hang on...what wool would you use? Let's hear it.

—I'd start with recycled wool, certainly, but later on, I would definitely use new wool...The son's face reddens with emotion. His heartbeat begins to race, his breath quickens.

—New wool? Do you know what that costs? And who are you going to buy it from? From that thief Paoli, son of a thief?

—No, Dad. I won't buy it on the local market, I'll get it directly from Australia.

—Oh! From Australia! Do you know where Australia is, Ivo? It's on the other side of the world!

—Dad, there are dealers in town. I've already spoken to them. You buy after choosing a sample, and all samples match the goods exactly. The Australians are honest people. They ship it from Perth or Melbourne or Sydney, I'm not exactly sure which, but the ship passes through the Suez Canal and…well, in a month and a half it arrives in Livorno or La Spezia.

—Australia…I'm…Ivo, you will make me use up what little money I have managed to earn…

—Dad, trust me.

—Trust me? How can I trust you? You don't even speak the language…What will you tell your customers? You need to know languages if you want to export!

—Dad, I've been going to Berlitz for a year, studying English and German. When I told you I was going out to play billiards with my friends, I was lying. I was going to Berlitz, until eleven o'clock at night. And now I know English fairly well. My German isn't quite as good because it's more difficult, but I'm more or less there. I couldn't hold a conversation about history or geography, but I have no problem discussing textiles!

The father turned slowly to his son, and in the far corner of his eye there was a flicker of consideration. Although he immediately started shaking that mane of white hair again, Ivo felt he had touched him: languages had been a constant concern for his father, who couldn't bear not knowing a word of English.

—Dad, listen to me. I've thought of everything. We go to the bank and ask for a loan —

—We ask the bank for a loan? As if we were penniless? Desperate? I would feel like a thief going to ask for money, I —

—Dad, let me finish. We ask for credit, or a loan, I'm not sure yet, and we'll build a big new warehouse: we'll have everything there, the spinning and weaving mills, then we'll buy more machinery and grow…

—Have you…No, but apart from the money, have you worked out how many people you would need to get all this off the ground? Do you know that once you've taken them on, you have to keep them, because there is no way you can fire them?

—But we wouldn't have this problem, Dad, because we'd be earning! Our problem will be hiring, not firing!

—Now, listen...

—Come on, how can I think about sacking workers now, when I haven't even employed them! And anyway, I know I won't have to get rid of anyone! Like you...

—Ivo—

—No Dad, listen to me. While we're building the warehouse, we'll stop making blankets. Or not. If you want, that is, if you prefer, we could continue, it's not a problem, it's up to you, but in the meantime, we'll start producing textiles. Immediately. We'll make the fabrics, flannel...even velour, everything. But my dream, the only way to start making money, Dad, would be to produce loden.

—Ivo—

—We buy a telex machine, take on some salespeople, and I'll go around the world doing sales.

—Ivo, Ivo, the world is so big—

—I know, Dad, but I like traveling, it's not a hardship for me. I like seeing new things, meeting new people!

—You like having fun, I know.

—No, Dad, no. I've had too much fun. I want to start working! I want to go abroad. To America even. I really believe in this, I do. With the money I make, we'll be able to pay off the new warehouse in five years, perhaps even earlier!

The father watches his son light up, his eyes laughing as he gesticulates and talks about his plan—the first he had ever suggested in all those years of respectfully working alongside him, without ever spending a minute more at work than was necessary, without ever suggesting something new. This is why. Now he understands. In this plan, he is an obstacle. His son wishes to build a new business, not expand the one that already exists. He wants his own business.

—Dad, I'm nearly thirty-two years old. If I don't do it now, I never will. I can't bear watching Franchina typing out those invoices in the office, answering five phone calls a day, one of which is Mom asking when to put the pasta on...

The enthusiasm that burned inside Ivo was bubbling over, impeding his sight, making his heartbeat race, loosening his tongue.

—Dad, we need to develop our business! The moment has come, not just for us, but for the whole city, for the whole of Italy! In the North they build factories like this every day, and not just in textiles! I've seen them. Brianza is one big building site, so are Bergamo, Brescia, the whole of Emilia. Work is growing, Dad, we can't stand still and just wait!

The invisible sun has fallen below the hills, the light slowly retreats, and it begins to get cold. The father buttons his suede jacket, shaken by the impact with a future that is too strong, too close. Ardengo Barrocciai breathes in the still air of that prickly, bramble-filled field, and wants to tell his son that he is too young, that he is not ready, that nothing he has learned over the years has prepared him for having his own business; that it takes experience to be a businessman, and you only learn by making mistakes; that passion isn't enough, and enthusiasm is worth next to nothing; that it is dedication and tenacity that make businesses successful; that despite all the work you put in, there is always a risk things won't work out and you will have to close, or claim bankruptcy.

He is about to tell him all of this, but then he remembers how unprepared he was when he first started making blankets, how he didn't even know whom he would sell them to, and how much desire and need he had to start working straightaway, and how much unshakable faith he had in himself, and how sure he was to be headed toward a future filled with success. How many years ago? Thirty? Forty? Is it really that many?

—Dad, you told me how Granddad was a cobbler, and that you were the first one in your family to do something different,

that you started making blankets against the wishes of everyone else, who would make fun of you and wanted to force you
to repair shoes! And I am so grateful to you, Dad, you have no
idea how grateful I am…You sent me to a good high school, and
thanks to you I've lived like a prince, then you gave me a job at
the factory, gave me my own office and telephone…but I can't
live wrapped up in cotton wool while the world steams ahead.
You understand, don't you?

Ardengo turns to face his son and sees him transfigured, his
features contorted, almost wounded by passion. How very far
away those Sunday afternoons just after the war now seem, when
he'd throw on an old hat, wrap Ivo up in a blanket, put him in
the sidecar, and they would ride around together on that old
English motorcycle, his BSA, even when it was cold. And how Ivo
loved it when he would accelerate and the motor revved! How
he laughed!

This must be how you become old: suddenly, at sunset, in the
middle of a field, wrenched by an invisible future, knocked down
by an audacious and infantile enthusiasm that is impossible to
share. He knew that the day would come when he would have to
pass the baton, but he didn't think it would be like this. He had
never imagined that he would feel so surprised, so useless, so
exhausted.

Ardengo smiles as he finally finds himself relieved of having to
keep his foot on the gas, free now to see all this as the completion of a titanic undertaking that was far too demanding for him
and that had continued for too long: a task that he was only able
to carry out by giving the very best of himself, each and every
day. He feels an enormous burden lifted from his shoulders—a
mountain of worries and fears and uncertainties and decades-
long suffering, all born of work, that had stopped him from ever
sleeping more than six hours a night and that made him jump
from his bed every morning at five, even during his rare and
brief vacations, filled with a nervous energy that came from God

knows where. He asks himself what life he has lived up to this point. If he has really lived.

Ivo notices that his father's eyes are wet. What are these, tears? He draws closer and would like to put a hand on his shoulder, but he cannot bring himself to. He has never done it before. And so he keeps on insisting. There is nothing else he can do.

—Dad, listen to me, please, I believe in this. This is a historic moment. People with small businesses can become successful managers, even industrialists. Like in America! We can build a new business, Dad, now, tomorrow, you and me!

He stops in front of his father, his legs are shaking.

—Ardengo, I promise I will make you proud of me!

The father, whose son has never called him by name, shakes his head just once.

—No, Ivo, I don't feel up to it. I'm too old.

—What do you mean "old," Dad! You're wise, not old. You would be so much help to me. We can build this new business together!

Ardengo embraces his son. He holds him close and speaks in his ear.

—Ivo, I'm not up to these dreams. I can't even understand them. I've done what I can. Now it's your turn. But remember, dreams won't get you anywhere. It is a very tough life. You need to work hard. All the time. Every day, even Saturday and Sunday morning, your work is never done, never ...

Ardengo is sorry to give this anxious list of cautions against life and its overwhelming force, but he feels he must. He would like to say so much more, and much better, but he doesn't know how, and he can't, so he just embraces that reckless son of his that he never felt so close to his heart.

—You build the new business, Ivo. If you need a hand, your Dad is here. You can be sure of that.

THE BEAST

IT WAS THE OPINION OF MANY that there was not an un-ranked tennis player in the whole of Italy who could beat Cesare Vezzosi, known as the Beast.

His farmhand's bone structure boasted broad shoulders and a narrow waist resting upon strong, sinewy legs that were just a few centimeters shorter than the canons of classical Greek beauty, but perfect for the short runs and rapid changes of direction required by that incredibly demanding game to which he had devoted himself.

Bradycardic, blessed with a right arm almost double the size of his left, Vezzosi would never tire and never even seemed out of breath, not even during the most testing games on the hottest days. This invulnerability would soon dishearten every opponent, who would often have to hear him moaning about not being able to enjoy playing a full five sets, rather than just three.

He had begun playing tennis late, at the age of twenty-three, and his style was self-taught. His forehand was short and snapped like a boxer's hook, always sending the ball down the line to torment the opponent's backhand, with just a hint of topspin. It was a shot aimed at accelerating the exchange, and it forced the rival into a continuous adjustment of his game, which invariably generated confusion and, eventually, an error. His backhand, on the contrary, was surprisingly elegant, almost pretentious. Always sliced and long, it was the Beast's favorite shot because its movement reminded him of a fencer's lunge and allowed him to place on the other side of the court a low, slow ball that was spitefully different in weight and rotation and speed from the snapped ball that came from the forehand—a ball that the adversary would quickly find impossible to attack.

Patient, infinitely calm, almost incapable of unforced errors, and impossible to call a mere baseline player given the intensity and speed of his game—of all the great champions, his style was closest to that of Jimmy Connors—the Beast went to the net only to shake hands with his defeated rival or to pounce on the drop shots with which his desperate opponents would try to break the spider's web of his rallies. Perhaps because of the short, hunched run it required to return, a drop shot would always irritate him deeply, and invited him to reply with another viciously diagonal drop shot that made it just over the net before falling dead on the court, impossible to reach.

Given his perpetual admiration of everything Anglo-Saxon, he only played with Dunlop rackets, making a point of distinguishing himself from the army of those using the more traditional, local, Maxima instruments, which, elastic as they were, would have been much better suited to his game than those rigid British tools. He only used strings of natural gut, always strung to a tension of eighteen kilograms.

Many of those who didn't know him would smile at seeing him enter the court with that disdainful half smile and his gunslinger's gait, and some would even stifle a laugh when he practiced his serve, undoubtedly the least effective shot in his repertoire.

Sadly, there was no real difference between his first and second serve, and Cesare Vezzosi could only dream of possessing the power of Roscoe Tanner or the Brancusian elegance of his idol, Adriano Panatta, with whom he once had the honor of playing a ten-minute rally, bursting into tears from the emotion immediately after, under the shower so that no one would notice.

So, seeing him contort himself in that confused, jumpy, almost comical twisting of arm and torso—the only result of which was an inoffensive ball floating slowly toward the other side of the court—his adversaries from outside of Tuscany assumed that they were up against a beginner or a "caveman," as he was disdainfully called by a once-ranked, well-known Roman player in that delightfully small tennis club nestled in the pine groves of the seaside town protected by the smallest mountain range in the world.

A furious Vezzosi, offended by the sniggering of the audience of layabouts the gentleman had brought with him, and incensed to realize that Arianna and Vittorio, who were sitting close by, had also heard the joke, subjected the Roman to a merciless defeat by 6–0, 6–0, and had that snob running up and down the court for an hour and a half, making him sweat like a bricklayer from the second game onward and taking great pleasure in keeping him on court for as long as possible, without conceding as much as a game.

His volley shots, which he rarely used in singles, made him an excellent doubles player. Like an Australian or South African, he volleyed on instinct, hitting short and nasty shots that felt like slaps, while his lethal smash had none of the baroque movement of his serve, but rather was a tennistic sublimation of the swipe of a billhook.

A conservative in tennis as in politics, he was always dressed rigorously in white from head to toe, and showed a strong preference for anything by Lacoste. He could not bear decoration or color in tennis wear, and if he showed great disdain for anyone who appeared on court with a white T-shirt adorned with stripes, lozenges, or patterns—he would tolerate the Fila's microstripes set that Borg wore—he refused outright to play anyone wearing a colored T-shirt.

He had equal contempt for left-handers, whose asymmetric game seemed to upset the abstract perfection of his idea of tennis, and disturbed his tactics. He so much enjoyed beating them that sometimes, in the changing room, he would ask them why on earth they had started playing tennis, if they could count solely on the hand of the devil.

After years of victories, Cesare Vezzosi barely signed up for tournaments reserved for nonranked players, partly out of boredom and partly due to his obvious superiority, choosing only to play the Tuscan championships, which he had won in singles uninterruptedly since 1969. While he was waiting to reach the age of forty-five to qualify for the veterans' circuit, he amused himself by teaching the game to Vittorio, and training with dedication every other day of the week at the newly opened tennis club, where he also hoped to be able to find work opportunities, given that in his fast-expanding town there wasn't a businessman, retailer, lawyer, accountant, or notary who didn't play tennis and wasn't more than happy to play for an hour and even lunch with Cesare Vezzosi, known as the Beast, the Best Unranked Tennis Player in Italy.

He had known Ivo Barrocciai for a long time, but only by sight. Their relationship had for years been limited to brief yet cordial greetings whenever they met, without ever speaking to one another or being introduced, because they both knew very well who the other was. This situation changed when Ivo—whose tennis was of purely aesthetic value and led to dozens of unnecessary errors and hazardous runs to the net following sliced serves that would have been much more effective on grass than on clay—began to stay for lunch at the club to avoid the tension that was now filling every moment he spent at home with his parents.

Thanks to his sunny character and the universally shared but momentarily unfounded certainty that he was on the verge of becoming a highly successful entrepreneur, Ivo was immediately given a place at the top table, the fulcrum of the club's social life, where Vezzosi held court — adored as he was by other members because of the very particular philosophy of that tennis club (this consisted in giving precedence not to the richest, who were instead bombarded with insults because they worked too hard and didn't enjoy life, but to those free spirits who best knew how to divide their time between tennis, friends, women, and very last of all, work) — and every day narrated the tales of victories past and present, both on the court and in the bedroom (Cesare had quite the reputation as a womanizer), and would always proclaim his battle cry to the hushed restaurant: "The same ones always win!"

One splendid day at the beginning of July 1973, following a long shower and a brief lunch of mozzarella and tomato, the Beast was making his way down the cypress-lined walkway that led to the parking lot, when he heard someone call, "Hey, Cesare!"

He turned and saw Barrocciai walking straight toward him.

— Hey, Ivo.

As Cesare instinctively tidied his damp hair to make himself more presentable to a potential client, Ivo smiled, came closer, and took his arm.

— Cesare, hi, I wanted to talk to you about work.

— Ah, well, if it's about work, Ivo, you'll have to excuse my hair. I've been meaning to go to the barber's to get it cut for a week now...

— Don't worry about that, it suits you. You're a handsome guy. Listen, I need to ask you something... So... I've been looking at a piece of land for a while now, and I'm having a nightmare with lawyers, subdivisions, maps... all things that I don't know the first thing about. However, it now looks like I'm finally able to buy the land, okay? And I think I've got it for a good price, but I'm not absolutely sure, and I would like your advice, Cesare, a little assistance, as I don't understand all that much about real estate …

—No problem. Tell me, how much are we talking about?

—Ten thousand meters.

—Ten thousand meters? Seriously?

—Yes. And I want to build the new factory on it.

—Good.

—Trouble is, Cesare, I don't know anyone in your field, and I never trust anyone. I can't help it, it's the way I am. And even if I don't know you all that well, I always see you here at the club and you seem to be a decent person. That's why I'm asking you …

—I see. Thanks.

—Am I wrong to trust you?

—Sorry? No, of course not!

—Okay, so, I don't want to go to those big companies, I've never liked them … I prefer small scale, for everything. And I'll tell you now, I can't pay a lot, or up front. But I will pay. I'll pay you your dues. Bit by bit, over time, but I will pay.

—I know you'll pay, Ivo. Everyone knows that.

—Thanks. I'm glad to have a good reputation. Now, Cesare, I've come to ask you if you're in. That is, if you would build the factory for me.

—Me?

—Yes, you. With your firm.

Having worked his way up through the ranks to become the head of works at one of the city's largest building companies, for a few years now Cesare had been working for himself, taking on a laborer and a decorator. But he had specialized in small apartments, the most lucrative part of that booming business. He had never built a warehouse.

—Of course, yes, I'd love to. Who's the engineer?

—No, no, I don't want an engineer.

—What do you mean, you don't have an engineer?

— No.

— Okay, so who's the architect?

— I don't want an architect either.

— But how…

— I need you to deal with those things, Cesare.

— But Ivo, you have to present your plans to the council. And they need to sign off on the project.

— Really?

— Of course. It's the law.

— The law…, the shitty law, always getting in the way…I want my factory the way I like it. Don't want someone else coming into my house and telling me what to do, understand? I've already worked it all out. It will be a beautiful factory. I just need someone very good to sort out the technical problems, and we're there. So, do we have a deal?

Cesare watched Barrocciai light up, radiant as a boy, standing out against a hundreds-year-old cypress tree, and the only thing he could do was reciprocate that contagious smile. He had just been asked to play a game against himself—against Cesare, not the Beast—and the playing field wasn't the 78-by-36-foot rectangle of red clay on which he had no adversaries, but that terrible, accident-strewn desert that he had always been afraid to face, harder than cement and more slippery than grass: work.

He immediately liked everything about the idea: the risk, the difficulty, the uncertainty of being able to complete it and the parallel certainty that, even if he didn't manage it, he wouldn't have to pay any great penalty. What really won him over, however, was that bold, injudicious young man who was making the proposition: son of the most respected and intractable manufacturer of blankets in the city, best known for his very flexible working schedule and his playboy antics, Ivo was clearly possessed by a fierce dream that was entirely invisible to everyone else.

It was a dream—it was clear from the dimensions of the warehouse he wanted to build, totally out of proportion with the small ambitions of the fearful mass of antlike owners of microscopic textile works that populated their city—that he had decided to dedicate his life to. A dream he planned to make true by spending a load of money he still did not have. Cesare now understood the irrational, courageous tennis Barrocciai loved so much to play.

—Okay, Ivo, yes. I'm in. Look, listening to you speak, I've thought of the perfect person to sign off on the project...

—Good. Come and see me in the office tomorrow, you know where we are, don't you? Around midday. You can leave your car there, we'll take mine and go see the lot, then we can start working it all out.

They shook hands in the tennis club parking lot, under the brilliant sun, surrounded by the gracious sound of tennis balls bouncing against natural gut strings.

—You're married to Arianna, right?

Cesare smiled, nodded.

—My compliments, she's a fantastic girl. We went to high school together.

—Oh, I didn't know.

—We weren't in the same class though. I'm older than her, by two years. She was always with Rosa. Rosa Gonfiantini, you know, the one who married my cousin Brunero. Do you know Brunero?

—Yeah, I know him. Of course I know Brunero, everyone does. He's...he's a little bit...

—Let's just say he's a bit of a prick. And that's being kind.

—Exactly.

—He's been copying me my whole life. When he found out I'm building a new factory, he decided he wants to build one for himself, right in front of mine...And how is Arianna? I haven't seen her for years.

—She's fine. She breaks my balls a bit to be honest, but she's a good girl, at the end of the day.

—Ah, okay. Say hi to her for me. See you tomorrow, Cesare. Bye.

He smiled and turned toward his blue Alfetta. For a moment Vezzosi regretted having said his wife was a ball-breaker. He'd never said that to anyone, and it wasn't even true. He shrugged, got into the car, and set off behind Ivo.

LET THE OTHERS CRY

ONE BITTERLY COLD DAY at the beginning of December, Vittorio came home late from school. He had stopped to collect the last chestnuts of the season along the way, filling the pockets of his trousers and his blue woolen overcoat.

A few weeks before, when he had taken a handful to Grandmother, announcing that he would like to eat them with his snack, she had cuddled him and explained that they weren't real chestnuts—the ones that are delicious roasted and that he liked so much—but the poisonous seeds of another tree, the horse chestnut.

—Vittorio, do you know that the chestnut tree is a noble one? Have you ever seen it? It doesn't grow in the cities, only in the hills, where the air is clearer.

She added with a smile that he was right to collect those horse chestnuts anyway, because even though they aren't edible, if he kept one in his pocket it would protect him *from colds and all other afflictions*. At that point, Vittorio asked her if the horse chestnut tree was magic, a cross between a horse and a chestnut.

His mother wasn't waiting for him at home, as she did each day. Instead, there was his father, looking very serious, who called him into the living room and made him sit on the sofa while he made himself comfortable in the armchair.

During the long silence that followed, Vittorio thought he was about to be severely told off, and was just about to say he had been late because he was collecting horse chestnuts to put them in his grandmother's pocket, as she had seemed a little under the weather lately, when his father raised his head and told him that Grandmother had been taken ill that very morning. The ambulance had come and taken her to the hospital. His mother had gone with her; this was why she wasn't home. This was why he was there.

— It's serious, Vittorio, very serious.

And he kept silent for a while.

— Do you understand, my love?

His father had never called him "love." Vittorio suddenly stood up:

— We need to go straight to the hospital Dad, we can't waste any time. I've got lots of horse chestnuts…

His father's face went blank and he looked away. Vittorio heard him inhale deeply and slowly exhale, and at that very moment, he realized.

— Is she dead, Dad?

His father walked over and held him tightly, without noticing all of the shiny horse chestnuts that were pouring out of the child's pockets and rolling across the rug. Even though Grandmother was Arianna's mother, when she had become a widow, Cesare had been more than happy for her to come and live with them, and he loved her, as much as was possible for him.

— Yes, Vittorio. I'm afraid she is. Grandmother has gone to heaven. She's in paradise now. With the angels.

He let himself be held for a moment, inert like a mannequin, then he feebly embraced his father.

—You need to be strong, my son. You must be strong.

Vittorio closed his eyes and saw Grandmother before him, resplendent and smiling, in her woolen cardigan with its tiny buttons, the lace collar, the flannel skirt, the fur-lined slippers she wore in the house because she always had cold feet, and all her silk shirts in pearl gray and pink and ivory, the flowery summer dresses she kept in the wardrobe with little bags of lavender and never wore because she was afraid of damaging them.

He remembered her beside him, just a few days ago, when the light had gone out in the house and in all the other houses, and the streetlamps had also gone out and the world had become dark and the house a cavern, and he had run to hide in the tepee in the middle of the living room and didn't want to come out, and Grandmother had kneeled down in front of the tepee and had started to talk to him in a soft voice while striking the head of a match along the strip of sandpaper, and when that crackling flame appeared, filled with miraculous colors — yellow, red, orange, even a shade of blue — Vittorio had left the tepee to watch the match head move closer to the candle's wick, and he had hoped that the wick was set alight before the flame burned its way up the match and caught Grandmother's fingers, because he had been taught that you should always be afraid of fire and that every flame, no matter how small, could catch things or even people, because everything was flammable: the house, the school, his father's car, the bus, the trees, the grass, paper, even his schoolbag and clothes were flammable — he himself was flammable.

They had gone into the lounge to sit on the sofa and wait for the light to come back on, that single candle their only light, and they had told each other silly stories to fight the evil enormity of darkness, always the same ones: either his adventures at school, or Grandmother's tales from the war about how she would run to hide in the ditches during the bombing raids, and so, bit by bit,

Vittorio's fear of the dark had vanished and he had begun to talk, and asked his grandmother why the light had gone, and she had explained that it was all the fault of those Arab sheikhs who were mean people, because even though they were already so rich, still they wanted to raise the price of oil, and Italy couldn't pay such a high price and it had to make savings, and so all the electricity had to be turned off, *because electricity comes from oil, my treasure, you burn one to get the other.*

Vittorio had asked if that was a blackout, because he heard them say on the television that the blackouts would always be longer and more frequent, and when his grandmother had told him it was, Vittorio had shaken his head and begun to cry desperately: he was such an unlucky child because just a few years after Man had walked on the Moon and Mankind was about to start colonizing Space and the Universe — and he would certainly have been one of those brave astronauts flying off to the stars — everything was about to move backward and they would have to renounce all scientific conquests and start lighting candles again at night and traveling in horse-drawn carriages because the oil had run out, and everyone would be poor and would have to economize on everything and stick to the old things instead of creating new ones. Grandmother had smiled and told him not to be scared because the world would go on.

—Vittorio, the world always moves on. Don't you worry, she had told him, drying his tears with the flower-embroidered handkerchief she always had in her hand.

—It has never been the case that children are worse off than their parents, that the future is worse than the present. It's not possible. It has never happened. Otherwise there would be no progress, my child, but there is progress, and there always will be. Don't you worry, Vittorio.

And he remembered her yesterday, just yesterday afternoon, when she'd prepared his afternoon snack, bread with a few drops of red wine and sugar. They sat at the Formica table of their small kitchen, just the two of them, bathed by the light of a single bulb hanging from the ceiling, barely shaded by a half cone made from beige paper, and as she smoked a Muratti Ambassador and he chewed, their microsounds had seemed to blend together, accompanied by the ticking of a large alarm clock, and Grandmother would puff on her cigarette each time Vittorio took a bite of his slice of bread with wine and sugar. When he had finished, his Grandmother with blue-rinsed hair had immediately started grappling with pans, cartons of milk, and slices of bread to toast in the oven because one slice of bread with wine and sugar couldn't possibly be enough for a growing boy. He also needed bread with oil and tomatoes.

Vittorio couldn't take his eyes off her as she meticulously rubbed the tomato into the slice she had carefully cut from the loaf of Tuscan bread so that its core would be of the perfect thickness: it mustn't crumble in the mouth, nor fall apart when soaked with tomato juices. Then she poured over more oil in a slow S-shaped figure, ensuring not a drop fell onto the plate, and added a pinch of salt, taking care to distribute it as evenly as possible.

From far away, from very far away, he heard his father's voice.

— Cry if you want to, Vittorio. Go ahead. Don't hold it in.

And then he saw Grandmother turn toward the cooktop and start staring at the milk, as if she could make it boil faster just by looking at it, because she was from a farming family and always said that if you drank it raw, you might catch a disease. And when he, a steaming cup of milk and coffee in his hand, had once again restarted their perpetual conversation and attempted to convince her of the truth of the theory of evolution, she had smiled as ever, shook her head, and stroked his hair and said that there was no way her lovely grandson had descended from apes.

On hearing these words, Vittorio suddenly felt lost and foolish tears began to roll down his cheeks. He stood up, his legs trembling, and told her, "Nonna, I'll never leave you."

For the first time in his life he had realized that Grandmother was an old person, and who knew how much longer she would be with him, and he had been terrified by the terrible thought that his time with her was not infinite, and that he should treasure each day, each hour, each moment with her. Because without her, he would be alone.

— Please don't die, he told her, and as an indecipherable smile appeared on his grandmother's face, he launched himself forward to hug her, that nine-year-old stick-thin boy with curls and tears streaking down his face, and she held him tightly in her arms.

— Look what a silly grandson I have, she whispered. Vittorio, don't worry. I'm not going to die, I'm a tough old bird.

And she took his face between her hands: those wrinkled hands with their delicate, almost translucent, blotched skin which he loved so much to pinch and then watch it remain immobile, a mountain range on the back of her hands.

— Listen to me, little one. I need to tell you something important. Listen carefully.

Vittorio nodded, lifted his chin, and fixed his gaze on the perfect sky of his grandmother's eyes, which watched him from just a few centimeters away.

— Even if I die, because everyone dies in the end, I will not leave you. I will always be with you, Vittorio. To protect you. And when I need to tell you something, I will come to you in your dreams. Do you understand?

—Yes, Nonna. Thank you, Nonna.

—And there is something else which is very important. Something you must never forget.

—What?

— Don't cry for me, Vittorio.

— Okay, Nonna.

—Actually, never cry.

She dried the tears from his reddened cheeks and kissed his forehead. Yesterday, only yesterday, just yesterday.

— Let the others cry. Don't you cry.

Vittorio nodded.

— Never, understand? Never.

THE GUY FOR THE
GOOD DAYS

—CAN I ASK YOU SOMETHING?

—Of course you can.

—Well, if one of these days I died while we were making love here at the Den...What would you do?

—Come on, Cesare, don't die...

—But if I did?

—The Beast is immortal.

—No, tell me. What would you do if I died here, in this bed? If I started to pant like a dog and beat my chest and scream for an ambulance and then I stood up and dropped dead on the ground, huh? What would you do?

—Idiot.

—No, really, what would you do?

—I think I'd be furious.

—With who?

—With you, Cesare. Who else?

—And what would you do?

—I don't know, come on...I don't know right now...But I'd do something...

—Like what? Would you insult me?

—I might slap you. Maybe a kick, too.

—Really? Where?

—Hmm...maybe in the butt.

—You'd kick me in the ass? When I was dead? Hard?

—No, not hard. A little kick.

—What?

—You'd leave me in a lot of trouble, you know...I might run away. Yes. Actually, I'd definitely run away.

—What? My Historic Baby Doll would run away crying, and leave the Tuscan unranked tennis champion dead on the floor?

—But Cesare, your Historic Baby Doll would be left in a real mess if you died here...What if the police found out that I was with you?

—Ah...

—Don't you think about me?

—Ah, so I die but I have to think about you?

—Of course. You always have to think about me. Always. Listen, Cesare, let's make a deal. Don't die please, okay?

—Okay, I won't die.

—Good.

—Let's talk about something else. What did you think about me the first time you saw me?

—What's with all these questions today?

—Tell me.

—No, I don't want to.

—Tell me.

—Do you want the truth?

—Of course I do.

—That you were old.

—Really?

—Yes...well, I saw you walking into that bar, and I knew

who you were, that you were a tennis champion, and I guess I'd thought you were younger.

—Was it because of my hair?

—What do you mean, because of your hair?

—Because I'm losing it?

—What are you talking about? You're not losing it.

—No, of course I'm not losing it, but…is it because I have a receding hairline?

—You haven't got a receding hairline. Cesare, poor baby, have I upset you? You're right, today I've been horrible to you, I don't even know why. Sorry, I didn't mean to say you were old.

—But why? I don't understand. How am I old? I'm only thirty-nine…

—Sorry, sorry, sorry, sorry. Will you forgive me?

—Of course.

—Really, please forgive me.

—I forgive you, I forgive you…

—Thank you.

—But do you know why I forgive you? Because it's not a problem. And do you know why it's not a problem? Because I don't give a fuck about anything you say.

—…

—Because I'm not old, got it?

—I know, Cesare, I'm sorry.

—No, you don't know. You can't possibly know. You're young, and you're a hairdresser. You know fuck…

—I'm not a hairdresser. I actually have my own beauty salon.

—It's the same thing.

—Come on, Cesare. I said I was sorry…

—No, listen to me. Because there might be a little bit of truth in it. I've had a difficult time. When I saw my first gray hair on the temples, three or four years ago. I said, "Shit, I'm old. I'm finished." I couldn't sleep, I would wake up during the night, and sometimes I wouldn't sleep all night, thinking about

37

all the opportunities I would miss because I was getting old. All the brilliant things I couldn't do anymore...

—But Cesare...

—Man, I felt terrible then...

—I'm sorry, Cesare.

—Don't interrupt me, please.

—Sure, I'm sorry...

—And then, one night, I wrote down everything I have, you know? From the first thing to the last. And I calmed down. Because I've got a lot going for me. I really have a lot. And the first thing I've got is my health. And physically, I couldn't be in better shape. Just have to get used to someone sticking a finger up your ass every so often...I mean the urologist, darling, of course, for the prostate. Because in the future I might have a problem there, like all men...

—But Cesare...

—And then, when that truly unpleasant sensation has passed...

—Which truly unpleasant sensation?

—What do you mean, which truly unpleasant sensation? The finger up my ass! Well, once that is over, so is everything else...and that is the most important thing. If that is okay, everything else is secondary.

—And what is the most important thing of all?

—Honey, as long as I fuck like I've done today, everything is fine. That's the most important thing. As long as I see you and I feel you come like you did today, like all the times you did today, I will never feel old, and I will never be old, get it?

—Yes, but—

—How many times did you come today?

—I didn't count.

—You see?

—Cesare, I don't want to argue, things have been so good. I thought you were joking...

—Well, you know, I *was* joking up to a certain point, if you were going along with it...

—...

—What are you doing now, are you going to cry?

—No, but...It's that I'm not okay, and you're being mean...

—What? What are you talking about? What's wrong? Are you feeling ill?

—No, you're being mean! I'm fine. I mean, my health is fine, but I...

—You what?

—I've got problems, Cesare...

—What problems?

—I've got my own problems. Personal problems...I can't do it anymore, Cesare...

—Do what?

—Anything. This.

—What?

—Doing this with you...We never see each other except here...

—Honey, we see each other as often and as soon as I can.

—Yes, I know, but it's not enough. I'm always alone...

—Find yourself a boyfriend, honey, what do you want me to say? I'm sorry...You certainly can't be with me. I'm a married man.

—I know, I know, but I'd like to spend more time with you. I—I can't go on like this, Cesare...

—Hang on a second. Stop. Stop everything. Stop the machines.

—Huh? What does that mean?

—Do you know who I am? Hey, look at me. Look at me. Don't you know who I am?

—Who are you?

—I'm the guy for the good days.

—What does that mean?

—It means that if one day you've got a problem and you're feeling bad and you need someone to talk to, I'm not that person.

Don't come looking for me. Don't even mention your problems to me. I have enough of my own. And if you ever think of telling me about them, if one day you're just dying to tell me about them...well, don't. Understand?

—Cesare...

—No, no fucking Cesare. Go take a walk, go for a drive, call one of your friends and go buy yourself a bag or a lipstick or whatever you want, and come back to me here at the Den when you're happy. And we'll make love. If I feel like it. And if you feel like it, of course. I'm not going to rape you. You know that I only like it when I can see you are enjoying it.

—I know Cesare, but—

—But what?

—No, nothing.

—Good, then. I'm the guy for the good days, that's all.

—Okay. I'm sorry.

—No problem. Just as long as we understand each other.

AN INEVITABLE MIRACLE

AS THE SUN SETS behind the skeleton of the house, the temperature suddenly drops and the breath of the boys on the field starts to condense. This causes the game to slow down and become erratic: passes lose precision, controlling the ball becomes difficult, stopping it is almost impossible. Two kids playing defense for the Green Zone pretend to smoke imaginary cigarettes. The game is drawing to a close.

They aren't tired, because no one that age is ever really tired, nor are they cold or hot: they are indestructible creatures, superior beings forged in iron and pride, and mercury runs through their veins instead of blood. So when the umpteenth attack of the Green Zone begins again, Vittorio gives chase to the short-legged, quick boy playing in jeans and plastic shoes who has already scored three goals, and they look like comets, their heads wrapped in smoky white breath as they run. No one wants to lose this match, which counts for absolutely nothing and has been played for over an hour now on a field where grass survives only in tenacious, isolated clumps on the four corners of the hypothetical rectangular pitch, leaving bare its hypothetical center and even more hypothetical penalty area, trodden into oblivion by an irresistible passion.

Two lines of single-story houses stretch out along the clearing, separated by a dirt track. Many seem to be still under construction, unfinished but already inhabited, with no sign of a plaster veil to hide the hastily thrown-together mosaic of perforated and solid bricks—it's the Green Zone, an entire illegally built neighborhood in glorious, continuous growth, right in the middle of an immense empty field full of brambles and punctuated by wild radicchio, which on winter mornings the dew would paint white and cause to shimmer like diamonds.

Arianna is there. The only adult present, she has stayed in her car, leaving the engine on, smoking and chewing peppermint-flavored Brooklyn gum and thinking of her mother.

She keeps seeing the radiant, weary smile with which, toward the end, her mother tried to hide the signs of the bastard disease she indignantly refused to give in to, even in the final days.

Her mother had fought with the strength and courage of a lioness, without asking or wanting anyone's help, particularly Arianna's. She had confided only in her doctor, who was her own age and had made a point of minimizing every symptom of the slow progress of the ordeal she was facing, forcing Arianna into the role of the weak daughter from whom it was best to conceal the depth and intensity of the pain and the truth, in an inversion of roles that pained Arianna but from which she did not have the courage to break, despite Cesare's pleas.

So, every telephone call her mother made to the doctor was followed up by another, wretched one of hers, in which she asked for a report on the progress of the disease. And every blood test result arrived in a crumpled envelope—"That's enough now! I'm going to make a complaint to the post office!"—because Arianna had already steamed it open and resealed it with great care, trying her best to avoid those cursed creases in the paper, in the hope that her mother wouldn't notice.

Besides her silent war against that cowardly evil, Arianna found herself fighting the opinion her mother had of her and, in some way, fighting her mother herself, who was always so sweet with her grandson and so harsh on her daughter, stubbornly refusing to recognize her as an adult, a wife, and a mother: a responsible person, finally, after the absolute irresponsibility she had shown by marrying a man who—her mother had wanted to tell her on the eve of their wedding, when an anxious Arianna desperately tried to obtain an embrace that would act as a blessing—didn't love her and was already cheating on her before getting married, just imagine what he'd be like once they had tied the knot.

Arianna lost all of those battles at the same time, when her mother—from the hospital bed she had ended up in after fainting in the kitchen, exhausted and worn out, pale as the moon but smelling, as ever, of Marseilles soap—asked her to comb her hair, then took her daughter's hands, thanked her for everything she had done as if she were a nurse, reminded her to always stay close to Vittorio, and then turned her sharp gaze to the ceiling as if she wanted to go and settle the score with the disease in the other life. She closed her eyes and didn't say another word. An hour later she was dead.

Chased by Vittorio, the boy in the plastic shoes has ended up over the baseline without having managed to pass the ball. He had stopped as he heard them shout "Out of bounds," and now he is just standing there, immobile, with one foot on the ball. A halfhearted objection is raised. Vittorio says, "If the baseline runs in a straight line from the post, the ball is outside the line and, therefore, out of bounds."

He is an excellent student, even if he spends most of his days in Mompracem exchanging stories with his fellow pirates under the shade of the fronds of a giant Ravenala palm, or exploring the Snaeffels crater in Iceland, or rounding Cape Horn, or invisibly crossing the seas on board the *Nautilus*, or perhaps flying to the moon in an aluminum spaceship shaped like a bullet, shot into space by a gigantic cannon powered by guncotton.

His team, of which he is captain and creator, is made up of six little boys who live in medieval palazzi in the historic center of the town, a far cry from the tiny houses of their adversaries, which look more like garages.

The captain of the Green Zone, Dino Citarella, would like to respond that, yes, the baseline is a straight line, okay, but it should also be an extension of the goal line and, as he now sees it with his back against the post, the straight line that starts from the goal should pass well to the left of the clump of grass the ball is resting on. He would like to add — because he is also an excellent student — that because the line extending from the goal line cannot be oblique, the ball is clearly and visibly in play: in short, it is in bounds.

But Dino is concerned that, if he says the word "oblique," his friends — all of them not excellent students — will think he has become some sort of a nerd who uses big words, and then he doesn't want to give in to those rich boys in their perfect set of white acrylic soccer uniforms with two diagonal blue-and-red lines that run from the right shoulder to the spleen and are the object of desire for the boys from the Green Zone, who play in their everyday shirts and corduroys and cannot understand how the other boys can be so rich as to own a football uniform that they only wear to play with them, on the field in front of their illegally built houses. Because they know their houses are illegal. They are told every day at school.

So, even though his father works for Vittorio's father and he has been asked — ordered even — never to argue with the boys who come from the center to play soccer with them, when Vittorio asks his opinion — from captain to captain — Dino looks at his friends, all lined up waiting for him to speak, and feels entitled to represent and defend them at any cost, and answers that it is in — fuck, the ball is in.

At that same moment, Arianna shakes off her anguished thoughts and finds herself in the smoke-filled interior of her cream-colored Renault 5, alone, at sundown, in the middle of the Green Zone, and decides it's time to go. She sounds her horn three times and all the boys turn to look at her as she struggles with the steering wheel during her maneuver.

Vittorio, gripped by the fear that his mother might get out of the car and start giving everyone orders, desperately proposes to kick the ball as high as possible, and start the last play after the rebound. Dino shrugs and agrees, because it's not just the rich kids that have to go home—everyone does. He can see his mother watching him from the window, undoubtedly on the point of calling him in because it is nearly dark, and for a reason that is as deep-rooted as it is incomprehensible in a land without crime, no boy can stay out after sunset.

So Vittorio picks up the ball and kicks it as high as he can, as if he were a goalkeeper, and everyone runs after it: eight, nine boys, as fast as deer, racing after the ball that falls from the sky and bounces on the barren land that is as hard as cement. And the first one to reach it as it comes down is Ricky Mariotti, a boy with blond angelic curls and angular features who hits it with a full-force instep kick that sends the ball even higher, aimed straight at the Green Zone's goal, which is defended by Tonino, the smallest kid of all. Tonino Citarella, Dino's brother, an eight-year-old who, until that moment, had only stopped the ball with his feet and shins, and had taken no interest whatsoever in the trigonometry-inspired discussion on the angle of the hypothetical baseline, instead remaining seated in front of the goal with his legs crossed, engrossed in his own Sumerian game of letting the dust run through his closed fists as if they were hourglasses.

The ball—a gnarled, rough, rubber sphere adorned with the word "Yashin" in honor of the great Russian goalkeeper of the 1960s whom none of the boys had ever seen play—rises so high that Arianna sees it trace an arch through the sunset burning brightly behind the low, distant hills. It's a brushstroke, a satellite, a signature that strokes the sky, and Arianna is inexplicably moved by the gratuitous beauty of the act, by the strength of the desire and the futility and the courage of that boy kicking the ball toward the faraway sky, as if laying down a challenge to it.

Tonino, called back by his brother's voice, looks up and sees the ball falling toward him, immediately understanding the perfection of its trajectory. He stands up with his fists still clutching the dust, and hopes with all his heart that the sheer strength of that projectile will take it over the bar, because, even if he jumps up with his arms out and his fingers stretched as far as they can go—which would mean interrupting his Sumerian game—there is still at least a meter of light between his zenith and the bar. He is not even actually a goalkeeper: he is only there because the real goalie had to go with his father to deliver bags of lime mortar to a factory, and so he, the smallest of all, was called in, incredibly proud to be allowed finally to play with the big boys.

Tonino watches that white meteorite hurtling toward him, and worries about how much it would hurt the palms of his hands to stop that speeding projectile in the freezing cold that had overtaken the Green Zone after the setting of the sun, and he decides to try and knock it away, but the more he looks at the ball bearing down on him, the more he is convinced that you can't stop a meteorite, and so he prays with all his might that the lob passes over the bar, also because he thought he heard them say it was the last play, so if the ball goes in, the other team would win and everyone would blame him even if it wasn't his fault.

In that ever-prolonged moment Tonino also has the time to think that if he had a stone he could throw it at the ball, because he excels at throwing stones—he has killed sparrows with stones, broken windows from thirty meters away—but the Yashin is coming in and it is already on top of him, and so he jumps as high as he can, pushing out his body and his arms, and extends his fingers as far as they will go, putting aside his idea of punching the ball away and the Sumerian game, without a thought to the pain that he is about to feel, determined to do what needs to be done.

Arianna smiles as she watches that courageous little boy levitate toward the ball. Forty meters away, Ricky Mariotti watches incredulously the perfect trajectory of the lob he had kicked so high only because he was cold and didn't want to run anymore but still wanted to win the game; and Vittorio stays perfectly still to watch that perfect kick, transfixed by the beautiful and rare and yet entirely inevitable event that is unfolding before his eyes—an inevitable miracle—and, like an old man, he asks himself when he will ever see anything like that again; and Dino, standing next to Vittorio, feels bad for his little brother, whom he had forced on the others when they had wanted to play without a goalkeeper and who will now be held responsible for that goal despite the fact no one could have ever saved it, except maybe Yashin, and yet he is heartened at the sight of his grasshopper of a brother stretching himself out to his limit, and his extended arm with a permanently grazed elbow isn't all that far from the Yashin that enters the goal, whistling like a missile, oblivious to every human desire or weakness, and immediately bounces and rises up once more, right over the lopsided wall of perforated bricks one meter behind the goal, and disappears from the boys' view forever, as if weren't a soccer ball but a lightning rod thrown to earth by Jupiter himself.

A brief moment of absolute silence falls over the Green Zone only to be broken by Arianna, who lowers the car window and shouts loudly for Vittorio as all of his friends start to cheer and run to embrace Ricky Mariotti, who stands transfixed in the middle of the field with his hands immersed in his blond curls, incredulous and ecstatically happy.

Dino watches silently as the six rich boys cram into the cream-colored Renault 5 that accelerates in the dust and whisks them away in the blink of an eye. As the car's rear lights grow dim and disappear into the darkness — because there are no streetlights in the Green Zone — he turns to his companions who stand in front of Tonino's goal, immersed in a cloud of white breath.

A single star shines in the dark blue sky, and Dino asks himself how that star could be Venus. Isn't Venus a planet?

—That was such a fluke!

—We can't tell anyone that we lost to the rich kids ... But, hey, they left us the Yashin! Let's climb over the wall and get it!

— How much bloody money have they got, Dino?

Tonino, still on the ground after his great dive, is relieved and shocked that no one blames him for the goal. He takes his brother's outstretched hand with a shy smile and stands up, shakes off the dust by slapping himself on thighs and buttocks, and then asks into his brother's ear, "Dino, what's money?"

AN OLYMPIC
SWIMMING POOL

IT MIGHT BE DUE to his humble origins, or to the fact he had been taught many of the lessons of life by his father's belt, but Pasquale Citarella was very easily embarrassed. At the slightest prompting, that portly, tireless, taciturn man would blush like a debutante: his face would flush, his ears would turn violet, and his gaze would fix on the reinforced toe caps of his work boots.

That morning it had already happened many times: When he arrived in the forecourt of Barrocciai Blankets in his farting Ape Piaggio. When he was forced to park in the only place his Ape wouldn't be in the way of the trucks constantly moving in and out of the court, which happened to be the narrow spot between two brand-new blue Alfettas that undoubtedly belonged to the company's owners. When he had to hide in the palm of his hand the Nazionale cigarette he had been smoking, and then extinguish it by scraping the end along the chassis of his Ape before putting the butt in his pocket, because he didn't want to throw it on the floor in that pristine forecourt. When he was obliged to introduce himself in his paint-flecked overalls to the skinny, supercilious porter who magically appeared the minute he had attempted to park between the Alfettas. When he had to explain to the porter that he was expected (that's what Vezzosi had told him to say) by Mr. Barrocciaio. When the porter corrected him with a sneer, telling him that the correct name was Barrocciai, with an *i* at the end, in the Tuscan style, not with an *o* as was more common in the South where he was from, in the heel of Italy's boot.

Pasquale was embarrassed once again and most of all when he was asked if he was expected by Mr. Ardengo or Mr. Ivo Barrocciai, because Vezzosi had not specified, and he had to answer that he didn't know. And he was also embarrassed when the porter abruptly ordered him to follow, led him up a steep flight of stairs, and then down a corridor of well-buffed blue tiles to an office where an elegant man with a great mane of white hair wearing a blue jacket, a light-blue shirt, and a yellow tie sat at a large desk. He had been speaking on the telephone in a foreign language, and as he heard the footsteps come to a halt outside his door, he turned to look at Pasquale with an inquisitive air before gesturing to him to stay put and keep quiet.

This series of successive embarrassments had not given his face the time to return to its normal color, and so the redness had fixed itself to his cheeks as if it were permanent. He tried to calm himself, but his heart was beating fast. He pretended not to look around him, his hands wrapped tightly around the cycling cap carrying the logo of a mortar company, waiting for that elegant older gentleman to finish his telephone call in that unfamiliar language, and he jumped when the man abruptly put the phone down and began shouting in a loud voice.

—Franchina! Franchina! Come here, quickly! And who might you be?

—I'm the painter.

—We don't need a painter. Absolutely not! Who sent you?

—I work for Mr. Vezzosi.

—Ah, you must be here to see Ivo, not me. Come, I'll take you to the provisional offices of Barrocciai Textiles.

The gentleman rose from his chair and led Pasquale along the corridor to a door that opened onto a steel platform that hovered above the empty space of the company's small warehouse, at the center of which was a cubicle made of glass, metal, and white plastic, divided into two sections.

In the first section, two young women sat opposite one another, each holding a telephone to her ear, on desks so close there was hardly any space to pass between them. In the other section, a younger version of Barrocciai the elder was gesticulating wildly in front of Cesare Vezzosi, who sat with his head down.

Ardengo began to walk down the narrow steel staircase, and Citarella followed. When they arrived at the cubicle, Ivo saw them and pointed them out to Vezzosi, who turned around and gestured for Pasquale to come and join them.

—They are always on the phone here, Ardengo said. He opened the door, let Citarella in, closed the door, then started back up toward the steel staircase, slowed ever so slightly by a mild limp.

Now alone before those opposing desks, facing the prospect of having to walk sideways like those figures in Egyptian hieroglyphics to get through the narrow gap, Pasquale froze and stood there listening to the two young women — one fairly robust with chestnut curls, the other blond and pale, prettier — talking away in two different languages. He couldn't move forward or backward, so he turned to look at the old Barrocciai cut diagonally across the warehouse floor and nod at Carmine Schiavo — the young, bearded, Castro-supporting warehouse worker whom Pasquale also knew because he too came from Ariano Irpino, his hometown in Campania. The old gentleman slipped past a pile of brown blankets stacked neatly on the shelves and stretched out his arm to touch them as he walked past. Was it a caress?

When he heard his name being called again by Vezzosi, Pasquale had to overcome his embarrassment and squeezed his way between the desks of the two young women, apologizing profusely and receiving death stares in return, finally arriving at the glass door that opened onto the partition of the cubicle that was Ivo Barrocciai's office, almost entirely occupied by a splendid desk in rosewood, so big as to arouse the suspicion that the cubicle had in fact been built around it.

Vezzosi gestured for him to come in, sit down in the uncomfortable plastic seat next to him, and keep quiet. Barrocciai was on the phone, his elbows resting on a large blueprint that took up the entire table.

—Thank you, sir. Thank you again... Yes, I'll get them to you right away. I'll send one of the girls... Yes. All of them, absolutely. I will send them all. Perfect. Of course. All of this week's invoices.

He rejoiced, clenching his fist in the air.

—Foreign, yes. They are all in German marks... Absolutely. I know, I know that foreign invoices are twice as valuable...

Vezzosi whispered into Pasquale's ear.

—Pasquale, once you've painted, you need to air out... Today at the Den I thought I was going to suffocate while I was screwing... He brought his hand to his throat and mimed being strangled to death.

Pasquale was so unsettled at hearing him speak in that way in front of a businessman that he could only nod. He had closed all the windows because he didn't want Vezzosi to find that small, unfurnished room too cold.

—One day I can lend you the Den, if you like. So you can finally get laid, too. Don't you have any pussy?

Pasquale shook his head, now overwhelmingly embarrassed.

—I thought not... Well, if one day somehow you should ever find some, you can fuck her at my place, okay? He stopped to stare at the painter.

Pasquale turned to look at Cesare, then nodded again.

—But wait, if you go there, your hair will be all over the place. And hers, too, because I bet you love hairy women…You'll have to wash all the sheets and pillowcases, or even boil them. No, better still, burn them…You'll need a flamethrower.

Vezzosi smiled with wolfish eyes and slapped Pasquale on the back.

—My father is well, thank you, very well indeed. Every so often he comes down to see what I'm up to. He was here a moment ago. He just left the office…Yes, yes, he's happy. Very. Perhaps even a little proud. Let's hope so…Thank you, sir. See you soon, all the very best…goodbye, goodbye…

Ivo hung up and pointed his index finger at Cesare.

—Sorry, Cesare. One more second. Gabriella!

The young woman appeared at the door, in the glowing health of her twenty-two years.

—Take all the invoices to the bank. They're going to advance them today.

—Fine. Listen, Ivo, there's another order from Austria. They want to try the loden.

—Excellent!

—Right, I'm off to the bank.

—Good girl.

The young woman smiled briefly at Cesare, threw an inquisitive glance toward Citarella, and left.

—We're going to have to start hiring people. And we'll need to rent a warehouse. Immediately. We can't go on working like this.

He looked at Cesare and pointed at the blueprints.

—However, Cesare, as for this, it's just not right. No, no…I'm sorry, but it's really not there. It will have to be entirely redone, from scratch.

—Ivo, just a second. Let's go over it together.

Pasquale leaned forward to look at the plans. He could tell it was a factory, a big one.

—Please, tell me exactly what it is you don't like, because I want to understand properly, and you need to be happy with it.

Barrocciai sneered.

—All of it…I mean, none of it. I don't like any of it at all. Come on, Cesare, it's not right. It doesn't say anything to me. It's a normal factory. It's the same as all the others. It's old, understand? I want my factory to be completely different. I want it to be new. I didn't buy all that land to build an old factory!

Vezzosi shrugged.

—Ivo, I've told you many times we have to talk about it, but you were never available, and so I had to work on my own initiative, to save time. I thought you were in a rush.

—Of course I'm in a rush. You can see for yourself that this new business has hit the ground running, and that we can't stay in this cubicle one week longer. We need to start building the new factory now, understand? But it needs to be beautiful, absolutely stunning!

Pasquale stared at him, astonished. It was the first time he had heard someone give so much importance to beauty.

—Okay, Ivo, let's start again from the beginning. I've spent three months on calculations and designs, but that's not important now. You want something new, and I'll give you something new. But please, Ivo, let's agree on some of the technical details now, okay? You want a warehouse that covers five thousand square meters, with an internal courtyard, right?

—Yes. But I want it on two levels, Cesare. I want two floors, not one. I want to go higher than the others, understand? In every possible sense. I want to see the horizon. A man's gaze must roam free, Cesare. If I have a wall in front of me, how many ideas do you think I'm going to get? So I want a building with ten thousand square meters of floor space. On the ground floor I need all the warehouses with the raw materials, and all the machinery, spinning, warping, and weaving. On the second floor, I want all the offices, the sampling department, and storage.

—Okay.

Cesare answered immediately, instinctively, hoping Ivo would not notice that he was startled by the enormousness of the challenge. A ten-thousand-square-meter factory! Over two floors! To be built by someone whose greatest achievement was a block of four apartments of fifty square meters each, which Pasquale had painted on his own!

Citarella saw that Vezzosi had leaned over to write on the blank sheet of a notepad:

TEN THOUSAND SQUARE METERS. OVER TWO FLOORS.

—But Ivo, if it has to be over two floors, then we will have to build elevators and freight elevators and perhaps even conveyor belts...

—Sure.

—How many?

—How many? Cesare, are you asking me? You need to tell me how many.

—Yes, of course. You're right. Okay. Yes.

There was a long pause during which the two men looked one another in the eye, engrossed in their own, very different thoughts.

—Ivo, I'm sorry, there's one thing I don't understand. If you put all the machinery and wool on the ground floor, you are going to have space left over, and a lot of it, because no matter how big you make the offices and the storage, they can't take up more than, I don't know, a thousand square meters? Maybe two thousand? What are you going to do with the rest of the space?

Pasquale saw Barrocciai stand up and begin to pace up and down the cubicle, his hands in his pockets, his head slightly bowed. He was wearing flannel trousers in a light-gray mélange, handmade leather shoes, a blue jacket, and a blue-and-gray-striped tie. Pasquale was very impressed by his elegance. He hoped that, one day, he too would be able to dress like that, perhaps for a special occasion.

Barrocciai didn't open his mouth for an entire minute, then turned his back on them and started to look outside the box, toward the gray wall of the warehouse, and Pasquale wondered what could that young man see, instead of the wall. Florence? Milan? England? America? The future?

—A swimming pool.

Pasquale turned to look at Cesare, who was staring straight at Ivo's back.

—Excuse me?

—A swimming pool, Cesare. I want a swimming pool on the factory roof.

—A grimace that was only vaguely reminiscent of a smile spread over Cesare's face.

—You mean a water tank? In case of a fire? Or some tank for rainwater, for the dye works...?

Barrocciai turned toward them. He was smiling.

—No tank, Cesare, no dye works. I don't want dye works. I want a swimming pool. Something I can swim in, in the summer. A place where I can bring my clients to sunbathe and be in peace.

—Sorry, what?

—I said it in Italian, didn't I? I want a swimming pool. On the roof of the factory.

—Are you joking? Are you pulling my leg?

—No, I'm not pulling your leg. I want a swimming pool.

— ...

— ...

—And how big is it going to be, this swimming pool?

—Big, Cesare. Very big.

—Yes, but how big? How long? Five meters? Ten?

—I want an Olympic swimming pool.

—An Olympic swimming pool? Twenty-five meters?

—No, Cesare. An Olympic swimming pool is fifty meters long, not twenty-five.

Cesare watched him silently for thirty seconds.

—Come on, don't mess around...

Pasquale Citarella smiled, full of admiration. He had immediately understood that Barrocciai wasn't joking, he really wanted an Olympic swimming pool on the roof of his factory—so this is what he saw when he was staring at the warehouse wall!

It was crystal clear. You could tell just by looking at him. His eyes were shining with the same look his father had had that day, when he had gone back to Ariano and told his family that they would be moving north, all of them, in a week's time. It was that look a man is rarely allowed to have in life, because life is a bastard and kicks you down every day, and wants to flatten you, knock you right to the floor, and it always wins and you always lose, but on those marvelous and incredibly rare days in which for some reason you wake up one morning and feel you are truly alive, and all around you the world is shiny and perfumed and you can see the future and you are certain it will be full of good fortune and wonderful things, and so you find the courage to say what you have wanted to say for the longest time, and you finally make that decision you have always been scared of making and from which you can never back down because there is no turning back from some decisions, and you accept all of the consequences, good or bad, certain that they will only be good.

You, Vezzosi, you just can't understand these things, thought Citarella as he saw Barrocciai move closer to Cesare, look him in the eyes, and place a hand on his shoulders.

—Cesare, listen to me. Are you with me or not?

As always, Vezzosi answered immediately, ever obedient to that ironclad impulse that obliged him never to let on he wasn't prepared for something.

—I'm with you. Of course I'm with you.

—So help me do what I want to do, please. I know it is difficult. It's difficult for me too. Look where we are now...And he
held out his arms as if he wanted to embrace the cubicle.

—Cesare, I need you to tell me now whether I can count
on you, or if I have to look for someone else. Because I want to
move on.

—No, damn it! Of course you can count on me.

—And on me, Barrocciai! You can count on me, and my entire
family!

Ivo and Cesare turned toward Pasquale, who had been unable
to stand in silence before all that passion. The three of them
looked at one another. They were about the same age.

—Thank you. What's your name? Sorry, I've forgotten.

—Me? Pasquale Citarella.

—Good, I'm Ivo Barrocciai. Thanks again, Pasquale. So,
Cesare: I want a factory over two floors, five thousand square
meters per floor. The machines all on the ground floor, the offices
upstairs. And above the offices, I want an Olympic swimming
pool, complete with diving board and starting blocks. On the
factory roof. Okay? Can you build it for me?

—Yes, I can.

—Are you sure?

—Yes, of course.

—But up until now you've only built apartments, right?

—Yes.

—No factories.

—No.

—So tell me why I shouldn't call someone else to build my
factory. Someone with experience.

Citarella swallowed.

—Why? What do you mean, why? Because we know one
another. Because you trust me, because I'm a serious man,
because...because quite frankly, Ivo, it hardly takes a Brunelleschi to build a factory, come on! I have seen plenty of them built

from scratch! And I can get help, if I need it. I will get some good people in ... and then there is Pasquale ...

—No.

—What do you mean, no?

—No. This isn't why I'm giving you the job. I'm giving it to you because I don't want someone with experience that breaks my balls, an old fellow who tells me what to do and tries to get me to change my mind.

—Of course, Ivo. You're right!

—I wouldn't have any fun.

—Exactly.

—Okay. So, when can we get started?

—Right away. It's going to cost you a fortune, Ivo.

—I know. It's not a problem. I'll find the money. You, Pasquale, are you a builder? Have you got your own business? How many employees do you have? Five? Ten?

—Mr. Barrocciai, sir ... Pasquale cleared his throat and turned bright red, his heart suddenly beating faster than ever, terrified by the possibility of being excluded from the project.

—Don't call me sir. From now on you will call me Ivo.

—Okay, well, Mr. Ivo, thank you. I'm ... well, to tell the truth, I work for Mr. Vezzosi, and I'm a painter, but I can do building work. No problem. I'll give it my all, Mr. Ivo, don't you worry. I can learn. It's not a problem at all. It'll be fine, Mr. Ivo. Don't you worry.

Ivo stared at Cesare for a few seconds, then burst out laughing and couldn't stop, and they all started to laugh so hard that Giuliana had to cover the mouthpiece with one hand and knock on the glass to tell them to be quiet, because she had to write down another order from Germany and she couldn't hear a thing.

MY LODEN

—BAROCCIAI, LISTEN TO ME. You're making a big mistake.

Leo Gabriel removed his glasses and laid them on the leather pad of his desk. He leaned into the back of his armchair and took a long deep drag on his Marlboro.

Having canceled three appointments at the last minute, he had finally agreed to meet Ivo in his small, elegant office with dark wood paneling on the walls, in Milan's Galleria Vittorio Emanuele.

The agent had grown fond of the voice of this Tuscan guy who, in their frequent telephone calls, had always been extremely polite in that cheerful accent of his, and so he had granted him a fourth appointment, to which Ivo had arrived with a two-liter bottle of fresh, fragrant olive oil the color of emeralds.

Leo Gabriel was universally respected in the world of textiles. Now close to sixty, thin, not short but gnomelike, and still blessed with most of the thick, straw-colored hair he had been born with, Gabriel was known for always being tough in his dealings, but honest and very, very good at his job.

Born into his profession, he had two lines of business that were both complementary and opposed. The first saw him as a sort of luxury wholesaler, selling classic imported fabrics from the finest English cottons for shirting to Harris tweed, from Irish linen to Shetland wool, from cheviot to moleskin, which he sold by the meter in his shops in Milan and Rome, and distributed to dozens of outlets throughout Italy and Ticino in Switzerland. His second line of business was, however, the one Gabriel owed his reputation and most of his income to: an established textile agency which employed a formidable, personally selected network of aggressive subagents who were bound by contract to dress and speak like him, and sold the best combed wool fabrics from Biella and the most elegant Como silks throughout Europe, Great Britain, and North America.

—Barrocciai. My name is Barrocciai, Mr. Gabriel. With two *r*'s.

To overcome the discomfort of hearing his surname being so horrendously mangled, Ivo cast a sidelong glance at the photo inside the large, ornate silver frame that occupied pride of place on the desk, facing the agent: two indistinct men in tuxedos were shaking hands, and the one smiling more happily was a young Gabriel.

—Yes, of course, please forgive me, Barrocciai. In any case, that is the reality of the matter. Loden isn't produced where you come from, and even though yours isn't that bad—

—Hold on, what do you mean by "it isn't that bad"?

—Well, it's a fine fabric, okay. It is a fine, shiny loden…and you certainly gave it a good hand, I'll give you that.

He delicately rubbed the fabric between his thumb and index finger, without rubbing the underside as is commonly done by the ignorant.

—What did you make it with?

—It's a rather original mix, Mr. Gabriel. Well, it's really a factory secret, but I'll tell you. There is Australian wool—no fleece, just carbonized skirtings—some twenty-micron noils, and polyester.

—Noils? Do you mean the waste from combing? The fluff that falls under the machines?

—Yes. That fluff is very fine, Mr. Gabriel.

—I see, Mr. Barrocciai uses noils for his loden. And you also use polyester ... How much?

—Thirty percent.

—Thirty percent? That much?

—Certainly. It makes the fabric smoother and more resistant, and it prevents creasing in the fabric. It's also far less expensive than wool.

Gabriel nodded and plunged the Marlboro into a decorated ceramic ashtray that was already half full with cigarette ends.

—Well, it's a fine fabric, but we sell very little fine loden, Barrocciai. You see, it's the more classic loden that sells best.

Ivo had moved to the edge of his seat, and was having trouble holding back from singing the praises of his brand-new quality, so much lighter than the one that was made in Tirol, and at the same time finer and shinier and more resistant to any mishandling: a unique article, with no market competitor and an excellent price for such quality, aptly baptized Ursula in honor of Ursula Andress.

Why wouldn't it work? Ivo could not make sense of it, but he chose to contain himself. He had come to hear Gabriel's opinion, not for a fight. He knew that it was futile, stupid even, to interrupt and, even worse, contradict someone whose opinion you have requested: it was best to keep quiet, listen, and then decide if the opinion was useful or not. But it took self-control. In some cases, such as this one, a great deal of self-control.

—You see, my dear boy ... Gabriel paused, lingering pensively over the lighting of another cigarette.

He was wearing a white shirt with finger-width blue stripes, red suspenders, a gray unbuttoned vest, light-beige corduroy trousers, and shoes of orange leather. *He definitely has a lover,* Ivo thought, *that's why he's dressed like that, and he's going to see her tonight.* The thought of Gabriel holding a voluptuous younger woman in those thin little arms made him want to laugh, and he had to fight hard to hold it in. The agent inhaled long and hard on his Marlboro, and continued.

—Let me explain, Barrocciai. You see, loden is not simply a fabric or an overcoat or a jacket or even, as many think — especially in America — a color. Loden is a concept. A way of life. It is the most Germanic — no, *Teutonic* thing in existence. It brings all the Krauts together, it's the textile equivalent of the Anschluss, understand?

—Yes, but Gabriel —

—Please let me finish. I was saying ..., where was I?

—At Anschluss.

—That's it ... Now I've forgotten what I was going to say. Ah, yes. Ideas regarding the nature of loden vary depending on the country. In Tirol, in Austria, and even in Bavaria, it's used for sports coats, whereas in Italy and Spain, my dear boy, loden is used for elegant overcoats, and is extremely fashionable among lawyers, accountants, barristers, doctors ... They even wear it to go to the theater.

—Yes, of course, but —

—And there is no explaining it, believe me. Nobody has ever done a marketing campaign to create this preference. To put it simply, it's what the market wants, and the market is unique in every country: whimsical, sometimes even irrational, but above all else, sovereign. Never forget that, Barrocciai: *sov-er-eign*.

Forcing himself not to interrupt the lesson, Ivo looked out of Gabriel's office windows. The Christmas of 1975 was on its way, and the Galleria was full of people going in and out of shops. From the way they stopped to shake hands, embrace one another, and exchange greetings, it seemed the Milanese all knew one another. Apart from one fabulous lady wearing a mink coat and another wrapped in an exquisite sable, everyone was wearing overcoats that were so beautiful they managed to lift Barrocciai's spirits. Even from behind the windowpanes, it took him no more than a simple glance to recognize which prized fiber had been used in those wonderful garments: alpaca wool in the warm colors of the sun-scorched Andes, the icy sheen of precious mohair, the comforting luster of cashmere, the dry, austere elegance of camel hair.

It was a fashion show, and the Galleria a monumental catwalk: you could admire all kinds of shapes and cuts in an astonishing display of total freedom of inspiration and style. All kinds of prints — even the most daring — were used to embellish overcoats, greatcoats, capes, jackets, stoles, duffle coats, and suits: dogtooth in all sizes and colors, Prince of Wales enlivened by the brightest threads, the subdued or bold tones of pinstripes, the splendor of fishbone in all sizes and combinations, the large chevrons, and then the old Scottish joke that is tweed, which looks rough but can be as soft as clouds, the jovial harlequin buttons of the knickerbockers, the light swell of mouflons, the simple elegance of all the loden mixes and the glamorous, inimitable richness of astrakhan.

Ivo Barrocciai adored Milan. It had always seemed to him an incomparably larger version of his hometown, moved by the same spirit and inhabited by the same sort of people, who unfailingly put work before everything else but, once work is over, dedicate themselves and their free time to live their city and her bars, restaurants, cinemas, theaters, discotheques, opera houses, museums.

He was always happy to visit Milan, and how he loved the industrious dignity of the people, their good taste and savoir faire, the elegance of their simplicity and the simplicity of their elegance, their capacity and desire to get to know and embrace the best the world had to offer!

He liked everything about Milan: from its subdued colors to its funny, musical dialect that wasn't so invasive as to demand recognition as a separate language, from the imposing facade of its Stazione Centrale to the polite lightness of the lines of the palazzi designed by modern architects. He liked the fact that the

Maestro Fontana had decided to live there. He liked the trees that seemed to be too shy to blossom, the wide, empty streets, the lovers walking hand in hand through Brera, even the fog. And, of course, the women, who summed up and personified all of this grandness: elegant, serene, and eternally wanting more from life. Not something better, because better would have been difficult and maybe impossible to obtain—just more.

In Milan—and only in Milan—Ivo Barrocciai could feel growing inside him the wild idea of throwing all caution to the wind and listening solely to the voice of courage urging him to be ambitious and tireless, and to live in full the blooming of that formidable Italy which drew its strength from Milan. In no other place did Ivo feel so perfectly understood. In no other place did he feel so strongly the roar of the enormous, invisible energy that created well-being and employment out of nothing through the honest, tireless, and unbelievably hard work of the many men and women who, each day, pursued their most private ambitions and the most material of their dreams.

Because cities dream, and Milan's dream was naive and grandiose and brilliant, and it told everyone that it was possible to change your life and your destiny if you were courageous enough, and it didn't matter where you started from, or whether your dreams were large or small, nor whether you were planning to open a business or a shop, a bar or a bank, a publishing house or a newsstand, a hotel or a gas station or a pizzeria. There was a need for everything and a space for everyone in 1975, in Milan, Italy.

—And then there is also the difference in quality and look, Barrocciai, and sometimes even in composition, when it comes to loden. You must consider these things. Though in Italy and Spain the most noble loden is favored, often mixed with alpaca, most of what is sold as loden in Austria and Bavaria is a rustic fabric, rough, almost spartan, made from pure wool and sold exclusively for men, not women. And so . . .

—So?

—So you will not be able to sell your loden to the Germans. Believe me, I know them. They wouldn't even consider it.

—But my loden is better than theirs, Mr. Gabriel! It even has cashmere in it!

—You put cashmere in there?

Gabriel furrowed his brow for a moment, surprised, before breaking into a faint smile.

—And why did you do that? There has never been a loden made with cashmere.

—Exactly. That's why I put it in.

—And why didn't you tell me this right away?

—To see if you could guess when you touched it.

—Eh, my boy. How much did you use?

—Ten percent.

Gabriel smiled incredulously.

—Okay, five.

The agent picked up the sample and touched it, stroking it against the grain and immediately smoothing it back. It returned perfectly to its original state.

—How much does it cost?

—Fifteen marks. Well, fourteen ninety-five.

Gabriel continued to stroke the sample.

—It's a wonderful sample, Barrocciai. I told you. Well done. And the idea of adding cashmere is not bad at all...

—So, Mr. Gabriel, what do you say? Will you represent me in Germany and Austria?

The agent lifted his eyes to look at him.

—No, Barrocciai. I'm sorry.

—Why not?

—Because I like you, and I like your fabric. But you cannot go against the market. If a fabric like this doesn't exist on the market, it is because there is no demand. That's the end of it.

—No, you don't understand.

Gabriel stared at him.

—What don't I understand, Barrocciai? Perhaps you could explain.

—No, I'm sorry, I meant that…well, the market isn't God, after all…I mean it's not perfect, Mr. Gabriel. The market is the people who go to department stores and shops, and even if they're traditionalists, otherwise they wouldn't be buying loden, they always find the same two or three garments on sale, in the same old style and the same old colors, and so they end up buying those. But it won't last, Mr. Gabriel. It isn't a choice.

Gabriel smiled and shook his head.

—I already sell my loden in Germany and Austria, Mr. Gabriel. Not a lot, but a little more each year, and I came to see you in order to grow my business, because the deutschmark is getting stronger by the day, as you well know.

The agent stopped shaking his head and nodded three times.

—I think loden needs a fresh look. It needs to be modernized. And it should also be sold for womenswear. But why are you still shaking your head? We need new fabric in this business, and new colors…The world is made of colors, why shouldn't we use them? And it's not just loden, all fabrics need to be modernized, Gabriel. Clothing will change completely. Fashion is on its way, believe me. I know it, I'm sure.

Then Ivo fell silent. It made no sense to keep on insisting: he might seem a naive young man or, even worse, a visionary. Someone in need. Someone who is begging. Finally Ivo realized he had no reason for coming to Milan. He shouldn't be speaking with agents, but with customers. He shouldn't send someone else to do his job. He should go to talk to the clients, to every client. Not just in Germany, everywhere. He should be traveling the globe, telling the story of the new fabrics and new colors. Determined, competent, passionate. As Ardengo used to say, with a boner. He didn't need to wait around for anybody to understand his idea. Gabriel was a big player, yes, but he was sixty years old: soon he'd be retiring to his villa on Lake Como to play grandfather. And then, if he had got it straightaway, it would have meant his idea wasn't so new, so revolutionary. And revolutions are made by hungry boys from the provinces, not sixty-year-olds with an office in the Galleria. Barrocciai smiled. It really is a wonderful life!

—Thank you very much, Mr. Gabriel. For your kindness and for seeing me, and for everything you have said. I will take heed. Many thanks again.

Ivo stood up and held out his hand, which the agent barely shook, caught by surprise. When he leaned over to put the Ursula sample back into the leather case, his disappointment had vanished, and in its place bubbled the excitement of having finally understood that — like the knights of the Round Table — he held his fate in his hands, and he was now certain that with the help of technicians, finishers, workers, artisans, and, most of all, the Bundesbank, everything would go just as he had planned. He wasn't afraid that for him to be right, everyone else had to be wrong — even the experts, even the very best, like Gabriel. It would go just like that. It was the age-old, never-ending struggle between the old and the new. Between progress and tradition. In the end, as always, the new would win. He would win.

—Excuse me, Gabriel, may I ask you a question?

—Of course.

—Who is in that photo with you?

—Which photo?

—The one on the desk.

The agent's gaze turned to the ornate silver frame. He smiled, reached out his hand, picked up the frame, and admired the photo as if for the first time, then he showed it to Ivo. It was a much younger Leo Gabriel shaking hands with Frank Sinatra.

—My compliments, Gabriel! Well, I'm speechless! Old Blue Eyes! Where were you? In Las Vegas?

—In Monte Carlo, Barrocciai. An unforgettable concert, believe me. Unforgettable. I still carry it in my heart.

They shook hands once again, this time with the strength of two lumberjacks.

—I wish you all the best, Barrocciai!

—You too, Gabriel!

When he left the office he found himself before the secretary—an attractive, German-looking fifty-year-old in a grayish-beige suit who must have been a knockout in the past and who was undoubtedly Gabriel's lover. With a broad smile, she extended his orange Casentino woolen overcoat with its wolf-skin collar. Ivo smiled as he put on the glamorous coat he had decided to wear to impress Gabriel, then effortlessly performed the perfect hand kiss.

—My dear, tell me: how long do you think it'll take me to get from Milan to Munich with my Alfetta, if I leave right away?

A GREAT SATISFACTION

SOMETIMES, when they managed to send the children to bed at nine o'clock right after *Carosello*, the popular reel of TV commercials, Pasquale would ask Maria to take a walk with him. She didn't always say yes. If it was cold or windy, she preferred to stay in and watch television or knit or sew, but she always encouraged him to go and get some fresh air.

She was not lazy, quite the opposite, but often found herself exhausted after a day working at home braiding the fringes on blankets, not to mention the help she gave Pasquale's mother with housekeeping. Furthermore, she was convinced that a strong young man who worked all day, like Pasquale, needed to get out of the house from time to time for a little breathing space, and she assumed he only asked her to accompany him out of kindness.

It was one of the few things that she hadn't understood about him at all, perhaps the only one of any significance. In those moments, Pasquale felt the strongest need to confide in her, and even if he never showed it, he was always disappointed when she declined his offer. In those cases, hoping she would realize how important her presence was for him, he shortened his walks to the short time needed to smoke one of his Nazionale cigarettes, piss in the ditch that ran along the dirt track in front of their house, look at the stars for a few seconds, then come back home.

He had fallen in love with Maria at first sight, the day she arrived with the rest of her family from Panni, another one of the small towns in the mountains between Irpinia and Puglia whose inhabitants had unfathomably decided to move en masse to the city that had welcomed and adopted Pasquale. At first, from a distance, it was her breasts that had bewitched him and left his youthful nights languid and sleepless, as he guessed for hours just how large and compact they had to be, impossible to hide even under those loose, punitive dresses her mother forced her to wear, and which Maria donned without protest, certain that the man of her dreams would be able to see past her appearance and fall in love with the girl who knew how to hide her best secrets beneath that flower-printed screen.

When they met at a parish dance, Pasquale was enchanted by her fine features, her melodious yet always quiet voice, the decent happiness he could see in the depths of her astute eyes, and that timid gaze ever ready to lower itself to the tips of her shoes, just like his.

Without actually looking like her—of course—Maria reminded him of Claudia Cardinale, but when Pasquale confessed it to his sister, she laughed and told him he was crazy. He was very upset, and blushed more than ever before. He had meant a character played by Cardinale in a film, or an expression or gesture, or even a simple look of one of Claudia Cardinale's characters, but his sister's caustic laughter told him that he might be the only one to see Maria as beautiful as she was. Poor fools!

He was so heartened by this incredible good fortune that he found the courage to declare his love—and how surprised Maria was when that small shy hulk of a man finally stopped throwing her all those smoldering looks and decided to make a move! They got engaged at once, and when Dino was already on his way, Pasquale took her to the altar with her enormous bump, and kept her always with him ever since.

Without Maria he would never have become anything or anybody: everyone said so. He had the strength and the desire to work, yes, and he would have never given up on anything, true, but Maria was honest and intelligent, and Pasquale had quickly learned to listen to everything she said, not least because she always spoke at the right moment, always and only in private. And even though she would never allow herself to give him orders or even advice, she was able to point out the pros and cons of every situation, showing as inevitable the decision that her husband — and he alone — should make.

Once, Pasquale — who held her in such high esteem that he would have been more than willing to take orders — asked for her opinion on the most important matter: how much land he should buy to build their house on, and where.

They had to choose whether to buy licensed land they could legally build on at eight thousand lire per square meter, or unlicensed greenfield land at fifteen hundred lire. Pasquale had just got back from a crowded meeting with a surveyor, who had explained to him and many other men from Ariano and Panni that it was illegal to build on greenfield land, but some of it would soon be declared in line with regulations because *people were arriving from the South in droves.*

He also said that the regulatory plan put forward by the local council already predicted that the city's population would continue to grow, even to double. All those people would need and want to build themselves a home, so the map already showed — he pointed to a number of very fine lines that snaked away from thicker lines — dozens and dozens of streets that did not yet exist. Two of these future streets — "fantasy" streets, he had called them — crossed the Green Zone, and so they could build without any fear!

Pasquale, full of enthusiasm, told Maria he wanted to start building their house right away. But how big should it be? And how much land should he buy? There were three of them at the moment, but they might become four, or five, or six...What did she think? Maria blushed, said it wasn't a matter for women, and went back to her sewing, concerned that speaking up over a technical issue so close in nature to her husband's work would have undermined him. So Pasquale made the decision alone, the wrong one. After many nights mulling it over, he bought too little land, and when the time came to lay the foundation, he realized that the house he wanted to build would never fit into the minute parcel of greenfield he had bought.

Maria saw him come home with his head hung low, his stomach in knots, humiliated by the need to return to the notary to buy yet another parcel of land because he had not made the correct calculations. Finally she realized he needed her—he really, desperately needed her, and for everything—and this sudden realization warmed her heart, and as she consoled him, Maria decided that from that day on she would no longer keep her mouth shut.

Maria couldn't bear the cold and hated even the mildest breeze. Going out in the winter was always a hardship for her, but on some clear evenings, when there were no puddles in the streets and the white moon shone brightly in the sky, she enjoyed putting on her coat and scarf to go for a quick starlit walk arm in arm with Pasquale, who was so pleased that he wouldn't stop talking. He was always defending Vezzosi, who was a bit of a rogue, yes, but also deserved gratitude for taking him on when he had only just started painting and didn't know anyone, and for ensuring he never went a day without work, and even though he paid poorly and late, it didn't matter, because the important thing was the certainty that there would always be a job waiting for him when he woke up in the morning.

Pasquale always told her how much he liked his work, that it wasn't as hard as people thought because once you had built up your arm and shoulder muscles, painting was not really that strenuous. He would explain to her, over and over, that you didn't use just your arms, but your whole body: your back, your legs, your knees, and your ankles. If you could stand up and move around while you were painting a ceiling or a wall, even if you were at the top of a scaffolding rig, you didn't get as tired as when you had to kneel down to finish a wall, or lean over a pair of shutters, or stay hours perched at the top of a stepladder—*that* was strenuous, even though it didn't seem so. It was staying still that could break your back.

He would tell her how the painter's greatest satisfaction was giving the final touch to the house, being the first person to see it finished because you were the last one to go in and work: the one who *signed it*, and in white, the perfect color that *cleaned the world and made it better*.

He would tell her how much he liked to be sent around by Vezzosi to paint rooms in which, just a few days later, families with children would live, and sometimes he would entertain himself by imagining the people who would live in those rooms that he was about to paint—the work they did and the life they would have, wondering whether it would be as happy as his.

He put his arm around Maria and they walked together on that dirt track in the cold silence of the winter Tuscan night. On their right was a row of newly built houses, some yet to be finished, all built by people who had arrived from the South like them. On their left a field that spread out for a good kilometer and ended with a long line of small warehouses that had just been built and had their lights on because there was always someone working in that tireless city of theirs.

And during those walks, Pasquale would tell her that she was worth so much more than he would ever be able to give her, and then, with his voice made hoarse by the cigarettes, he would go back to explaining how painting a warehouse was much easier than painting a house, because if the paint dripped it didn't matter so much. And he would say how wonderful it was for him to walk into an empty warehouse knowing that a full day of calm, quiet work was awaiting him, together with the great satisfaction of seeing that huge space slowly turn white and light up because of him, becoming bigger and more beautiful and losing that horrible, dirty gray that is always a sign of poverty and neglect. Each time he said the word "poverty" he would always add how happy he was to have put it behind him, *that nasty son of a bitch*, to have eliminated it from the future of his family, and then he would fall silent as if he had completed his mission, and would stay quiet for a while before asking her if they could go home.

It was as if every time Pasquale mentioned poverty he would lose all of his strength, sapped by the fear that it might return, and he would almost be faltering by the time he took his final steps toward the house. Then he would throw himself on the bed and fall instantly asleep, with his clothes on, and Maria would delicately undress him, tuck him under the covers, kiss him on the temples, and stroke his hair, because she knew that his work could not be as easy as he described it. Then she would fall asleep, serene, next to her man.

THE EXTRA MAN

SO, CESARE, as you might have noticed, there are a few changes here: my father has retired and left me the firm, and Barrocciai Blankets no longer exists. We now have Barrocciai Textiles, and I'm the owner and the director ... Thank you. Thank you. We've moved to these old offices. The girls are still down in the cubicle sorting out the old company's final orders, then I'll take them on. Last week I hired ten people, and next month I'll hire two more. The company is taking off, Cesare, and it's going well, but we have a lot of expenses and I no longer have a problem with space, so we need to slow down on the project for the new factory. That's why I called you in. I'm already full up to my eyeballs with the banks, so we must slow down ... No, Cesare, don't laugh, it's not a joke and I haven't said we have to *stop*, I've said we need to *slow down* ... And that's a joke anyway, because we've been talking about it for over a year and you still haven't shown me anything, not even one drawing ... Yes? Really? Is that right? And you didn't tell me anything? Where is it? Let's see it then, damn it, I've been waiting for a year! You should have told me right away about the plans, Cesare! We need to celebrate! Now, let's have a look and see if I can understand anything from all this ... This is where the offices will be, correct? The stairs look a little small though. I want a staircase to my office, in white Carrara marble. Immaculate, it must be...Well, let's make it in travertine, then, but it must be beautiful, Cesare...I'll also need an elevator, I think, in case I break my leg or end up in a wheelchair. Why are you looking at me like that? You've got to think of everything. Hey, I'm going to be spending my whole life in this place! Not a private elevator, I want one that the employees can use, too...No, Cesare, no. Not a service elevator. A real elevator. Beautiful. But it doesn't have to be luxurious, it needs to be useful. Nothing in this company must be a luxury. Have you put in air-conditioning? Because we'll need it. Otherwise in summer everyone will be dripping with sweat and nothing will ever get done...I want it in the offices, in the sample room, and in the spinning and weaving sheds, too...Ah...No, I've never actually heard of a textile factory with air-conditioning in the technical sheds either. Let's put that on hold for the moment...This must be the main technical area, correct? The forecourt must be visible from my office, I want to see everything: people coming and going, the trucks loading and unloading. I'll be able to see everything?... Good. Which one is my office? This one? It's too small. It doesn't matter if it's forty square meters: it's too small. I want an office the size of a tennis court to make up for the two years I've spent in that cubicle. Come on, I'm joking! Cesare, you've gone pale...But it needs to be bigger than that...And where is the pool?...Oh, I see. I thought it was the roof. Well, I guess it *is* the roof. But it's huge, Cesare, it's...huge. It's really fifty meters long? And no one will be able to see me swimming, right? No, because all of the lots around mine have been bought, and Brunero has bought one too...He'll build a tiny little warehouse, I'm sure, he's so fucking tight...There's an incredible energy in the city, Cesare. Everybody has so much work, they're giving it away. I've been told of a barber who last year opened a spinning firm that works twenty-four hours a day, every day, even Sundays, and he's just bought himself a Mercedes...No, not the Pagoda, the 200 diesel, in beige. I bought a Pagoda...Yes, really. Yes, the Roadster. No, I'm not joking. Thanks. I'll show you later. I keep it in the warehouse, under a tarpaulin. Well, I use it to go to the seaside, but only when the weather is good and I can put the roof down...You should see how good it looks: I never had such a beautiful car...Metallic light blue, leather seats. It was a moment of madness, Cesare, it cost me a fortune, I don't even know if I can afford it...Everything I have is in the company's name. I have next to nothing in my bank account, I'd bet there's more money in your account right now than in mine. Anyway, let's get back to us. I want total and absolute privacy in the swimming pool...Also for the customers who will go up there to relax once they've signed their orders. It's a selling point, you see? Not a luxury. Luxury at work is for fools...Okay, are we done? Is there anything else? No? Well, I like these plans. When can we start? Because, as I told you, I have a lot of expenses, and I'm a bit tight with the banks...How long do you think it will take?...Yes, where do I need to sign?...There you go. How long to get it signed off by the council?...Three months? Is that all? It doesn't seem long enough. Let's say six. And how long will it take to build?...No way, Cesare, come on...Ah, just the walls...One year still doesn't seem long enough...But then I'll have to take all the machinery there, move over all the systems...I'll be in by '77, I imagine, not before. Maybe even '78. It's a big job, Cesare. And have you worked out how much it's going to cost me?...Go on, tell me. I know it's a lot, tell me, come on...Shit! Including the swimming pool? One and a half billion lire? You're going to cost me one and a half billion? It's too much. It's way too much, and I need to take it easy now, Cesare...Slow down, I told you. I can't take all that blood out of the new firm now...No, no, Cesare, listen to me. Ivo Barrocciai doesn't have problems with money, and never will, okay? Don't forget that. Never. Look, I want to be straight with you...The other day I saw the bank manager and told him I wanted to start building the new factory, and I would need a billion. I thought a billion would be enough, damn it...Okay, he looked me in the eye and said, "Barrocciai, you go ahead, don't worry, I'll straighten it out with Rome." I left the bank walking on air. It's like this, you see: if you have money and you've got ideas and you want to work, they'll lend you the money...No, I'm not scared of debts, not at all. I'm growing, and I'll keep on growing. I'll pay all that money back, that's not a problem. With German customers paying within ten days and the banks charging interest every six months, I'll have everything paid back in no time. You can set your watch by the punctuality of German payments, Cesare. I've got work coming out of my ears, yes, but it's not enough. I want more. I want this to be an important company. I want to employ lots of people. Not like my competitors, who are scared of their own shadow, always scrimping and saving, working in pigsties...They don't even produce samples. I want to employ all the workers I need, and then one more. Because that's how I create value, understand? I add it to the world instead of taking it out, and when it's created, the value comes back to you...No, Cesare, I'm not a philosopher, I'm an entrepreneur. I do it because the day will always come when you need an extra man, and that day all the money you've spent over the years comes back to you. I know it sounds crazy, but it's crystal clear to me. Think about it, Cesare, I'm always abroad selling, and while I'm in Germany, or America, or Japan, or Cape Town in South Africa, my business needs loyal, honest, tireless workers, people who care about the business as much as I do. They're the ones who'll keep it going. I call the shots, of course, but they're the ones who do all the work, and if they aren't any good, if they don't give their hundred percent, if they don't want to stay that extra hour, the company won't go anywhere, you see? You know that the most beautiful fabrics in the world have always been invented by the workers, not by the stylists, right? They handle your fabrics every day and start to wonder whether they would become softer or shinier with a different setting of the machines, and one fine day they try it out without asking for permission, and out comes the right fabric, one you can then sell the world over. But if you've never spoken to those guys, if you've never asked them how they are or wished them a merry Christmas, if you've treated them badly or paid them poorly or late or unwillingly, if you've treated them like they treat them in those huge metalworking firms in the North, there's no way in hell they're going to try out that idea they had, or do you a favor. It's teamwork, Cesare, always. And I want to be the captain. I want to be great, and I'll work as much as possible, and I'll do whatever it takes! ... Come on, that's enough with speeches. Today is a great day. The new factory is getting started! ... No, no! Go on, Cesare, go on! No slowing down, I take it back! We start immediately. Let's get started! In fifteen days' time, actually in a month, I'll give you the first payment. I don't know how I'll do it, but I'll get it to you. Ah, another important thing. I want a line of cypress trees from Bolgheri all around the factory. Male cypress trees, not female. The ones as straight as spindles. They will be my fence, because who's ever going to steal from me, Cesare? Write it down on this sheet of paper: *Bolgheri cypress trees. Lots of them. Male.*

AN IRON SUPPOSITORY

IT IS A CLEAR SUNDAY MORNING in the dry November of 1976, and the sky is filled with fluffy clouds vainly trying to hide a furious, distant sun. The midnight-blue Alfetta with only one window open — the rear one, so Arianna can smoke — sits haughtily in the middle of the field, right in front of the white-and-red tape trembling in the breeze to keep the onlookers three hundred meters away from a big hole in the ground that is carefully surveilled by two police cars with flashing lights and two fire engines. Because the hole isn't really a hole, but a mere graze no more than forty centimeters deep, the dozen men fumbling about in it seem to be caught in quicksand.

Some fifty curious onlookers stand around Barrocciai's Alfetta. They have arrived in dribs and drabs to watch the show: all men but Maria Citarella, who arrived sidesaddle on a Lambretta driven by her husband, who parked fifty meters away out of the usual embarrassment and walked slowly to the car, waving shyly in the direction of the Alfetta's windshield, which the sun had transformed into a mirror.

He can't bear the sight of all those layabouts who have come to enjoy the show dressed like hunters, with cameras and binoculars around their necks—one even has a video camera. He grumbles, shakes his head. If he could, he would kick them out of the field, which, after the graze, is now officially his building site.

Inside the car, the only sound is the barely audible chewing of Arianna's peppermint gum.

—You know, it's infuriating. I mean, it was dropped from a kilometer, it hit the ground without exploding, and it hasn't exploded for thirty-four years, but now they say that *the slightest vibration* could set it off at any moment! And why do they have to explode it here? Why can't they take it away? Eh, Cesare?

—...

—Cesare...

—Yes, Arianna?

—Ivo asked you a question.

—Oh, sorry Ivo, I was thinking about something else. What did you ask me?

—Cesare is always thinking about something else. He's been like that for a while...

—What are you talking about, Arianna? I don't...Sorry, Ivo, what did you ask me?

—Are we absolutely one hundred percent sure that this thing isn't going to be a problem for the building site?

—No, Ivo, it's definitely not going to be a problem at all. They explode it, they leave, and we can get back to work.

—So, no damage?

—No damage. We'd only laid a few fixed cables. And we would have to dig for the foundations anyway.

—But it's insane! I buy land and they find a bomb in it from the war! Brunero must be laughing like a madman...You know what, Vittorio? It looks like a suppository. I've seen it. It's exactly the same shape. Absolutely identical. Just imagine an iron suppository, all rusty, about a meter and a half long. You see, champ, or, rather, Little Beast?

At hearing himself being called *Little Beast*, Vittorio rolls his eyes and snorts silently. He should have never signed up for those under-twelve Tuscan championships in the first place, and then he shouldn't have won it without conceding even one set, dressed like Bjorn Borg, so no one would be calling him Little Beast now. He is very tired, having spent most of his immense twelve-year-old's night reading *Foundation*, the first book of the *Foundation* trilogy by Isaac Asimov.

—Really?

—You know, Ivo, Cesare said, there are lots of unexploded bombs around. They often find them when they start digging, and not just here, everywhere the war was fought. Even in Germany, France, Britain...

Far away, the sound of a helicopter.

—Of course, if no one checked whether the bombs dropped from the airplanes exploded or not, you can't even sue the manufacturer for the unexploded bombs.

—Pardon, Ivo?

—No, I was thinking that...well, if a bomb doesn't explode it's defective, right?

—Well, yes, in a way, I suppose. But it's a blessed defect, isn't it? If it doesn't explode, it doesn't kill anyone or destroy anything.

—Don't start being a pacifist now, Arianna, you and your friend Kennedy!

—Pacifism has nothing to do with it.

—And Kennedy was hardly a pacifist.

—You see? Ivo understands. It has nothing to do with pacifism. You really are unpleasant sometimes, Cesare...

—But Arianna, it wasn't really about the war. I was just thinking about the business side of it. If the bomb is defective and doesn't explode, but it's been paid for, someone is making money, right?

—I'm sorry, Ivo, but I don't understand.

—Let me give you an example. If you build an empty bomb, without any explosives inside, it's going to cost you less than a real bomb, okay? And if no one can check whether or not the bomb has exploded, because they were all dropped together from dozens of airplanes at the same time, then someone can rip the government off and make money from it, right? That's what I was trying to say.

Arianna sees Vittorio shaking his head in mute disbelief, and an incredibly loud, inhuman voice amplified by a megaphone announces, "The bomb will be detonated in a few minutes' time," and advises everybody to "maintain a safe distance." As if in response to the warning, Arianna gets out of the car, followed by the others a few seconds later.

Silence has fallen over the field. Arianna leans on the bonnet of the Alfetta and tugs gently at the belt of her long, soft, cream-colored coat. It feels like an embrace. She smiles at the thought that Christmas would soon be upon them, with the gifts, the roasted chestnuts, the pipers coming down from the mountains, the new movies...It might even snow.

—Cesare, Arianna! The sky this morning looks like it's made out of wool! Look at those clouds, aren't they flakes of carbonized Australian fleece?

Amused, Arianna turns toward Ivo, who immediately answers her smile with a slow, warm, intense one directed right at her, and her alone. It lasts three seconds, no more, then he slowly turns to look ahead, toward the hole. Arianna is surprised, but also somehow rewarded that a handsome man like Ivo—a successful man, a man of industry—would smile at her in that way. She hasn't been looked at like that in years. She turns toward Cesare and finds him deep in conversation with the painter from the South. He didn't see anything. But, then, what was there to see? Nothing happened, nothing at all. It was a smile, just a smile.

A dozen men exit the hole and move quickly away from it. The breeze suddenly picks up and Arianna closes her eyes, holding them shut until she hears the sound of helicopter blades. Vittorio points it out to her. It's a green military thing, floating unnaturally in the air, twenty meters from the ground. Then, the voice from the megaphone: *Ten. Nine.*

—You should put on your glasses, Ivo says to her as he slips on a pair of mirrored Ray-Bans.

Eight. Seven.

She smiles at him.

—I'll take the risk.

Six. Five.

And Ivo thinks how beautiful Arianna still is, and turns once more to watch her furtively. Even though she is looking straight at the hole, Ivo is sure she knows he is staring at her, and she likes it.

Four. Three.

And Arianna thinks that it would be wonderful if all the defective bombs that hadn't exploded during the war had been made that way on purpose, if they were *created* that way by some kind of a small clandestine army of pacifist saboteurs—because of course she was a pacifist!—present in all nations, all unaware of each other's work but guided by the same convictions: good gnomes who, while they built bombs, made one out of ten innocuous—or one out of eight, perhaps—by disarming it in some undetectable way that they alone knew about, and in a way that no one else could ever discover, like pulling out a hidden wire or undoing a special screw, making the bomb nothing more than an enormous piece of iron, dangerous only if it landed on your head.

And what a wonderful film they would make from the story of these men who sabotaged silently and secretly, risking imprisonment or even death on the spot, always quietly reciting the same words or even prayers as they sabotaged—enemies of their state only because they were devoted to a higher idea, the idea of peace!

Arianna pulls her coat around her, holds on to Vittorio, and closes her eyes.

Two. One.

THE SMELL OF THE NEW

IF YOU LOOKED AT PASQUALE CITARELLA—not an inch over five feet six, a Nazionale cigarette hanging from the corner of his mouth, shoulders and legs curved by all the weight he lifts every day, sky-blue eyes fixed within a square face that never failed to appear friendly—he wouldn't seem very different from all the other fathers who, exhausted and sweaty and dusty, returned to the Green Zone to join their families for dinner.

That evening, Pasquale was once again the last one to return home after a spectacular sunset had celebrated the end of a tedious February day, leaving behind an immense Prussian-blue sky. Many of the other fathers had already gone out to the bar, where they would spend a few hours blowing off steam talking about all the trials and tribulations of their working day, and spending the last shred of energy left in their strong hearts. Later, Pasquale would go too. He would order a glass of wine and sip it while listening to the others, or watching them play cards.

That evening, however, Pasquale had parked away from the bar and hesitated for a few seconds before opening the door of his Ape. Even though there weren't any thieves in the Green Zone—the only suspect had literally been kicked out a few months before, after a bicycle had disappeared—he had taken a suspicious look around before getting out and walking toward the house. So tightly was he holding the handles of a supermarket plastic bag from which the sleeve of a tartan shirt protruded that the knuckles on his right hand had turned white.

As he arrived at the three steps that led to the door of the house in the street's half-light, Pasquale struggled to enter because he did not want to release his grip on the plastic bag, and so had to perform a partial, painful contortion of his body to get his left hand into his right-hand pocket, where he had his keys. When he finally managed to extract them, ripping his pocket in the process and peppering his efforts with a series of whispered curses, he failed to find the right key among all of those on the key ring, and had to clumsily try at least three of them with his left hand before finding the right one.

When the lock finally gave way and the door burst open, he closed the door behind him and allowed himself to smile. He took a deep breath to fill his lungs and let it go very slowly. Suddenly reenergized, he climbed the stairs two by two, went directly into the bedroom, and called out to his wife.

—Maria, come here!

—I can't right now, Pasquale. I've got water on the stove!

—I said, come here now!

She grumbled under her breath, but within a minute she had calmly arrived from the kitchen, climbing the stairs with the economy of time and gestures of someone who has to climb them many times a day. Then she stopped on the threshold of the bedroom, her heart suddenly pounding, a hand over her mouth, unable to say a single word.

On the double bed they had just bought, on the lace blanket her mother had sewn for her as part of her wedding trousseau, was a mountain of money. Banknotes of all sizes: five thousand, ten thousand, fifty thousand, even some of those large one-hundred-thousand-lire notes she had only seen in the movies.

Her husband was plunging his hand into them and holding them up, then watching them float slowly down back onto the bed.

—Oh my goodness! What have you done, Pasquale?

—Maria, this is our money!

—What?

Maria couldn't take her eyes off the pile.

—Where has it come from? Who gave it to you?

Pasquale didn't reply. He was watching the falling money, mesmerized. He struggled to raise his gaze from the banknotes and looked at her for a few moments without saying a word, then smiled.

—It's the down payment for the work on Barrocciai's warehouse. Vezzosi gave it to me. We will build the biggest, most beautiful factory in the city. What am I saying, in the whole of Tuscany! Even the Milanese will be jealous of us, Maria!

—How much is there?

—One and a half million lire.

Maria, who could not even begin to imagine such an amount, ran her hands through her hair and left them there.

—What do you mean, Pasquale, a million and a half just for painting?

—Maria, I'm not just the painter. I've been made site manager.

—Site manager? Do you even know how to do that? You're a painter, Pasquale!

—I'm a bricklayer, too.

—A bricklayer? Since when? Who taught you?

—I've seen them work, Maria. It's not difficult. I know how it's done. It's not a problem, as Barrocciai always says.

—Pasquale…

—Maria, listen to me, don't worry. It's really no problem at all. And then I can learn on the job. You don't have to be Brunelleschi…Come on, Maria. Touch it.

The woman shook her head, as if he had asked her to stroke the head of a vicious dog.

— Come on, Maria. Sit down.

Her eyes sparkled.

— Oh my goodness...

She sat on the bed.

— Touch them.

— Can I?

Her husband smiled, and she stretched a hand out toward the banknotes: at first she just stroked them, then, encouraged by his amused smile, she took two of the newest notes in her fingers and rubbed them together, and was taken aback by the consistency of the paper and the faint sound of friction.

She brought them to her nose, closed her eyes, and inhaled an odor she had never experienced before, one that was like no other. It was a strange smell, the sum of others, many others, and while the strongest was certainly a potent chemical scent, like acid, she could also make out a vague, far-off perfume.

That money smelled of damp, of ink, of plastic, of sweat. Of darkness. Of lost sleep and fatigue. Of recompense. Of merit. She told herself that it must be the smell of work: that immense and far-away world which, until that moment, she had never dared hope to come into contact with. But then she realized she was wrong. It wasn't the smell of work. It was the smell of the *new*.

She opened her eyes and wanted to tell Pasquale, but he was so pleased with himself, batting his eyelids and playing his childish game of sinking his hands into the banknotes, that she decided to keep quiet.

— It's not all ours. Some of it will have to go for tools. But it's money, Maria. Real money, our first real money.

Dino and Tonino came in, beckoned by their parents' voices, and reacted just as their mother had done, stopping still on the threshold with their hands over their mouths. Pasquale burst out laughing and his heart started to beat faster, and he was certain that he had never been so happy in his entire life. And then a bright white light suddenly shone in his eyes and he became entranced by the pinwheels circling inside that light, and he felt as if he was falling, and then found himself sitting in a cinema, all alone, watching a film, the film of his life.

There he is in 1959, at nineteen years old, newly discharged from military service, leaving the train station with a suitcase in his hand, whistling to himself like Buster Keaton. He makes his way toward the city center, where he sees a textile mill, walks inside, and asks if there is any work. He is hired on the spot. They tell him to put his suitcase in the corner and show him to a gigantic loom.

There he is just a few months later, he has a problem with his boss and resigns, leaves the mill and walks to the one next door. He asks if there is work and they hire him immediately too, and there he finds himself once again sitting by a loom.

There he is trying to earn a little more, learning how to paint from Michele Russo, who has also arrived from Ariano Irpino. He quickly realizes that he prefers painting to sitting at a loom, and so he resigns from the second textile factory and starts work as the assistant to old Russo, painting the rooms and warehouses and apartment blocks that spring up around him like mushrooms.

Maria arrives in 1964, and they manage to get married just before the arrival of Dino, and he moves from the attic he lived in with his parents and sisters to the attic of another house, bigger and more spacious. Tonino is born in July 1966, and Pasquale decides to work on his own, while she will start working from home. This means cycling up to the factory that produces blankets, loading the blankets onto the handlebars, taking them home to get rid of the knots and braid the fringes, being paid thirty lire per braid, and then taking them back to the factory and picking up more, every day but Sunday.

There he is, painting an apartment all by himself and dreaming of buying himself land and building a house on it when he meets Vezzosi, who hires him on the spot and offers to pay his overtime in the form of a *work discount*, which means sending over two builders on Saturdays and Sunday mornings to help him build his house in the Green Zone. There he is in February 1968, he is entering his own house with Maria and the children — it is a *baiadera*, the curious, inexplicably Spanish name that is given to a small, single-story house by the inhabitants of his ebullient city.

Pasquale is now twenty-eight, has a job and a house of his own, and can afford to go to the cinema with Maria once a week in his white shirt. And at the cinema he sees a world full of things he doesn't have and he wants them so much, and when he goes home to his *baiadera* he no longer feels the relief of having left the attic or the pride of owning his own home. Instead he torments himself because his family doesn't have a telephone or a car or a dishwasher, and now he pities the neon circle that hangs from the ceiling to light their minuscule kitchen, the Formica table, the fridge with its iron handle, the sofa in artificial brown leather, the doors with ribbed glass, and the tiny black-and-white Telefunken television! But he says nothing to Maria and doesn't lose heart, and tells himself that it is neither a fault nor a sin to be born poor, but you have to do everything you can to get out of poverty, and so he accepts every job he is offered, and paints more than he has ever done before and never sleeps more than four hours a night, and is always the first person to arrive on site, which is just one of the hundreds and thousands of building sites throughout Italy where millions of people work because there is an Italy to be built — not to be restored or refurbished, *built* — and the air itself smells of paint, gasoline, plastic, and rubber.

There he is one evening, going home and saying to Maria that the *baiadera* is too small and that they need to add another floor, and she raises her eyes from the blanket and tells him he is right, and seeing her in agreement with him, full of desire and hope just as he is, Pasquale gets all fired up, and the next day calls Moreno Barbugli and Franchino di Oste to tell them they must build another floor, but it needs to be done right away because it has to be finished by September, or it'll be raining on Maria and the children, and so they call Claudione and Claudino, and here they are, all five men, working like demons all through August, and when they finally finish it is only mid-September and it hasn't rained even once, and Pasquale Citarella has a two-story *baiadera*!

They celebrate with the rabbit stew that Maria cooks so perfectly, then open a flask of red Chianti given to him by Vezzosi, and some of the wine ends up even in the children's water, and they chirp excitedly and run up and down the stairs over and over, and Pasquale is so moved by their joy that he must make up an excuse, get in the Ape, and go for a drive so that nobody sees him cry, and while he travels through the dirt roads of the Green Zone, tears running down his unshaved cheeks, he starts to tell himself that perhaps there is a real hope of making something important for his family now, thanks to his work, but when he reaches the new ring road and all the cars and trucks and motorbikes overtake him because no matter how hard he presses on the accelerator, the Ape cannot go faster than forty kilometers an hour, Pasquale decides — he actually shouts it in the cab — that the time has come to buy himself a car, because he has dreamed of it since forever and now it is time to stop dreaming, because dreams grow old and die if you don't make them real.

There he is in 1971, on his pale green Fiat 128, celebrating with the family with a trip to Montecatini to taste ice cream.

There he is in 1974, giving his father the contract for the small apartment he bought for him from Vezzosi on the promise of paying it off in work over the next few years, and there he is in 1976, doing the same thing for Maria's father, who was also living in an attic, but that was yesterday...

Then he heard Maria calling him from afar and the film suddenly ended and he found himself again in his room, sitting on the bed, with his alarmed wife holding his face in her hands and telling him something he couldn't understand, and next to her the boys were looking at him too, their eyes wide, and they also were telling him something he could not understand, and at that moment Pasquale knew that this was how he would die: all of a sudden he would detach from life and would never say or hear anything again—he would just float in the same mute, distant peace in which he was floating now, and then he would close his eyes.

But then he smiled, said hello, and the three of them threw themselves around his neck, embracing and suffocating him, then they all fell onto the bed and the money, laughing like madmen. When the boys had finally calmed down and returned to their room, Pasquale said to his wife, "Okay, put it away now."

Maria turned to look at him and was about to ask him how and where, but as she saw him counting the notes, carefully dividing them into three piles and then tying them with elastic bands, she realized she didn't have to ask. She had to know how and where to hide the money from thieves.

Then Pasquale told her he needed to call home down south right away because he needed help, and would get her two brothers and even his cousins to come up, because there was plenty of work for all of them. Upon hearing the best news she could ever wish for—she was very close to her brothers and couldn't bear anymore the thought of them spending their days at Panni's Bar Centrale—her eyes filled with tears, and Pasquale saw her standing in the middle of the room, wearing her tomato-flecked apron and crying with her hands full of money.

—If only you could see how beautiful you are, Maria. You look like the Queen of Sheba!

HE LOSES HIS HEAD

AFTER MAKING LOVE, they slowly get into the car. It is a beautiful spring evening, and the breeze blowing through the open windows carries the intoxicating scent of flowering jasmine.

Cesare Vezzosi is happily exhausted, his body invaded by endorphins, his muscles finally relaxed, as he has just left between the sheets all he had. Every so often he looks at her. Satisfied, voluptuous, softened by sex, she keeps her eyes closed while the wind ruffles her hair as if in a caress, and he couldn't be any happier or more proud that she is his girlfriend and his lover, his little hairdresser, his one and only Historic Baby Doll.

Cesare smiles as he catches the pine scent of the shower gel they just washed themselves with, stroking one another, free from the wild urgency that had governed them just an hour before.

He is comforted by the quiet, subdued rumble of the silver Alfetta 1.8 he has just bought: it suggests that a vast and radiant reserve of energy is ready for him, but even if speed is for Cesare a synonym of life itself, this is not the right time to accelerate anything.

He takes a deep breath and tells himself that it might even be possible to live a life better than his, yes, but he just can't imagine how. He looks at her. She has opened her eyes and stretches out a hand toward his oversized right arm.

Infinitely confident, Cesare asks, "So how's your sex life, baby?"

—Perfect. With you it's always perfect.

—No, not with me, with the others. Your sex life without me.

—Ah, she says, turning her gaze away from him and toward the road ahead. That one... Well, it's okay. Not like with you, of course, but it's full enough...

A slap. No, a punch. No, a hammer blow. A shot. His lungs and his stomach melt, and a void opens inside him. The gentle breeze from the car windows becomes an arctic wind that cuts his skin, and he can no longer smell anything. Cesare takes his foot off the accelerator and the engine hiccups, unable to sustain fifth gear with the motor running so low. It would have turned itself off if he had not automatically pushed the clutch.

The suddenly stuttering motor causes her to turn and look at him, and all she sees is Cesare staring at the emptiness in front of him, his hands gripping the steering wheel, his mouth half open, his hair ruffled by the wind, the neck of his shirt suddenly slipped back onto his shoulders.

—Full? Cesare manages to ask, his heartbeat pounding, his face contorted in a ridiculous grimace. How is it full? What does that mean?

—You asked me a question and I answered...

—Yes, but what... what did you say?

She looks him straight in the eyes, until he has to shift his gaze to check the road ahead. Then she says, "I have a boyfriend."

—I don't believe you, he announces immediately, and smiles, because it's not true and it can't be true. But then he turns to look at her face — surprised and worried and sincere and young, suddenly way too young — and he stops smiling.

—No. I can't believe it. It's not possible. It's not true. I can't believe it and I don't believe it.

She continues to stare at him.

—It's not true. You would have told me, I know ... I'm sure ... No, I'm not going to believe that.

Then he remembers to change gear, and when he turns to look at her again, he finds her pressed up against the door, as if to distance herself as much as possible from that moment, that conversation. Maybe even from him.

—Really, I don't believe it.

—Cesare, I've got something going with one guy, okay? But it's nothing serious, really. There's no need to worry ...

Dozens of responses start to amass in his head. Dozens of wrong and useless responses, because everything has already happened behind his back, and who knows how long it has been going on. Weeks? Months?

—But why didn't you tell me? Why ... how ... why should I find out like this, by accident, just because I asked that stupid question?

—I didn't tell you because it's not important, Cesare, and it's probably going to end soon. And I'm sorry, but it was you who told me to find myself a boyfriend ... What's wrong now, Cesare? Are you angry?

At that moment he realizes he will never, ever get used to sharing her with someone else; that from now on he will say and do a lot of stupid things; that this is just the beginning of a shitty time and it's going to be a very long shitty time; that he will have to start talking to her differently now, and that will be a mistake; that he will have to start behaving differently toward her now, and that will be another mistake; that he will only make mistakes with her from now on, one after the other, and he will promise her things he never promised before, and it won't work, and he will beg her, and that won't work either.

Nothing will work anymore, and he will need her at times and in ways and circumstances in which he had never needed her before, when there was no doubt that she would always be there for him. He will find himself wondering at the hidden meaning of every word she says from now on: every question, every expression and pause, every sign of uncertainty and reluctance, every smile and sigh will become infinitely more significant than before, and he will begin to interpret them as if they were messages from another world, and when he will not hear from her for a few days, life will become very difficult, because he loves her and he is totally unable to react to this situation, and always will be.

—No, I'm not angry, he says in a voice just that bit too high, because I don't believe you. It's . . . it's not possible. If it were true I'd be angry, of course. You are too important to me. But it's not true. I know it's not true.

The silver Alfetta stops in front of her house, and in a sudden moment of clarity Cesare realizes that their future largely depends on how they leave things tonight, the words they say, and so he summons up all of his strength and manages a smile that looks a little like one of his own, but it immediately crashes against the new expression he sees upon her face: a mix of surprise, uncertainty, fear, and yes, unfortunately, satisfaction.

—Come on, it's not true. I don't believe it.

And then again, hating himself while he says it, yet feeling entirely incapable of stopping himself, "Tell me it's not true."

The Historic Baby Doll looks at him for a moment, opens the door, gets out of the car, and puts her face into the frame of the lowered window.

—I'm sorry, Cesare, but I don't understand you. I really don't. Good night.

Cesare nods and barely manages to whisper a goodbye. He starts off slowly, looking at her in the mirror as she becomes smaller and smaller before disappearing altogether.

NEW YORK CITY

—HELLO?

—Mom?

—Who's speaking, please? Who is calling at this time of night? Who is it? You're scaring me, who is it?

—Mom, it's me...

—Ivo! Where are you? Your voice sounds so far away...

—Mom, I'm in America!

—In America! Have you already arrived? Are you well?

—Yes, Mom, everything is fine.

—How was the journey?

—Well, I'm a bit tired...With such an early start and all the flights, I've been traveling for nearly a whole day.

—My goodness, all that time on an airplane! What did you eat?

—I'll tell you, Mom, I always like the food on the plane.

—*Ardengo, pick up the telephone!* Ivo, are you at the hotel?

—Yes, Mom. I'm at the hotel. On the thirty-fifth floor.

—*Ardengo, Ivo is calling from America!* What time is it there? Here it's midnight.

—It's six o'clock here, Mom.

—In the morning?

—No, Mom. In the evening. Pass me Dad.

—*Ardengo!*

—Mom, please, don't shout!

—He won't come otherwise. He's gone half deaf. He's down in the basement, watching television. *Ardengo!* Ivo, listen, how can it be six there if it's midnight here?

—It's the time difference.

—Yes, I know. Your father told me. But I don't understand. I don't think he does either. What is this time difference, Ivo? How can it be?

—Mom, the Earth moves around the sun, and as it turns, in some parts of the Earth it's day and in other parts it's night, and so it can't be the same time for both us, because I'm on the other side of the world, you see?

—Hmm...Well, now that you've arrived in America, you can come back here. Your room has been cleaned and dusted. I've ironed all your shirts and picked up your trench coat from the dry cleaners. What are you doing there? Come home, understand? Otherwise I worry.

—Mom, don't worry. I'm fine.

—Hello, Ivo. I was in the basement. Please excuse the heavy breathing, I ran.

—Hi Dad...

—Ivo...

—Dad...

—Tell me, Ivo...

—Oh, Dad...

—Yes...

—Dad, this city...this city is incredible...

—Really? Tell me about it.

—You would not believe it. The skyscrapers...

—What are they like?

—They're...infinite, Dad. I don't know if I can even describe them...But just think that today it was foggy and the tips of the skyscrapers were lost in the clouds...And the streets, Dad, the avenues that run through Manhattan...If only you could see how beautiful they are...They're enormous, Dad, wider than our highways...

—My goodness, Ivo...

—Next time you have to come with me.

—Yes, I owe America a lot! And you too! We all do!

—I know, Dad. I know...

—They freed us from Fascism and poverty!

—I know, Dad!

—When they passed through Narnali with their tanks and trucks, they would throw us chocolate and candies!

—...

—Ivo...

—...

—Ivo...are you crying?

—...

—Just look at this fool. He's in New York City and he's crying!

—It's so...overwhelming, Dad. It's truly overwhelming...

—Go on, Ivo, it's fine.

—It's such a great moment for me...Being here for the first time, Dad, and on business, not as a tourist...I only hope I'm up to the challenge. I really hope I'm as great as you and Mom, and all of you...I wanted to tell you that...

—Stop it, you fool, or you'll have me crying too. Tell me about Fifth Avenue!

—Yes, Dad. Fifth Avenue is beautiful, but I have to say I was more impressed by Sixth. They call it Avenue of the Americas! All the skyscrapers are full of offices, and there are so many people working in them! So many people from every possible race and color...And, I've even seen Radio City Music Hall!

—My God, Ivo, you're making me jealous!

—If you could only see how badly they dress, all of them!

—I knew it! Americans always dress badly!

—It's like they couldn't care less. I'm sure some of them dress badly on purpose!

—And Broadway, have you seen Broadway?

—Yes, yes, I was about to tell you! So, Dad, Broadway is a diagonal street, sorry, a diagonal *avenue*, it cuts through all the others, which are straight. I've even been to Times Square!

—Broadway! My son is on Broadway!

—Oh Dad, if you could see how spectacular it is!

—Hey, behave yourself, it's full of prostitutes there!

—Prostitutes, Dad? Who cares about prostitutes! Who has ever gone with one, anyway? Park Avenue is fantastic, too, perhaps the most beautiful … It's all residential, and also the widest because traffic moves in both directions, and instead of guardrails they have long flower beds, and inside the flower beds there are sculptures by great artists, even Pablo Picasso! But if you could see these apartment blocks, Dad! Outside there are doormen in uniforms with braids, and limousines as long as boats, with their motors always running, waiting for the ladies or the gentlemen … But out on Park Avenue people are very elegant, Dad. Ladies in furs, dogs with dresses, and all the governesses pushing children in carriages and strollers …

—It's like you're showing me a photograph, Ivo! It's like I'm there!

—But Dad, listen to what happened to me. I walked the whole length of Park Avenue, it goes on for miles, and at one point I noticed that there weren't any more limousines, and that the people weren't as elegant, the opposite actually, and the apartment blocks were ugly and low, badly kept, and I started to see so many black people, all standing around in groups on street corners, and they were giving me strange looks. Dad. I'd ended up in Harlem!

—In Harlem? Ivo, are you mad?

—Yes, in Harlem, in the midst of total poverty, and I was very sad to see all those men without a job, and I thought that a textile mill there could solve all their problems...I'm sure they would be happier making textiles than selling white powder in the middle of the street. Anyway Dad, you really need to come here, and with Mom, too!

—Hmm, she doesn't travel well...She's scared of airplanes, you know that. Her feet swell.

—It's not true! Ivo, don't listen to him! My feet do not swell up in the airplane!

—Quiet, Fosca! Eavesdropping, are you?

—I don't eavesdrop! I answered the call from my son and I stayed on the line! I want to hear about Ivo in America too! He's my son as well! And you're wrong, Ardengo, it only happened once, that swelling, when I went on honeymoon to the Canary Islands!

—Ivo!

—Yes, Dad.

—But how have you managed to see all these things already, if you only left the house this morning?

—Well, the highway was full of trucks so I barely made it to the airport in Milan to catch the flight to London. And even in London I was very lucky to get to the plane at the last second, and I arrived at JFK in the early hours of the morning. I went straight to the hotel, took a shower, and since it's Sunday and I don't have anything to do until tomorrow morning, I pulled on a pair of comfortable shoes and set off to explore the city!

—Ivo, I don't understand. You arrived there in the morning?

—Yes, nine a.m.

—Nine a.m.? That's impossible! The flight takes eight hours...

—I flew on the Concorde.

—Concorde?

—Yes, Dad! It's fantastic, like traveling in time!

—Are you mad? How much did that cost?

—Eight million lire.

—Just for the flight?

—Yes. A round-trip flight, obviously.

—And did you go first class?

—Concorde is all first class.

—Why did you spend all that money, you fool?

—I wanted to make the right impression when I got to America, Dad.

—What? I don't understand. Who? Who did you see?

—I did it for myself. I wanted to start on the right foot. It's a question of personal pride, Dad. And without pride I can't work. I know I could have taken an Alitalia 707, in economy. I would have had a tiny seat at the back of the plane next to the toilet, thrown in with all the tourists—it would have cost me less than a million lire—but I'd have arrived in New York exhausted and depressed. No enthusiasm, no nothing...

—Ivo, I don't understand you...

—Dad, the clients need to be shown a movie. You have to arrive in their offices looking like a million dollars, with your hair perfectly in place, fresh from the shower, smelling of cologne, super elegant, and you have to make it clear from the beginning that we Italians are the best in the world at making textiles, and no one else even comes close. And that we don't only produce fabrics, we create fashion, we *are* fashion, we're the real designers—otherwise they won't buy anything from you... Dad, you have to go to the clients with a boner, like you say, and if you've flown second class and you've slept in a little hotel room, you have no boner, and there's no movie to show, and you don't sell a damn thing, you see?

—But you've spent a fortune, Ivo, for Christ's sake! Which hotel are you staying in?

—I'm at the Hilton! On the Avenue of the Americas! I'm on the thirty-fifth floor, and from the window I can see the whole city right down to the new Twin Towers! I know I'm spending a lot of money, but these are business expenses, the company pays for it all, and at the end of the day I don't need to justify it to anyone, especially since this is all hard-earned money...

—I know, I know Ivo. That I know...

—I'm like you! Honest to the core! And I just wanted to give myself this much. I wanted to see if I could do it, see if I could have this victory...

—It's a very costly one though.

—But I'm not doing this for the money! I'm not interested in money. I'm doing it for me, Dad. I understood that today, while I was on the Concorde. It's all or nothing.

—Hmm...

—And I'll tell you, I enjoy spending my money. I might be a fool but it's the right thing to do. If you've got it, you should spend it, otherwise the wheels don't turn. The day I start saving is the day everything will be over.

—Listen, Ivo, talking about spending money, today I went to your building site! You know it's Melchiorre's field?

—Melchiorre? Who's Melchiorre? How was the building site?

—Well, I just saw a few plastic cables...Citarella was there with his hands in his pockets, looking really sorry for himself. He's good, that guy. Vezzosi was nowhere to be seen.

—Ah...

—Anyhow, there's no rush to get into the new building, Ivo. Don't you worry. You're fine at the blanket factory, and you don't have to pay rent. You just have to think about selling...

—Dad, I've spent the last month going around the world selling.

—I know, I know...Who would have thought that my son would become such a hard worker?

—Please, Dad, could you go and check on the building site now and then?

—I don't want to overstep the mark...

—No, go, please go and check up on it. Put your foot down. You be the boss.

—Okay. Listen, when are you going to see your clients?

—Tomorrow. My first appointment is at eight a.m. They're all in the same area. Then I'm going to Montreal, in Canada.

—Bravo!

—I'm always on the offensive Dad, and even if I don't sell anything this time, I'll sell next time! It's not a problem. This city is full of excitement, of ferment, of expansion... It's another world, really... Okay, Dad, now I have to say goodbye to you and Mom. But I want to thank you for everything.

—For what?

—For everything, Dad. For everything. For my whole life. Thank you.

—Ivo, it's your turn now!

—Ivo, come back soon! We'll be waiting for you!

—Okay, Mom. Bye everyone. And good night. Sorry about calling so late, Dad, but I wanted to tell you all about it.

—Not a problem, son. Good night!

—Ardengo, you need to wish him good evening, not good night! It's late afternoon there! There's a time difference!

—Okay, Fosca, I know... This woman is getting worse every day.

—If you don't know something, I'll tell you. Good evening, Ivo. And send us a postcard with the Statue of Liberty!

—Of course, Mom.

—Ah, Ivo, make sure you go to the Empire State Building! Right to the top! And then tell me what it's like! It's always been a dream of mine!

—Yes, Dad, I'll go and then I'll call you!

—Bye then, Ivo, bye!

HE COMPLETELY
LOSES HIS HEAD

HE COULDN'T STOP THINKING ABOUT HER.

Her cheerfully calling the Other to plan their evening together, then asking the girls in the beauty salon to blow-dry her hair and fix it with hairspray before running home, chased by their compliments, to carefully choose her lipstick and try on shirts and tops and skirts and dresses until she finds the right ones.

Her smiling in the mirror and spraying onto her neck little bursts of Shalimar, the perfume that he — poor idiot — had given her, that heavenly perfume he liked so much, the one that smelled of the plastic dolls are made from.

Her leaving the house and greeting the Other with a chirruping "Hi" and a kiss, and getting into his car and spending the trip to the restaurant looking at him as if bewitched, then sitting at the table and flirting and blushing more and more with each glass of red wine and each compliment, and after coffee she wants to make love, and she tells him, and when they leave the restaurant, she pretends to be a little more tipsy than she really is, and lets him take her by the hand and open the door for her and kiss her, and at that point Cesare's imagination mercifully came to a halt and refused to go any further.

It was like being stabbed repeatedly, as his thoughts gave him no respite. They only stopped at sunrise, when he would fall asleep for a few hours, and then they would immediately resume upon waking. He could not understand how this had happened. When, and why, and where was he at the moment the Historic Baby Doll decided to open herself up to another. He couldn't believe that she needed more sex — not after all those afternoons they had spent making love with an intensity that each time left them exhausted, soaked with sweat, legs trembling: her lying there with her eyes closed, trying to catch her breath; him listening to the wild beat of his heart, watching the ceiling, infinitely proud to discover himself a great lover.

So what had happened? What could she possibly be missing?

As is always the case with winners, Vezzosi did not know how to lose or deal with the consequences of a loss, and so he spent his days fumbling about, lurching between wild mood swings.

Half the time he was apathetic and full of angst, while the rest of the time he became the Beast, spouting expletives for the smallest of reasons, punching the dashboard of his Alfetta, kicking his office door, revving the motor like a madman every time he got in his car, and if someone dared to look at him the wrong way, he would immediately invite them to pull up and get out of their car.

Defenseless and dazed, furious and weak, Cesare only managed to get to the building site once, with Citarella, to lay the fixed cables that had been cleared away by the blast, but upon seeing the mess in that field he lost heart. The task of building such a big and beautiful factory on that bombed-out field seemed impossible, the fruit of the unbridled ambition of an impetuous young man who, sooner or later, would pull out and leave him to deal with it all. He told Pasquale he wasn't feeling well and that he would call him.

He spent his days in the office with the light off and his head empty, his right hand resting on the telephone waiting for the only call that didn't arrive. And every so often he promised himself to call Citarella to tell him he'd be at the site the day after tomorrow, but he didn't do it out of fear the call would tie up the phone line he needed so desperately to keep free. He always went home late, after dark, kicked about by his guilt.

Even his appearances at the tennis club grew rare, and when he found himself struggling to beat one of the juniors, he feigned tennis elbow and announced to his friends at the top table that, as a result, he would not be back in time to play the tournaments and team competitions that year. Then he stopped going to the tennis club altogether.

He spent the nights walking through the house in his underwear and socks, brooding and recriminating. He convinced himself he had never truly been understood. Not by anyone. Ever. He was a decent, sensitive man, he told himself, full of noble sentiments that he had always been forced to hide beneath a warrior's armor.

What kind of Beast am I, he muttered in the dark living room, surrounded by framed photos of his victories. A soldier in ferocious times, that's who Cesare Vezzosi was, forced into inexcusable hardships by having to spend every day in the arena, constantly surrounded by opponents as hungry as himself, if not more so, painfully misunderstood even in his own home, where he had to make do with pretending to feel passion for a woman who did not love him, and whom he no longer loved.

In the depths of one of his darkest nights, he decided he would have to confess to the Historic Baby Doll that he loved her, and could not live another day without her. Yes, he had to tell her everything. Every single thing.

Tell her that when he left the Den after making love to her, he felt like a lion and the whole world was his for the taking. That being next to her made him forget all those years of listening to his heart beating slow, of wearily taking care of his family and work, of being celebrated for victories that weren't real victories.

Tell her how he was certain that, as an old man, he would end up on a balcony watching people passing in the street below, alone and absentminded, with a white shirt open down to his stomach in the summer and wrapped up in plaid in the winter, and that he would only smile at the rare moments when he remembered those afternoons spent making love with her, when they were young and crazy and didn't realize that the life ahead of them was bright and free like the Autostrada del Sole.

The morning after, he woke up and drove to the office at full speed. When he arrived he had to get rid of Citarella, who had dropped by again to ask about the building site: "Don't come around here no more!" he yelled to the painter, and walked into the office slamming the door behind him. He then waited for the cathedral bells to strike eleven, put the telephone in his lap, and dialed the number for the beauty salon.

After three rings the Historic Baby Doll answered with her shrill voice, "Excelsior Beauty Salon, good morning," and, overcome by emotion, all he managed to say was his name: "It's Cesare." She asked him where he had been all that time and when could they meet because *she was dying* to be with him, and Cesare barely managed to contain himself, his heart suddenly pounding in his ears, his dick already stiffening in his trousers, so immediately happy that all he could stammer out were a few truncated words, and he had to force himself not to throw in a tattered "I love you."

The few hours that separated him from the appointment grew interminably long. Lunch at home seemed never-ending, and his excitement brought him to apply the immortal rule of Porfirio Rubirosa, the one that recommends an early afternoon wank to those who have an important appointment in the evening. But when the Historic Baby Doll finally entered the Den without apologizing for being late—it was already nearly five o'clock—Cesare embraced her warmly, without giving her time to even take off her coat, and when he caught the scent of her hairspray he was so moved and turned on that he started to kiss her with all the passion he had never shown her, and touched her most intimate parts with a delicacy that soon became frenzy, and screwed her better than he had ever done, and she had never reached orgasm so many times, and so completely.

When they had finished, the Historic Baby Doll curled up like a cat next to his undersized left arm and showered him with caresses and kisses. He smiled with his eyes closed and enjoyed each of those endearments, which he had hardly been able to bear before, and began to fantasize about how she would react to the declaration he was about to make. Would she cry, overcome by joy? Or maybe she would faint out of happiness? How do you revive a woman who has fainted? Is it enough to slap her delicately, as in the movies?

He smiled and was about to start talking when she spoke.

—You weren't really angry the other night when I told you about my boyfriend, were you, Cesare? Because I thought a lot about it, and I don't want you to be angry when you're with me. Never, never, never. For me, you are and always will be the guy for the good days. At the beginning I was upset, I really was, but I eventually understood: you're right, that's how it should be, and so I want to be the same for you. Your girl for the good days...

Suddenly filled with desperation, Cesare had to close his eyes, and when he reopened them—who knows how much time had passed—she was watching him, worried, her large eyes blinking.

At the sight of the uncertain smile that unfolded across her face, Cesare forced himself to smile and told her that no, of course he wasn't angry, and she was right. Of course she was right. He drove her home and waved at her as she got out of the Alfetta, cooing. Then he set off and drove aimlessly along the roads that slowly started to empty, knocked out by the heartbreaking notes of Fausto Papetti's saxophone.

It was over. She was leaving him. She would have given him time to get used to the idea: another fuck, maybe two, and then it would all be over. Cesare burst into tears like a child, sobbing and hiccupping. He had to stop in the middle of an elevated supermarket parking lot that he couldn't even remember driving to, and it took him the whole of Papetti's tape to get himself together, while mothers and small children walked past the Alfetta in droves, laughing and pushing their clattering shopping carts filled with stuff, without so much as looking at him.

He decided he couldn't let it end like that. And like all desperate people, he raised the stakes. The next day he rang the Historic Baby Doll and invited her to Monte Carlo for the weekend. Taken by surprise, not least because Vezzosi had only ever invited her to the Den, she answered how that would be wonderful, really wonderful, but that she wasn't sure if she could come. What would she tell her boyfriend? Cesare swallowed hard and insisted, and the Historic Baby Doll got nervous, cut him short, and told him she would let him know. The next morning, however, she called him early to say that she would come. The night before she had argued with her boyfriend, and then she had never been to Monte Carlo and had always wanted to go.

Cesare had to spin Arianna an acrobatic excuse that she accepted without comment, fixing her gaze outside the window: there were problems at the building site, he told her, and they needed to visit a specialist in avant-garde masonry in Milan, but given the commitments of this famous expert, he could only meet him in the late afternoon on Saturday, and then, given how late it would be, he would sleep in Milan rather than driving back through the Apennines at night, which is always dangerous.

And so Cesare Vezzosi and the Historic Baby Doll left for Monte Carlo late one Saturday morning in a newly washed Alfetta, under freezing rain that followed them all the way there, and when they got to the hotel, there was a note for her at reception saying she had to call home immediately: her mother had suffered abdominal cramps that morning, just after they left, and so the Historic Baby Doll had to spend hours on the phone organizing help for her, while he watched the rain beating against the glass of the only window in that hotel room with a street view, which they had been forced to accept instead of the room with a sea view that Cesare thought he had booked, and about which he had boasted the whole journey.

All these circumstances made the Historic Baby Doll nervous. At dinner, she didn't at all like the bouillabaisse he had ordered for her, or the Beaujolais he had chosen to accompany it—"You don't drink red wine with fish, Cesare, come on!"—and then she became very irritated when, having just set foot in the casino, Cesare immediately took her away because his old employers were sitting at the roulette table, squandering some of their undeclared earnings on gambling and prostitutes, half a dozen of whom encircled them hungrily, giggling like hyenas, each (Cesare couldn't help noticing) undoubtedly and painfully more beautiful than the Historic Baby Doll, who, with the worry over her ailing mother, the strain of the journey, the squalor of their room, and a total lack of comprehension of how gambling could be fun, had taken very little care over her clothes and makeup, and had eventually decided on a sequined dress that was too tight, making her look both chubby and shiny.

So they went back to the hotel at half past ten, after a brief and tense walk along the seafront, which was being blown about by a cold wind that had no place on the Côte d'Azur in late spring, and they began to bicker over nothing until, at a certain point, the Historic Baby Doll fell silent and refused even to take his arm, bitterly resentful of having gone on that disastrous trip and plagued by guilt over the lie she had told her boyfriend.

Once they reached the room, after begging and pleading, Cesare managed to convince her to give herself to him, but partly because of the general anxiety and partly because of the bouillabaisse, he was not able to pleasure her, and to the frenetic babbling of excuses that flowed from his mouth, she responded that there was always a first time for everything.

So, at half past eleven, they miserably began preparing themselves for their first night together, and in the silence that had now grown impossible to break they had to take notice of all the odors and noises that followed their time in the bathroom. She pulled on a ridiculously long, pink nightgown with lace trims and hoisted the covers up to her face, turning her back on him and falling asleep almost immediately. Vezzosi stayed awake until dawn, watching the ceiling and listening to the yelping of cats scrapping in the alleyway. Even with her next to him in bed, he was already looking forward to seeing her again.

Totally incapable of breaking free from the maelstrom, over the following days he began to assail her with very affectionate, very badly judged phone calls. He no longer cared that the Historic Baby Doll had given herself to someone else: he was now fighting with the sole intention of delaying the moment of final separation, trying to keep alive the hope of fucking her just once more, if only to free himself from the thought of that unthinkable, shameful *défaillance* that continued to burn in his memory.

She always answered the phone, but no longer wanted to see him. She hated being begged, as he had lowered himself to do, and she always declined. Politely, of course. But she declined. Every time. And the day he sank to the level of inviting her to meet him for a coffee, the Historic Baby Doll lost it and asked him where the Beast that she liked so much had gone, and when Cesare — whose poor heart had fired up after that blow — answered that the Beast was on holiday, and that it was Cesare, her only real boyfriend, who wanted to see her if only for five minutes, and a coffee would be fine because couples always drink coffee together, the Historic Baby Doll's voice hardened. This was also a first.

—Cesare, we have never been a couple, she said to him.

—We have never spent enough time together to build a lasting relationship.

—We had a great time, but it's over now. Let's try not to hurt one another. You've got everything you could want from life, Cesare. Don't insist.

And she hung up.

He remained immobile for a few minutes, staring at the receiver, incredulous, his mind blank and his soul stripped bare, and he died. The Beast took his place, furious.

Don't insist? he asked the thin air.

Don't insist? he repeated, louder.

DON'T INSIST? he shouted and stood up, smashing the receiver into the telephone and breaking both parts, then he pulled the cable out of the wall and threw the telephone toward the window of his office with all the strength of his oversized right arm, shattering the glass. He grabbed his appointment book and, hemorrhaging obscenities, ripped out the many pages in which he had written her number and destroyed them in the paper shredder, hoping that sooner or later he would forget that crude sequence of odd numbers that had been etched into his mind.

Then he stopped and burst into tears.

THE ARMY OF DREAMERS

ARIANNA HAD WOKEN UP before dawn and couldn't get back to sleep, so she had lain in bed without moving for an hour, not to disturb the snoring Cesare beside her. At seven o'clock she silenced the alarm clock, slipped out of the bed, and strode down the corridor to wake up Vittorio. She opened the windows of his room, chose his clothes, and made her way into the kitchen to prepare breakfast. She laid the table with a checked cloth, biscuits, melba toast, and butter and jam, and waited for her two men to arrive. They sat themselves at the table without saying a word, picked at their food, sipped their coffee, and then left with a few mumbled words of farewell, leaving her a prisoner of the empty, terrible freedom she had never wanted or asked for.

She stepped into the shower, washed her hair, applied the conditioner, and carefully rinsed it out. Then she wrapped herself in her bathrobe, dried her hair — first with a towel, then with the hair-dryer — brushed it, and then slowly dressed in a striped top and a skirt, only to find that it was still the early morning of a day in which she had nothing to do.

No visits to pay or errands to run. No shopping to do. No reason to go to the grocer's or the bakery or the butcher's shop. No laundry to do. Nothing. Her family did not need her anymore.

It was no longer necessary to support her husband, as had been the case in the early days of their marriage, when he would always moan that he couldn't stand working for others and not for himself, or when, after setting up his own business, he realized that his competitors were much better prepared and had much better connections than him.

On the contrary, after the injection of enthusiasm for the unexpected assignment he had been given by Barrocciai, she was wondering if she shouldn't start keeping an eye on him to make sure he didn't cheat on her, if only it were possible to keep an eye on a whirlwind: he left in the morning with a frown on his face and was back in the evening with the same frown, and though he never told her anything about his day, he was always ready to criticize the meal—he who had never given much thought to what he ate.

Vittorio devoured his pasta and his grilled meat every day, without saying a word. He behaved well, he didn't even curse. His hair was always tidy and he liked to dress classic. He didn't hang out with the wrong crowd, never drove a scooter, and spent his afternoons closed in his room, reading science fiction. All the advice Arianna felt obliged to give him every day felt increasingly empty and comical, even to her. It was as if she had trapped herself in the caricature of the dumb mother who fails to recognize how much, and how well, her son has grown.

At parents' evenings the teachers gave her very little time, sometimes she didn't even get the chance to sit down. The boy was forever distracted, but he studied hard, got an A plus in conduct and was equally good in all other subjects, and he would certainly pass his ninth-grade exams with an A or an A plus, and they all recommended he go on to high school and then university, thank you and goodbye.

She was no longer needed.

When she turned on the television, she found herself looking at the whistling color test screen, so she switched it off and opened *Letter to a Child Never Born* by Oriana Fallaci, but only managed to read a few pages. She was listless, tense. She went back to her room and lay down on the bed, with Cesare's raspy voice from last night's argument still ringing in her ears.

If you're bored, Ariannina, it's only because you don't appreciate everything I've done for you...

Work? What do you mean, work? I don't understand.

A shop? No way.

Who buys costume jewelry? No one!

I don't want my wife to work, people will think we haven't got any money.

No.

I don't want my wife working as a shop assistant.

You'd be seen as a shop assistant, Arianna...

You need money to open a shop, you know that?

No. The answer is no.

You'd lose it all.

You've got no business sense.

It takes a professional to open a shop, not a bored housewife...

I'm not cruel. I'm your husband, and I'm protecting you.

From failure, Arianna. From certain failure.

You aren't good at that sort of thing.

At being at home, yes.

At being a lady. Because you're a lady, not a shopkeeper.

You're good at spending money, not earning it.

You're not talking to me anymore?

Why?

Well, good night, Arianna.

Tomorrow when you wake up you'll see I'm right.

She turned in toward the blankets' embrace, fully dressed, closed her eyes, and basked in the memories of those days when she knew what to do every morning and never had enough time—those few months in 1963 in which she had gone from being a girl to being a bride, a wife, and a mother.

Bitten by a sudden enthusiasm, she jumped up from the bed and ventured down to the basement to get the projector. She carried it into the house and placed it on the dining room table, then she went back down to the basement for the box of home movies, and after many fruitless attempts that pushed her to the brink of tears, she miraculously managed to project the film of her wedding—ten minutes of brief, blurred scenes of men and women walking around in a garden, all shot by her father. She was so much younger and more beautiful, very happy and very pregnant, always smiling at the camera, waving every so often.

She remembered every moment of that hastily organized, poorly thought-out wedding. Everything.

The two frosty dinners during which she and Cesare told their parents everything. The identical stares, hard as nails, that the two mothers gave her right after being forced to embrace and pretend to be happy, while the fathers became emotional—especially Cesare's, Giuliano, who hadn't even finished middle school, and had to say: "Regrettably, Arianna, you are a good girl," and "Regrettably, you are in love," and "Regrettably, now this child is going to be born," and "Regrettably, it is with great pleasure that I say yes to this very good marriage," because he didn't know what "regrettably" meant.

The floods of tears of the morning of the wedding. The apartment invaded by smiling neighbors and Mozart's *Jupiter* Symphony, which her father had insisted on listening to at full blast. Getting dressed in the living room, continually interrupted by the arrival of crying friends. The unknown, adult Arianna she saw in the mirror staring at her, dressed implausibly as a bride. The car ride to the small country church. The terror of being late. The immaculate and heavenly scented tuberose that adorned the altar. The guests who watched her, surprised and amused because Cesare hadn't arrived yet.

The cross-eyed priest who, after half an hour's wait, had limped over and told her to have faith and not worry, because the wedding day was never an easy one for a man, and he had seen many grooms arrive late, but not one who didn't arrive. Cesare's guilty face when he had finally, after forty-five minutes, entered the church almost running, out of breath and unkempt, smiling vainly and apologizing to everyone without even attempting to explain the reason for his lateness. The slow, dignified "Yes" she had said when the moment arrived, and the pathetic mumble that had fallen from the mouth of the man who was about to become her husband. The first kick of the baby who still had no name but had wanted to make his presence felt during the ceremony—because Arianna wasn't even twenty-two years old when she had fallen pregnant, one summer night in Viareggio, on the beach, under a sky streaked with falling stars that she had watched the whole time, her eyes filled with stifled tears while Cesare fumbled about on top of her, repeating over and over how she drove him mad with desire.

When Arianna moved on to the wedding album, she realized she remembered each photo perfectly. There was just one of them she couldn't remember much about. It was the last one in the album, and the only one taken by Cesare. In that small, creased, slightly blurred black-and-white image she was composed and truly beautiful as she rested her bouquet of orange blossom wrapped in tulle on a coffin covered in the American flag: her only memory of when, on a November Sunday in 1963, still wearing her wedding dress, she had insisted on taking her bouquet to the American consulate in Florence, where a memorial was being held for John F. Kennedy.

She removed the photo from the album and put it in the best frame she had—a rectangular one in silver, a wedding gift—then placed it on a low table in the living room, next to a photo of Cesare lifting a cup. She couldn't remember why she had wanted to mark the happiest day of her life with an homage to a dead man, to dilute her joy with the pain of the people of another nation.

Arianna had liked Kennedy, of course. She found him intelligent and fascinating, but only about as much as everyone else, because everybody liked John F. Kennedy. So why? Why this single act of rebellion, the only one of her entire life, just before leaving for her honeymoon? Why give her bouquet to a dead American president rather than throw it to her friends at the party? She couldn't remember. Maybe she didn't know. Maybe she hadn't known even then. Maybe it had seemed the right thing to do, and no one had stopped her.

But then, on that desperate morning she had woken up to, she asked herself if that dream of a candid future she had hoped for since she was a child had not disappeared along with Kennedy: being the mother of a large, happy family in which everyone depended on her for everything, with lots of children to take to play at the beach and photograph in the white light of that infinite summer in which the Kennedys seemed to spend their days.

Because since she had been married, Arianna had never had another dream. Not one. All she had left were her ambitions. Cruel and cutting, impossible to control, they had slowly taken her over, forcing her to crave beauty and money and the cold well-being these bring — a bigger home, a new car, more elegant clothes, longer holidays in exotic locations, a costume jewelry shop. And then they left her there alone, locked away at home in the middle of the morning of an empty day, smoking a cigarette while looking at a painful photograph, asking herself what in her life had gone wrong.

She quietly started crying, then the telephone rang, startling her. She ran, cleared her voice so her husband wouldn't realize she was crying, sat on the bed, let it ring a few more times, and then picked up the receiver.

—Hello?

—Arianna?

—Yes?

—Hi, Arianna, sorry, it's Ivo. Am I disturbing you?

—Ivo?

—Yes, hi. Hello.

—Oh. Hello, Ivo, how are you?

—Good, thanks.

—I'm sorry, Cesare is not here. He left early this morning.

—No, Arianna...I didn't want Cesare, I—I actually wanted to talk to you...because there's something I wanted to tell you. I hope I'm not disturbing you...

—No, no...Don't worry, tell me.

—No, it's that...All right, okay, I'm abroad. I'm in Montreal, in Canada, and it's early morning here...Well, very early...The sun isn't even up, and I think the time difference has got to me this time, because I woke up at four a.m. and now I'm here calling everybody because I just can't get back to sleep, and...well, I just wanted to call you and say hi...

—Ah.

—I hope you don't think I'm being inappropriate...

—No, why should I? We've known each other for a long time, haven't we?

—Yes, exactly, it's just that—yes, of course that's true, but there's also something else I wanted to say to you. The thing is that seeing you the other day after such a long time had a strange effect on me, a very strange effect because...well, you really are beautiful, Arianna. Very beautiful indeed...Time hasn't passed for you, it really hasn't...

—Come on...

—I swear, honestly...You're magnificent.

—Now you're making me blush...

—Am I making you feel uncomfortable, Arianna?

—A little, Ivo, yes...

—Oh, I'm sorry. I hope it's bearable though...

—Well, I don't know. Let's assume so...

—I'm sorry, but I just had to tell you, and...All right, I'll say goodbye now and I'll go bother the receptionist to see if they'll serve me breakfast...But it was good to hear your voice and...Just know that I've always been a big fan of yours, ever since school. There's no one else like you, Arianna. You are special.

—Thank you, Ivo, but I'm totally normal. Believe me.

—I don't believe that for a second. Good morning from Montreal then!

—Bye, Ivo.

Arianna hung up and looked at the telephone for a few seconds, as if it could reveal the true story behind that phone call, then she took her bag and went out, a curious smile on her face.

A CRUMB OF LOVE

CITARELLA'S APE SLOWLY ADVANCES along the tortured dirt track that cuts the field in two. He has to drive in a zigzag to avoid the myriad potholes that would instantly shatter the fragile suspension of his Ape, and the feverish concentration his task requires absorbs Pasquale so much that he only notices at the last moment that, on the other side of the field, right in the middle of the lot in front of Ivo's, there is an enormous yellow cement mixer surrounded by a dozen workers and a wildly gesticulating Brunero Barrocciai.

Shocked by this unimaginable sight, Pasquale loses concentration and allows the back wheel to slip into one of the holes, causing the Ape's suspension to hit the ground with a loud crack. Brunero and the workers all turn to look at him, as he realizes with horror that he cannot get the wheel out of the hole because it isn't really a hole but a puddle of mud, and accelerating does nothing more than send dirt flying in all directions into the frozen January air.

Trapped, his face now tomato red, Pasquale turns toward the group and sees Brunero giving him two thumbs up like Fonzie, then saying something to the workers. There is a loud collective chuckle and three men detach themselves from the group and move toward him. He doesn't know any of them, they can't be local. Florence, it sounds like from the accent.

They don't even give him time to get out of the Ape. They easily lift the vehicle with him inside and place it down on the track, and one of them—a bearded giant—smacks the roof of the Ape, undoubtedly leaving a dent, before making his way back toward the cement mixer. Pasquale sets off slowly, trying to preserve what little dignity he has left as he pulls into Ivo's lot, which the rain has transformed into a vast quagmire. He stops the Ape in one of the few grassy areas, turns off the motor, runs his hands through his hair, and grips it tight, his fingers entwined in dry, jet-black locks.

What should he do now? Get out of the Ape and walk around pretending he came there for a reason? And what is he supposed to do after walking around, all alone in that abandoned field, with no tools? He doesn't even know why he has come.

He had been waiting for months now for Vezzosi's Alfetta to appear on the dirt track. Once he even dreamed of him: Vezzosi was arriving triumphantly, standing on the hopper of a bulldozer and barking orders at a crew of steelworkers who followed him on foot, shouting his name and waving their welding torches: "Vez-zo-si! Vez-zo-si!"

Cesare hadn't been seen on site since the morning they were supposed to mark out the new cables, a few days after the bomb. He had arrived an hour late, with a three-day beard, and had spent a long time staring at the bomb-scarred field without saying a word before suddenly leaving, muttering something about a terrible throat ache. He never came back. He made a few appointments he never kept and eventually even stopped answering the phone, forcing Pasquale to drive up to his office where, however, Vezzosi had always refused to let him in, ranting through the intercom about a nervous breakdown and how he required assistance in his hour of need. He went on stammering that he had helped Citarella when he was *walking around barefoot begging for work*, and that *he must never call him again under any circumstances, and especially never come to his office and ring the fucking bell because he was going out of his mind and all he could think about was this woman who had left him*—some kind of history teacher, if Pasquale had understood correctly.

Money wasn't the problem, because Barrocciai didn't seem in any way concerned about the state of the site either, and continued to pay his wages regularly. At the end of each month Gabriella would call him, and he would go to the old firm to collect a white envelope with cash inside.

What was killing him was having to stay at home and put up with Maria's silence and her concerned looks—and thank God he had managed to find work at a twisting mill for her brothers, who had come up from Panni to work on Barrocciai's factory!

Citarella couldn't and didn't want to take other jobs because he had given his word to Ivo, and so he had repainted his *baiadera*, his father's apartment, Maria's father's apartment, and Barbugli's one-story *baiadera*.

After all this relatively unnecessary painting, however, Pasquale found himself with nothing to do, and had to lie to Maria for the first time in his life. He announced that the building site was finally open, and each morning he woke at seven, left the house, and spent the day at the field. If it rained, he would sit in his Piaggio Ape doing the crossword, otherwise he would walk up and down the abandoned lot, chat with Melchiorre, watch the clouds chase each other across the sky, and measure the land with giant steps, ever deluding himself that Vezzosi or Barrocciai were about to arrive.

Pasquale despairs. Of everything. Of making such a fool of himself with the Ape. Of having to spend his days in a field. Of lying to Maria. Of being paid good money to do nothing. He even despairs of Brunero starting to build before them, because he certainly is not the boss or the owner of anything, and has nothing to do with the rivalry between Ivo and Brunero, but he cares for his employer's business as if it were his own.

But most of all he despairs at having put all his trust in such a foolish project, and he despairs of himself, of having even thought he could become a site manager when he only knew how to paint. He had let his pride get the better of him. He had been hypnotized by the thought of all that work, by that bag full of money. He had wanted too much and now would have nothing.

Pasquale looks at the empty quagmire from which such a wonder was supposed to spring forth and for the umpteenth time he is dismayed by the obscenity of all that waste — Barrocciai had paid hundreds of millions of lira for those ten thousand square meters of land left to radicchio — and he smiles bitterly as he remembers the words he said to Barrocciai in that cramped cubicle: "Everything will be fine, Mr. Ivo. Don't you worry. It'll all be fine."

Where was that Pasquale? Where was that young man who would have never given in to despair because he had a family to support, and no other choice but to hold on in the face of all adversity? He feels a knot of anger rise up in his throat, and shivers, but the very moment he is about to collapse, he grabs hold of the image of that optimistic and courageous young man who didn't have a penny to his name but dared to encourage a businessman, and for a moment he smiles, and with that smile he remembers the story Maria used to tell the children at bedtime when they were little: *that every smile is a brick you use to build a house*, and so a new, fragile chain of positivity is born in his heart, and if Maria is the first ring of the chain, Pasquale realizes that he must be the last one — the guy who lays that brick, or no one else will.

He is deeply, deeply moved, and tells himself that to restart that courageous enterprise from scratch someone must go beyond the call of duty, and it must be someone who feels a little love for the project, "just a crumb of love," as Barrocciai used to say, and that person could only be him. Him and no one else.

So he gets into the Ape and sets off without so much as a glance at Brunero's workers, who clap at him as he passes by at a snail's pace. It takes him twenty minutes at full speed to get to Barrocciai Textiles, where he quickly overcomes the obstacle of the frosty kindness of the new girl sitting at reception, who vainly tries to stop him, explaining that Mr. Barrocciai is leaving for Frankfurt and cannot see anyone.

Pasquale is already racing up the stairs, two at time, unstoppable, and the plebeian noise of his steel-toe-capped boots drowns out the clacking sound of the typewriters and fills the factory's quiet halls. He stops in front of Ivo's office, the one that belonged to Ardengo, pokes his large head into the room, and sees Ivo giving orders to three young secretaries. He clears his throat and Ivo raises his eyes, a gesture immediately mirrored by the young, doelike women, each more graceful than the next, who all turn to look at him. Pasquale's face instantly turns the color of a boiled lobster, but he still manages to speak.

— Ivo, I need to talk to you.

— I can't now, I'm leaving.

— It's important.

— Pasquale, I can't right now…Wait a moment. So, ladies, I think I've answered all your questions. Where are the samples? Ah, here they are. Good. You've got the phone number for Frankfurter Hof. Leave me a message at reception and tell me everything that happens today, but remember I won't get it until this evening, because I'll be going straight from the airport to the customer, and it's going to be a long trip and a long meeting. If there's a real emergency, like the whole place going up in flames, first call the fire brigade, then call me, okay?

The ladies nod and stand up to leave the office, but the door is blocked by Citarella's Quasimodo-esque form.

— Ivo, I need to talk to you right away.

—Pasquale, I've told you. I haven't got time. I need to go to Pisa to get the plane to Frankfurt and I'm already late. Speak to Cesare. We can sort things out once I'm back, okay? In three days' time.

—Ivo, Brunero is laying his plinths today.

Barrocciai stops, flanked by the girls who follow the conversation, turning their swanlike necks from right to left, as if watching a tennis match.

—What does that mean?

—He is laying the foundations, Ivo. He's starting to build. Before us. And if he starts first, he will finish first . . .

—How can he be starting before us? It's not possible. What does Vezzosi say? Where is he? What is he doing? I haven't heard from him in months.

Citarella shakes his big head, just once. Ivo stares at him.

—Ladies, please go back to your desks. Gabriella, close the door. So, Pasquale, tell me . . .

—The field was leveled out after the blast, Ivo, but we've done nothing since. We haven't even relaid the fixed cables.

—How? In all this time? And Vezzosi?

—Vezzosi isn't well. He's had a nervous breakdown and can't come to the site. And without him, we can't do anything.

—A nervous breakdown? Why? What's happened?

—I don't know, Ivo. He's shut himself in his office and won't even answer the telephone. He must be worried about the build . . .

—About the build? He hasn't even started.

Citarella shrugs.

—I just don't understand, Pasquale. I know I should call him, but . . . Guys, I just can't do everything by myself. I mean, I have to do sales, building the factory is your job. I — But tell me, what's the story with Brunero?

—This morning he was there with his workers and a cement mixer. Ready to start.

—This is incredible. This is…Can't you get things started, Pasquale? You're the site manager, aren't you?

Pasquale looks at Ivo, and hopes he remembers that he is just a painter, so he will not be forced to repeat it.

—Laying the plinths is difficult, Ivo, and I don't feel I should go over Vezzosi's head while he isn't well…And then he told me the building has been designed in a particular way, because you wanted the factory to face — was it the sunset?

Ivo closes his eyes for a few seconds, then grabs the telephone.

—Gabriella, get me Andrea Vecchio.

He hangs up.

—He's my Sicilian friend. I met him in Taormina having dinner at the Miramare, with Lo Turco. He was with his wife and I was with—who was I with? I can't remember right now. Well, we were sitting nearby and so we started to talk, we drank Malvasia from Salina and became friends. He's a great guy, Vecchio. He builds all sorts of things, from what I've understood…big projects. Roads, bridges…a factory is nothing for him. He's an incredible guy. The Mafia were threatening him and he told them to fuck off. I don't know if you understand, Pasquale: *the Mafia*…They were setting fire to his diggers, and he reported them to the police. He's like that. He began working in factories and moved his way up. Like me, like us…

The telephone rang.

—Andrea! Hello, how are you, my friend?…Good, good, and you? Everyone well at home?…Yes, of course, of course I'll be over soon, but first you need to come and see me in Tuscany…Actually, Andrea, can I ask you something? It's very important. You remember the factory we talked about over dinner?…Yes, yes, the crazy one, that's it. With the swimming pool on the roof. Yes, the Olympic swimming pool. Look, I'll be straight with you: something has happened, I won't go into details over the phone, but I need you…Yes. Now. No, we haven't started yet. Yes. From scratch, Andrea, from scratch. There was a problem with a bomb...No, nothing like—no, no, really, absolutely...Don't worry, Andrea, it wasn't an attack, it was just a bomb left over from the war...Yes, work has stopped. Stopped dead...The plinths? To tell you the truth I don't know. I'm traveling the world and can't follow the work personally...I know, I know...Pasquale, are the steelworkers already on site? Andrea is asking if the cages have already been built.

All Citarella can do is close his eyes.

—It seems they haven't, Andrea. But the cables have been laid, right? Pasquale? No? Not even those? Andrea, my friend, we are seriously behind schedule. We are actually standing still, to tell the truth, when we should be moving fast. You remember Brunero?...Yeah, the one who left me his hotel bill at the Miramare. That stingy scumbag, yeah...Yes, exactly, the cretin with the good-looking wife. He bought the land next to mine and has now started to build before me. Andrea, you know what that means, right? A challenge, yes. You're right, it's unacceptable...Really? I can't believe it. Tomorrow? Really? You'll be here tomorrow morning? Well that's incredible! What a great friend you are! No, don't you worry. Andrea, I just need you to get things started and then I'll sort myself out. But thank you, thank you so much! I'll get my representative to meet you at the airport, Mr. Pasquale Citarella. Yes. Pasquale, tell me your office phone number.

Pasquale, taken by surprise, stares at him for a moment, then gives Ivo his home number—Maria would answer the call and would know what to say.

—Andrea, I'm afraid I won't be here tomorrow as I'm leaving for Frankfurt, so you will need to talk to Pasquale...Of course, I understand. Yes. Absolutely. I'll book you a nice hotel, and if you can stay an extra day I'll take you to dinner in Florence, to Sabatini's, where they do steak just the way you like it. Okay then, bye, and thanks again!

Ivo hangs up and looks at Pasquale.

—Perfect. We're all set. Tomorrow afternoon you go and pick him up in Pisa with my Alfetta. He told me his flight gets in around three, but check with Alitalia. Do everything he says. He is a fantastic guy, and a real friend. We are all set, Pasquale. I've got to run. Bye.

And he races out of the office.

JUST LIKE THAT

WHEN PASQUALE CITARELLA and Andrea Vecchio arrive at the building site, tightly squeezed into the front seats of the Ape, they are met by the taunting of all twelve of Brunero's workmen, lined up along the edge of the lot.

—Look, the *Marocchino** is back!

—Hey, there's a new one today! So, two *Marocchini*!

As they drive past, Vecchio silently watches that row of young, sturdy men—three of them are players of Calcio Storico, the medieval game that is played every year in Piazza Santa Croce, right in the center of Florence, by the city's toughest—as Citarella turns purple with embarrassment for himself and for Ivo and even for the city that adopted him, because it is a shame that this Sicilian gentleman, who arrived at the airport with two bags full of exquisite almond biscuits, should be welcomed in this way. He is so agitated that he accelerates on the dirt track to move away from those thugs, but is unable to avoid a series of violent jolts to his poor Ape, which provoke another round of jibes.

---

* *Marocchino*, literally "Moroccan," is one of many pejorative terms used by northern Italians to designate those from the South who arrived in droves to provide a workforce for the postwar economic boom.

When a defeated Citarella finally reaches Ivo's lot and stops his Ape on the dry grass, Andrea Vecchio gets out and starts walking slowly toward Brunero's workers, with Pasquale rushing after him.

The Sicilian is not an inch over five feet three, his thick, chestnut-colored beard merging with thinning brown hair that has been carefully combed backward, wearing a suede jacket over a blue lambswool sweater, a white shirt, flannel trousers, and stitched English shoes. He quietly approaches the group of workers while the young men continue laughing and joking around the largest of them all — the bearded giant whose hand had left a dent on the roof of Citarella's Ape and who now stands with his arms folded, in his shirtsleeves despite the cold.

— Good morning. I would like to talk to the site manager.

— That's me.

The giant is well known throughout Florence and the whole of Tuscany for many fistfights and various prevarications which have earned him the nickname Mazinga, after the colossal robot from the Japanese cartoons. Vecchio stretches out his hand and Mazinga, taken by surprise, bends down to shake it.

— My name is Andrea Vecchio, and the gentleman with me is called Pasquale Citarella. We are two *Marocchini*, as you say. I am Sicilian, and Pasquale here is from Campania. I have to say this is a new definition for me. In other parts of Italy we are called *terroni*,* and I was used to that name. But it's not a problem. Your term, *Marocchini*, is fine with me. It has its exotic charm. I'll keep it in mind. Now, I'd like to place a bet with Mr. Brunero Barrocciai, who, I have been told, is your employer, and an acquaintance of mine...

Andrea's calm voice stops and, as he looks each of those young men in the eye, his serene gaze seems lit by an internal flame, as if a furnace was burning inside him.

---

*This is another pejorative term, perhaps the most common of those used to insult the Italians who live in the South. It is impossible to translate literally, but a very rough meaning could be "people who live by the products of the earth."

—I can't see him here, so I will make the bet with you. I see you have already laid a dozen or so plinths.

—Eight.

Citarella notices that after Vecchio made it known he was a friend of Brunero's, the men started to look at him differently. They have tensed up and no one is laughing anymore. Many now keep their sinewy arms folded on their chests, as if to protect themselves from the slow words of the Sicilian.

—Good, you are at an advantage then, looking at the cables you've laid…Even if some have lost tension, and will certainly need to be tightened up…

Vecchio points to the farthest side of the rectangle marked by the fixed cables, and all the workers immediately turn in that direction, while Mazinga keeps his eyes on the Sicilian, almost folding his neck because of the disparity in height.

—Your factory…or rather, the factory you are starting to build…It'll cover about two thousand five hundred square meters, correct?

Mazinga nods.

—Two thousand five hundred square meters, that's right.

Vecchio smooths his thick, chestnut-brown beard, then smiles.

—So it will be smaller than ours, much smaller. Exactly half the size, because ours will cover five thousand square meters, and on two levels, making it ten thousand square meters in total, while yours is only on one level, I suppose…So I would like to make a bet with Mr. Brunero that we will finish before you. Even though we haven't started yet. Are you in? Or rather, can you ask him if he accepts?

Vecchio takes his wallet from his inside jacket pocket, pulls out ten banknotes of one hundred thousand lira each and puts the dishcloth-sized bills in the enormous hand that Mazinga, upon seeing the money, has automatically stretched out.

—If you win, Brunero keeps the money. If we *Marocchini* win, however, he will give me two million, and I'll take him out for dinner the next time he comes to Taormina. Agreed? We'll see you soon then, Mr....

—Franchi! Mazinga proclaims, a bright, childlike smile suddenly lighting up his warrior's face, and he shakes the hand Vecchio is holding out. "Lorenzo Franchi! I will make sure I pass it on to Mr. Brunero, Mr. Vecchio. Good day to you. Wish the gentleman a good day, boys."

Eleven mighty throats enunciate their respectful goodbyes, as Vecchio turns and makes his way toward Ivo's lot, followed like a dog by Citarella. In the distance, slowly winding their way along the dirt track, two brand-new trucks—one full of steel and the other of steelworkers—and an immense cement mixer advance toward Ivo's lot.

—You put them straight, sir!

Citarella plods merrily through the wet grass, five or six meters behind Vecchio, who suddenly stops, not in the slightest bit bothered about muddying his English brogues.

—Eh, Pasqualino, let's just say that where I live I've had to deal with characters a little more troublesome than these idiots...From your accent I can guess that you're not from here. Where are you from?

A relieved Citarella tells him everything. The whole story.

About his father who worked on the railways in Ariano Irpino, and who one day said goodbye and left for the North.

About the phone calls he made once a week to the public telephone box, and how all five of them would immediately leave the house, with their mother in front and him at the back because he had to make sure that his little sisters didn't fall in the street and scrape their knees.

About that special call that his father made one day, saying that he had found a job at a brickworks and they were paying him forty thousand lire a month and so now they could come, too.

He told Vecchio everything.

About his father coming home and saying that up north there was work for everybody and they all had to go there right away, and so they sold their house and the wheat field and left.

About the journey, with his father traveling by train and he, his mother, and his sisters squeezed into the cab of Nunzio's small truck—Nunzio being a man from Ariano who worked as a driver for a furniture company in Florence, and rather than going back with an empty truck, he had filled it up with their things, which really weren't much at all: a table, the mattresses, the suitcases, and his father's Lambretta.

About how they ventured over the twists and turns of the mountain roads because they couldn't take the highway or the police would have stopped them and sequestered Nunzio's truck.

About how they arrived in Ancona at dawn and he saw the sea for the first time and swam in his underpants and the water was warm and calm and shimmering, and a silver-colored fish had darted around his feet.

Everything.

About how they finally arrived after a full day's travel, and how immense that city had seemed to him! All of those houses! Those enormous sheds! And that omnipresent noise that Nunzio said was the sound of the looms, which he said were black machines made of steel and as tall as a man, and made textiles.

He even tells Vecchio his secret, how he had decided the minute he arrived that this was his city, not Ariano, and how he would always strive to be worthy of living there: he would be good at school, and after school he would go to work to help his family. He tells him how he made this promise to himself, at ten years old, in the cab of Nunzio's truck. He crossed his fingers in front of his mouth and swore it.

Vecchio nods and stays quiet for a few long seconds.

—That's a great story. And it does you justice. But tell me, Pasquale, what's going on here? How did Ivo think it would be possible to make this project work? Has my friend lost his mind? Who is the site manager? Where is he? It can't be you...

—No, Mr. Vecchio, I'm the painter.

—So where is the man in charge, then? Tell me. I don't believe he's ill, it's not possible. Men don't have nervous breakdowns. Where is he? What has happened to him? Did they get rid of him? Was he stealing?

—No, sir. He lost his head over a woman. A history teacher.

—And he has stopped coming to work?

—He says he can't. He's lovesick.

The slowly approaching convoy has been joined by another titanic truck carrying a digger, and it goes slowly along the narrow, uneven track with the grandeur of a military parade, paralyzing Brunero's workers and leaving them speechless in the face of its unstoppable advance.

—Hmm, love, women... But now you have to explain to me what the hell this sunset business is about. This crazy matter that Ivo wants to watch it from his office, because I just can't understand it. In which month does he want to see it? Are you aware here in Tuscany that the sunset moves in the sky during the year?

Pasquale, Ptolemaic to the core and never fully convinced that the Earth isn't the unmoving center of the universe, shrugs his shoulders.

—Let's assume, then, that my friend wants to see the sunsets in May and June, when they are long and beautiful and heart-wrenching, and their beauty will console him while he is still working at eight o'clock in the evening. Which means...

That formidable little man looks at the sky, takes out a compass, stares at it, looks once more at the sky, and holds out an arm with his finger pointed upward.

—The factory will face *this way.*

SKIPPING SCHOOL TO READ

HIS MOTHER BURST INTO THE ROOM like a drill sergeant, throwing open the door and excusing herself for not having heard the alarm clock. While she opened the shutters and the window to let light and air into the room in an Apollonian attempt to cancel any trace of the night, as if darkness was dirt, she told him anxiously that it was late and he had to be quick, and ran off to prepare his breakfast, without even looking at him.

This was a stroke of luck, because as he languidly drifted in and out of sleep before his mother's invasion, Vittorio had been engaged in yet another attempt to have his first wank. He had managed to preserve from a dream the image of a girl with red hair and freckles who smiled at him and touched him right there. Upon finding his dick erect, he had started to jack off furiously, and at the very moment his mother had entered his room like a tornado he was starting to feel the far-off warning of a new, profound languor, and he startled, full of fear and shame and anger because once again he would not get to the anxiously awaited emission of that "sticky, transparent liquid," as it was described by his friend Fede, who swore he had reached that crucial moment and had felt "a really strange feeling, difficult to describe but really, really cool, and afterward you feel all weak and tired and loose, but it's really, really great."

While his highly efficient *corpora cavernosa* emptied of that untimely influx of blood, Vittorio gave himself a swift, catlike wash so he would be ready to show up for breakfast as relaxed, distracted, and virginal as ever, dip a biscuit in his milk, say good-bye to his mother, and walk to school without showing any suspect swelling beneath his fly.

He could have taken the bus, sure, but there were problems with the bus. Every time Vittorio set foot on one, he was assailed by a thousand illogical and invincible fears: that the bus would miss his stop and keep traveling toward the unknown; that the bus would stop where he needed it to stop, but he wouldn't be able to get off, blocked by a wall of people who refused to move aside and let him get past; that the bus would never stop anywhere, because the driver had lost his mind—and what could he say to the driver, when there was even a sign that forbade you to speak to him?

He also had a mortal fear of the ticket inspector, a figure whose semblance he could scarcely imagine, having never actually seen one, and so, like a hare, he lived in constant fear of an unknown threat, and his fear was reinforced by the intimidating tone of the signs stuck to the bus windows: those terrible yellow stickers, always picked at the corners by nervous young nails, which warned that there would be "spot checks" on passengers to make sure they were "in possession of a valid ticket," and threatened exorbitant fines.

He was also scared there might be bullies on the bus, or a madman, or "someone with bad intentions," as his mother always said. But above all else, he was scared of getting off the bus at the wrong stop and finding himself in a neighborhood he didn't know and eventually getting lost in that city of his, which seemed to grow and change every day.

So, no bus. Every day, unless there was torrential rain, Vittorio walked to school and walked back home. He didn't mind it. He had more serious problems. That morning in particular he was tormented by the certainty of being ill, very ill, and smiled bitterly at the idea that upon seeing him walking to school in his loden, his flannel trousers, and his Clarks desert boots badly misshapen by hundreds of soccer games, no one would have guessed his tragic destiny.

Because after months and months of fruitlessly choking the chicken, one day Vittorio had locked himself in his room and consulted the encyclopedia under *Penis*, *Testicles*, and *Sperm*, until he had discovered with horror the existence of *anorgasmia*, a very rare pathological condition which he was immediately convinced he suffered from, because not only did he fail to produce "the sticky, clear liquid," but he hadn't even arrived at the "really strange feeling, difficult to describe but really, really cool, and afterward you feel all weak and tired and loose, but it's really, really great"—and what a slap in the face it was for him to discover that many men suffered from premature ejaculation!

He was bursting with desire just like any other fourteen-year-old, his stomach tied in knots every time he saw a photo of one of those statuesque actresses who shone in his masturbatory pantheon, and he found his dick standing to attention at least three times a day, and yet he was unable to emit his seed joyously like every other creature of earth, sea, and sky, and had to keep on reading about wild fourteen-year-old kids who were impregnating their classmates up and down the country, from Veneto to Sicily!

If entrusting his father with the news of that rift in his masculinity was out of the question, how could he possibly tell his mother? How could he explain to her the symptoms of this incurable disease, and the circumstances in which he had discovered it?

Hammered by insurmountable doubts, Vittorio pushed on through the labyrinth of medieval alleys that would lead him to school, and immediately found himself part of a loose, boisterous procession of kids. That morning, rather than entertain him, the unapologetic collisions, the cigarette smoke, the cries and the squeals and the shrieks of the girls, melted in a great clamor that reverberated off the palazzi and deafened and upset him. Vittorio slowed his pace and let the most raucous group overtake him, quietly accepting pushes and insults, and when he found himself at the back of that human river, among the slowest, with the most timid and silent girls, he slowed even further and let them all overtake him, even the late ones running along, sweating and panting, until he was the last. The last one of all.

Vittorio stopped in the middle of the empty street and smiled. If he hurried — a short run would have been enough — he still could have managed to arrive on time, sit at his desk, and follow the geometry lesson of the first hour — that morning the teacher would explain the parallelepiped. But he waited. He inhaled deeply and exhaled slowly. He counted to ten, then to twenty, then to fifty.

There was no way he would make it on time now. He was skipping school for the first time in his life. His classmates had all done it, even some of the girls. He hadn't. Vittorio smiled and smelled the still air of the city center, which seemed fresh and sizzling with adventure. A burgeoning sense of immense freedom and happiness was growing in his chest. He could do whatever he wanted. The world was his.

On his right he saw a narrow street with two tiny sidewalks interrupting the irregular pavement of ancient stones, and he walked down it with the spirit of Livingstone. After fifty or so meters, he found a small bookshop and stopped to look at its minuscule window display. At the center of it was an old seat, with three extremely elegant white books written by a certain

Samuel Beckett leaning against the backrest. The small space around the seat was occupied by tiny heaps of science fiction paperbacks whose titles could only be read by twisting one's neck, and the flaming covers of Marvel comics were scattered all over.

Vittorio went in. There were two small rooms: the first was lined with wooden shelves that smelled brand-new, and stacked on them was the complete series of *Spiderman*, which began with the very first editions, the ones he shared with Dr. Strange — the wizard of Greenwich Village, whose sensational girlfriend Clea had bright white hair and was a sorceress, the niece of the terrible sorcerer Dormammu. Alongside *Spiderman* were other collections: *Daredevil* with the Silver Surfer, *The Fantastic Four* with Warlock, *Thor*, *The X-Men*, and the full series of *Conan the Barbarian*. The second room was dedicated to science fiction, which occupied the entire wall in front of the till, behind which a thin man with a stubble was reading *The Exorcist* by William Peter Blatty, framed by a smaller shelf full of books on theater.

Vittorio spent a few moments in ecstatic contemplation of the completeness of the range on those shelves, which stretched all the way to the ceiling, split more or less equally between the white spines of novels published by Editrice Libra (*Children of Tomorrow* and *Quest for the Future* by A. E. Van Vogt, *City* and *A Heritage of Stars* and *From Atoms to Infinity* and *Ring Around the Sun* by Clifford Simak, *The Forgotten Planet* by Murray Leinster, *Tunnel in the Sky* by Robert Heinlein, *The Left Hand of Darkness* by Ursula Le Guin, *Deus Irae* by Philip K. Dick and Roger Zelazny, *The Three Stigmata of Palmer Eldritch* by Philip K. Dick, *The Dreaming Jewels* and *The Cosmic Rape* by Theodore Sturgeon, *The City and the Stars* by Arthur C. Clarke, *Drinking Sapphire Wine* by Tanith Lee, *Nine Princes in Amber* by Roger Zelazny), and the golden spines of those published by Editrice Nord (the *Riverworld* cycle and *The Maker of Universes* by Philip José Farmer, *John*

Carter of Mars by Edgar Rice Burroughs, *Stranger in a Strange Land* and *Citizen of the Galaxy* by Robert Heinlein, *The Man in the High Castle* by Philip K. Dick, *Dune* and *Dune Messiah* and *Children of Dune* by Frank Herbert, and enormous science fiction anthologies of the golden years of science fiction and the Hugo Awards), while the fantasy section stretched out over the bottom shelves, which, at a glance, seemed to contain all the books of Conan, Kull of Atlantis, and Elric of Melniboné, and all of Lovecraft's short stories.

Seeing all of those legendary works on display, even those he had heard so much about but had never managed to find in the bookstore specializing in best sellers where his mother always took him, Vittorio was thrilled and went to introduce himself to the shopkeeper. He announced his name and held out his hand, scaring the man half to death, because he had just arrived at the point at which Father Merrin knocks at the door of Regan's house and the Devil welcomes him by hideously bleating his name from inside the infested room, as violent thuds shake the walls.

In a rush of complete sincerity that he was sure could be forgiven within the walls of that bookshop, he confessed to the shaken shopkeeper that this was the first time in his life he was skipping school, and asked if he could stay there reading until lunchtime.

He explained how he didn't have any money with him, but that afternoon his mother would come and buy all the books and comics he had read, even the ones he was only halfway through, and that over time he would have bought all of those books anyway, from the first to the last. The shopkeeper nodded, eager to get back to his book: there was no problem at all, he could read as much as wanted, and he immediately lowered his eyes back to the pages of *The Exorcist*.

Vittorio returned to the large bookcase, removed his loden, set it down, cracked his knuckles like a billiards player and picked up the largest book of all: *Asimov Presents the Hugo Awards 1955–1975*. He scanned the index in search of the most promising title, sat on the carpet, and began to read the first short story: "'Repent Harlequin!' said the Tick-Tock Man." It had been written by a certain Harlan Ellison.

IN A LIFETIME

BEFORE FALLING ASLEEP, Arianna had asked him if the next morning he would take her to visit the building site, because Ivo's factory was the talk of the town and so many people were asking her how the pharaonic work was going and she never knew what to say because he never told her anything. And when Cesare had answered that it wasn't the right moment, Arianna had asked if there was perhaps some kind of problem at the site, and then she went on, saying how she didn't believe that there was a problem, but that lots of people had been bad-mouthing the project, claiming that it was too ambitious and that they would never be able to finish it because Ivo was a megalomaniac who would soon run out of money. And even though she knew that all those words had been put in their mouths by that envious Brunero, and she didn't believe those stories, not even for a second, she would have really loved to see the building site, because she was so proud that her husband was the director of *such an important enterprise*. Then she had fallen silent for a few seconds before telling him that she loved him very much and she always had, more than anything else in the world, and that for her nothing had changed since their wedding day and she wanted to spend her whole life with him.

Cesare had answered immediately that he loved her too, of course he did, and he too wanted to spend his life with her, but it was best to wait a few more weeks before visiting the site, because right now there were so many people working on it — steelworkers, carpenters, crane operators — but he was more than happy to show it to her. Then he had done the right thing: he had called her Baby, and Arianna had melted and started to speak in baby talk, telling him it was such a long time since he had called her Baby, and then she called him Great Businessman. She had said it just like that: "Good night, Great Businessman!" Then she had kissed him on his forehead, wrapped the covers around herself, and after a few minutes was asleep.

Cesare fell asleep, too, right after her, but his sleep was as fragile as a Eucharistic wafer, and he woke up startled by the distant chiming of the cathedral bells, panting like a dog and convinced he hadn't slept a wink.

He wondered what time it was and whether he could wake up, because waking up would have been his saving grace, but he was afraid to go to the window and draw the curtains just to find out that he was still a prisoner of the deepest night.

So he waited for a minute, then braced himself, drew back the covers, put his feet on the ground, stood up, and pulled back the curtain. The sky before him and to his right was still dark, punctuated by small stars that shone palely around Venus, but on his left the night was growing soft, revealing the jonquil dawn that was about to break — the wonderful reward for whoever had survived the night, that rare marvel that the ill and lovers know well because no sunrise is more beautiful than the one you see from a hospital window, or you glimpse behind the hair of a woman in love who has held you all night long.

The dawn isn't sunrise, he remembered. His father had taught him that. Dawn is the glow that lights up the sky, but you still can't see the sun. Sunrise is when the first ray cuts through. Cesare smiled. The night was over. He decided to get up and leave the house immediately. He dressed in the dark so as not to wake Arianna, left the house, climbed into the car, and found out it was almost six o'clock.

He began to drive around the empty streets with his lights on, his mind empty and calm, and when he saw the sign for a bar, he went in to have breakfast. He found himself in the midst of a group of workers who were devouring frittata sandwiches and talking at the same time, showering the place with bits of bread and frittata while the suffocated and growling cacophony that emanated from their full mouths filled the bar's air, mixing with the smoke of the cigarettes they all seemed to be smoking, from the barista to the last customer, and the continuous thundering produced by the coffee machine in frantic activity.

As soon as he had swallowed the blistering *ristretto* he had almost lost his patience waiting for, Cesare paid and left the bar. He got back in the car and, as if by magic, the streets were filled with cars and vans and pickups and trucks and scooters which seemed to have left the same immense depot at the same time, and were now shooting past his Alfetta as if it were standing still, honking to spur him on — one man with a hat and a mustache even leaned out the window to shout *There's no time to lose.*

Having nowhere to go, Vezzosi was happy to follow the furious flow of traffic until seven o'clock, when he went to a phone booth, put his coin into the slot, and called Citarella's house. After two rings Maria answered, and behind her he could hear the voices of the children asking questions. She told him, without her usual affable cheerfulness, that Pasquale had already gone to work, so Cesare said goodbye, hung up, got back in the Alfetta, and sat there with his motor running while the traffic brushed past him cruelly.

After the harsh ending, Cesare was still suffering the loss of the Historic Baby Doll, but a little less each day. It was a minimal, constant reduction: the fruit of the hidden work that an ancestral impulse for self-preservation had activated to ensure his survival after so many signs of impending physical and mental collapse. Undetected, totally unbeknownst to him, many small dykes had been built inside his mind to stem the impetuous flow of the great river that was his desire for the Historic Baby Doll, turning it into many innocuous streams of tepid and inoffensive nostalgia, saving him from the blind suffering that had overtaken his life for months, and bringing to light the problem of the construction of Ivo's factory. Arianna's questions had just been the icing on the cake.

He had to get things started once and for all at the building site. Of course, you needed a serious leap of imagination to call that bombed-out field a building site! Who knows what Citarella had been telling his wife all that time, what lies he had invented to explain where he was going every morning at sunrise! The poor man!

He asked himself how much time had passed since the last time he had shown up there—how many months—and then he remembered all those mornings he had woken up and shut himself up in the office, staying in there all day without ever once thinking about work. He remembered he had once told Citarella to deal with everything—yes, but how? What was he supposed to do? He was just a painter! And with no plans! He had never given Citarella the plans! Where were they? In his office! He had to get them at once, he couldn't lay cables without plans! And he had to go straightaway, or Arianna would find out he had done nothing in all these months...There was no time to lose: he had to sort out the fixed cables and lay the plinths, today, immediately! He had to call the steelworkers...

Cesare started the car and left for the site, then he remembered the plans were in the office, so he headed back there, revving each gear to the red. He arrived, ran up the stairs, opened the door, and only then did he realize—and become horrified at—the foul air, the lowered blinds, the chaos, the dust, the broken telephone, the shattered glass of the window. There was nothing left on his desk, the papers and ornaments lay on the floor in a swollen, indistinct mass where he had sent them with a desperate sweep on one of his darkest days. He knelt down and, sorting through the papers, finally found the plans for the factory—all of them crumpled, some worse than others. He collected them under his arm, left the office without even locking the door, got back in the car, and headed full speed toward the building site.

He had suffered a nervous breakdown, he told himself. A big one. This is what had happened. A huge, terrifying nervous breakdown—one of those monsters that brings you to the point of no return, with a loaded revolver in your hand. It wasn't his fault, it could happen to anyone. He had lost his head completely. He had disappeared from the world for months and months. He could have ended up drooling in a straitjacket in a clinic with bars on the windows. But he had recovered. He was himself again, now, and he needed to make up for lost time.

But what had happened at the site? Why hadn't Ivo asked him anything about the factory? Why hadn't he complained at all? And why had he kept paying him every month, without delay or comment? And what had Citarella been doing all that time? Who had paid him? He certainly hadn't. And what had happened with that Sicilian friend of Barrocciai's, the consultant? Citarella had told him about this guy. What kind of consulting had he done? Maybe he was an estate agent, or a buyer…Yes, that was it, Ivo had decided to sell the land because he had finally realized it was impossible to go on with that ridiculous plan, and because he did not want to lose face in town, he had found someone from outside to do the dirty work…Maybe he had already sold the land: that's why he hadn't been in contact, and of course people were talking about the building site…Why would he even lay the plinths if he had decided to sell? But then why had Arianna told him that it was a pharaonic work? How could it be pharaonic if it hadn't even started, if they hadn't even laid the foundations?

And why was everyone in town talking about it, then? What were they talking about, an empty field? What was going on?

As he asked himself these questions, poor Cesare hadn't noticed that he was already on the dirt track that led straight to the site and had in the meantime earned itself a name, judging by the sign that declared it VIA NICOLA TEMPESTINI. Because it was still a dirt track, yes, but it was now perfectly flat and covered with a thick black gravel that made it easy and almost comfortable to drive on. Only when a bulldozer crossed the road and forced him to slam on the Alfetta's brakes did Cesare manage to escape the foul labyrinth of his thoughts and realize where he was.

Dumbfounded, he counted five structures being built: four were small sheds of a thousand square meters each, and the larger one couldn't have been much more than two thousand five hundred. Then he realized that those five factories were just satellites orbiting the main planet: a much, much larger building whose first floor was almost completed, as thirty-two huge pillars had already been erected and a floor slab laid, and it was flanked by a thirty-meter crane that was raising a huge bucket filled with concrete to finish laying the pillars for the second floor, the ones that would support the roof.

He stood with his mouth wide open for five minutes, taking everything in, then he found the courage to creep toward the building site and park his Alfetta next to Citarella's Ape. When Citarella heard the noise of his car, he turned, saw Vezzosi, and immediately detached himself from a group of workers and rushed over to greet him, a broad smile on his face.

Cesare got out of his car, and before he could open his mouth and say something desperate and cutting to Pasquale — something like how it wasn't right that they had done all that work without him, and if he thought he could do without Vezzosi he was in for some serious trouble because Ivo had entrusted the project to him, and Citarella should never forget he was just a painter and he should never try to bite off more than he could chew; and he should get respect, because Cesare Vezzosi deserves respect even if he hasn't been at the building site for a long time, because he had been ill with a terrible nervous breakdown and you don't take advantage of those in need, and anyway, he wanted respect because he deserved respect, Goddamn it—Citarella embraced him with the strength of a Marsican brown bear and, deeply moved to see him so lost and fragile, whispered in his ear

—Thank you for coming back, Vezzosi. Thank you so much. I was completely lost here. Thank goodness you've arrived. We need you, right away.

He took Cesare by the arm and led him to the group of workers, to whom he was introduced as Mr. Vezzosi, the man who had designed the factory, and everyone greeted him immediately, calling him sir, and Cesare suddenly found himself faced with a rather inconsequential dispute—a banal misunderstanding between the steelworkers and the carpenters which he resolved in an instant, and the minute he saw the workers going off in three separate directions to carry out their duties, Cesare felt a sense of pride that he hadn't felt for a long time.

And then he smiled, and told himself that he hadn't smiled in a long, long time.

A COOL MORNING

IT IS A COOL NOVEMBER MORNING when Arianna walks into a grocery store and sees Ivo buying a handful of truffles. She moves closer to greet him, he sees her and his face lights up. He embraces her and kisses her on both cheeks—they are cool from the wind—and his right hand brushes against her waist for a second.

He holds the biggest of the truffles under her nose, and when she smells its rotten, irresistible strength, Arianna starts laughing and says she cannot understand how people can eat those things. Then she asks someone to serve her and gets distracted, and only when she has finished does she realize that Ivo is still standing next to the checkout, chatting idly with the shopkeeper—asking over and over whether those truffles really are from Alba. She wonders for a second whether Ivo might be somehow waiting for her, because he suddenly cuts the conversation short when he sees her moving closer to the cashier.

Arianna has two full bags, and he offers to help her take them to the car because his hands are free: he only bought the truffles! They leave the shop together, and when they get to her car, Arianna can't find her keys. They aren't in her bag or in her coat pockets, and it starts raining. Ivo, shopping bags in hand, offers to take her home, if she'd like, or — he adds, faced with her silence and a helpless look — at least to give her some shelter.

Then the rain begins to pour and the decision is made for them. Laughing, they take refuge in Ivo's car — a blue Mercedes Pagoda whose interior still smells of leather. Ivo turns to place the bags on the backseat and the rain starts beating down like a drum on the roof of the car and the water streams down the windows and suddenly they can't see anything. It is as if the out-side world has disappeared and only they were left.

Arianna senses the intimacy of the moment and moves imme-diately to break it: she strokes the dashboard and compliments him on the car. Ivo thanks her and says that, thankfully, work is going well. Then he compliments her on the brown velvet jacket she is wearing under her trench coat and starts telling her all about velvet. He explains that no one really knows its origins, and everything they know about it comes from art and literature, but everyone agrees that the most beautiful velvets in history were made during the Renaissance in Lucca, Florence, and Venice, and how there were many types of it: cut velvet, patterned velvet, *fer-ronerie* velvet, curly velvet, brocaded velvet, *ciselé* velvet, but the most beautiful was *velluto allucciolato*, a velvet that took its name from fireflies because it had a double weft and one of them was made with a bouclé streaked with the finest thread of gold, which shone in the light of the candles. Then he tells her, passionately, about how during the Renaissance velvet was made from silk, and it was dyed red using ladybugs, which were immersed in boiling water and then dried in the sun, and it was dyed blue with indigo, which takes its name from India. Arianna listens to him without saying a word, her eyes bright, and Ivo asks her to imagine the sumptuous elegance of those Florentine women dressed in silk vel-vet, the only fabric in the world that can be both shiny and opaque.

—Just imagine a great ball at Palazzo Vecchio, Arianna. In the Salone dei Cinquecento. Lorenzo the Magnificent sitting on the throne wearing a vest of *velluto allucciolato* and admiring the greatest Italian masterpiece of all time, perhaps the only real one: the idea that life is worth living only if it's ennobled by art, by paintings, sculptures, songs, poetry...

The heavy rain and the smell of the truffles hit Arianna as she looks ahead in the sudden silence, then Ivo whispers that she is so beautiful, and that he has always had a soft spot for her, ever since they were at school, and Arianna smiles and turns and looks at him — she just looks at him and says nothing, then the smile disappears from her face and she doesn't know what to say or do, and Ivo draws close and kisses her, very slowly, on lips that immediately open, as if by reflex, and she closes her eyes and their tongues touch. They kiss for a long time, slowly, then he touches her breast over her clothes and she startles, and his hand quickly enters her cleavage and slips knowingly toward her bra, and Arianna quivers because she hasn't been touched like that in years — not with that desire, that hunger — and she feels her nipples grow hard between his fingers, then Ivo's hand suddenly moves away and reaches between her legs, it lifts her dress and moves upward until it gets to her underwear, and in a moment — truly a moment, the length of a breath — he moves it aside and his finger slips inside her, and she is wet, so very wet, and for a moment she is ashamed to reveal herself so wet, but then he starts to move his finger and doesn't stop, he doesn't stop, and after a while her back starts to arch, and when she feels another finger enter inside her, she feels as if she is rising, soaring, and she breathes in deeply, breathes out, moans, and comes, squeezing her legs tight and holding Ivo's hand inside her for a few precious seconds, before slowly opening them again. They hadn't stopped kissing, not even for an instant, and it is still raining hard, and he starts to stroke her there again and she feels everything starting again, the ascent, faster this time, and Arianna comes again, with a startle and a sound she has never heard leave her mouth: it is a yelp, both defeated and victorious and unnecessarily smothered, and it really doesn't matter that it's morning and the car is parked right in the middle of the city, it doesn't matter at all, and then she breaks away from his hands and from his mouth and leans on the door of the Pagoda. She looks at him in the eye for a brief moment and then moves close to him, strokes him, gives him a brief, feather-light kiss on the lips, and then bends toward his trousers. She opens his fly and touches his hardened penis, and begins what Ivo will remember as the best blow job of his life — he who had already received his fair share of blow jobs and would receive many more in the future.

Barrocciai closes his eyes and breathes in deeply, but then he thinks how he must remember everything, every tiny detail, and so he forces himself to open them again. He strokes her hair with his right hand while he uses his left to turn the lever on the seat in order to recline it, and some time passes, though Ivo cannot say how long, then she gives a faint sigh, and when she draws a perfect arabesque with her tongue he can resist no longer and comes inside her beautiful mouth, exhaling a long prehistoric grunt as Arianna continues and doesn't stop until he is completely finished, then she sits up and looks ahead, and at that very moment it stops raining.

SHE WOULD NEVER FORGET

LATER, AT HOME, Arianna could barely remember a thing. Not how it started, nor what had made her decide to do what she had done. She could only remember minor details: the white-and-blue pattern of his underpants, the smell of those leather seats, the scent of the truffles, the sound of the rain on the car's canvas roof. She wondered if other details would come back to her in the future, but in her heart she knew they wouldn't. And yet she would never forget what had happened, no matter how many years she still had to live.

Having never been unfaithful to her husband, and having never even imagined betraying him, Arianna did not know how she was supposed to feel. She was somewhat concerned someone might have seen her get into Ivo's car and then leave it twenty minutes later, all disheveled. However, it was highly unlikely. No one had dared go out in that downpour. The rain had been her accomplice: it had emptied the streets and turned the car windows into impenetrable screens.

It had happened, she told herself, and it would never happen again—of this, at least, she was certain. And she didn't cry and didn't feel lost or wounded or empty or shattered or, even marginally, a whore — she only felt slightly surprised that one of her few fantasies had become a reality.

Arianna took a long shower, but not even for a split second did she think that a shower was necessary to cleanse her of what she had done. She just sat on the floor and, for ten minutes or so, let the water hit her back and head and shoulders and stream down her body, without a thought in her head. Every so often she smiled. Then she dried herself, put on her gray Champion sweatsuit, and started to prepare Vittorio's lunch.

Ivo was both enthusiastic and troubled. A blow job from Arianna had been a dream of his since high school, and the sheer thought of it had led him to exhaust himself for years with long and extremely detailed wanks, but he kept seeing her getting slowly out of the Pagoda with the tiny ladder in her stockings that had occurred during that wild frenzy, and seemed to him like a wound. A wound he had caused.

He imagined her despairing, crying on the sofa and staring at the blank screen of the television, unable to restart her life after that first infidelity. Because Ivo was certain of that. Arianna had never cheated on Cesare. Never. And yet, how to explain the speed with which it happened, the decision that led her to bend over him and take him in her mouth, the way in which she had carried it out without the slightest hesitation and, more than anything, the total absence of any reaction after, apart from that fleeting smile? She hadn't even said goodbye. Not a word.

He wondered what had happened. Whether he should call her, speak to her, or see her, or not. What was best? Should he make it plain, right away, that what had passed had been nothing more than a moment of madness, or should he try to see her again and try to fuck her and then maybe start an affair? Because he really, truly liked Arianna...And what about her? What did she want to do? Why did she give herself like that? Did she do it on purpose? Had he fallen into a trap? What if she wouldn't leave him alone and started calling day and night? What if she told poor

Cesare everything and they got divorced, and she got it into her head that she would marry him? Because no one would agree to such madness! He never wanted to marry anyone; he was already married to his business! And so? What was best? To disappear, of course. It was better just to disappear. Arianna would understand. And if she didn't understand, he would explain everything at the right time, if needed. He would be kind, but firm. Of course, he said to himself, if he wasn't meeting with Cesare right after lunch, everything would be easier. Much, much easier.

THE INFINITE ABSURDITIES
LOVE CAN DRIVE A MAN
TO COMMIT

—Ivo, Vezzosi started, entering the office and sitting down on the black armchair right in front of Barrocciai's large rosewood desk. Shut the door. I owe you an explanation.

In his uneasiness, Ivo misunderstood and thought Cesare wanted an explanation from him, so he went pale and stood up. As he grasped the door handle, he wondered for a second if he shouldn't start to run down the corridor and throw himself down the steel staircase to the factory floor, where Carmine and the other workers could defend him. He told himself he had to remain calm at all costs. He took a deep breath, exhaled, shut the door, and turned slowly toward the desk. He sat back down and, memorizing the exact position of the letter opener, leaned forward to prop up his elbows on the desk, then he put his hands together and rested his mouth on them pensively.

—I'm sorry, Cesare, an explanation for what? I don't understand.

—You know very well...

Ivo gripped the side of the desk as hard as he could with both hands, as if he were strong enough to throw it at Cesare before making a run for it.

—It's very good of you to say that, however...and I do appreciate it a lot. But I also feel it's my duty to tell you about something personal that has happened to me over the last few months... Something that nearly ruined my life...Seriously...And I want to give you an explanation. No, I *owe* you an explanation.

—Are there problems on the site, Cesare?

—No, it's all running smoothly now, don't worry about the site. It will all be ready very soon...I just need to ask you a question, and you need to answer honestly. As a friend.

Was he playing with him? Cesare wasn't as ebullient as usual. He looked worn out, tired. He had bags under his eyes. Ivo let go of the desk and leaned back into the armchair, as if to distance himself as much as possible from the matter, regardless of what it might be.

—As a real friend...

—Of course, Cesare...

Then Ivo changed his position again: this time he leaned forward and slowly placed his hands on the chair's armrests, with a gesture that could be seen as an attempt to get closer to Cesare and whatever he was about to ask him, but was actually a way of ensuring he could stand up faster if he needed to escape.

—So, I've been having an affair, okay? With someone younger than me. Beautiful...Well, I think she's beautiful. Not drop-dead gorgeous, you understand...but she is fine, believe me. And she drove me wild, pure sex...Before you ask me, you don't know her. She's a simple girl, has a beauty salon...She's a hairdresser basically...And everything has always gone really well, no problems at all...You know, one of those perfect relationships where she never breaks your balls and such. Until one evening, as I'm taking her home, I joke and ask her if she has a boyfriend, and when she tells me she does, well, Ivo, I lose it.

Totally. Completely. I went out of my mind, and I had a very hard time...Really, really hard.

Ivo loosened his grip on the armrests.

—I know that it doesn't make sense for me to feel bad because she has a boyfriend, and you should know that I had even told her to get a boyfriend. And then I'm married...I have a family, a wife and a son, and I have my work. I have a life...I know, I know all of that...

—Exactly, Cesare...

—Yeah, yeah...Even though, Ivo, let's be honest, my son was an accident. I wasn't married, I wasn't much more than a kid myself, and it was the only time in my life, the only fucking time, I came and did not go and piss before fucking her again...You get me? Anyway, I started to suffer real bad because of this girl, okay? Real bad. Real real bad. And for a while. For a long while.

—For how long?

—A long time, Ivo. Months.

—Months?

—Months. I've had a nervous breakdown, Ivo...I lost it completely. You were always abroad, but you must have noticed that you didn't hear from me...Ivo, I don't know how long I've been in my office in the dark, sitting next to the telephone. Of course the building wasn't getting anywhere. It's lucky Citarella was there, and thank God you called in your Sicilian friend...He must be one hell of a guy. I'd like to meet him...

—I'm sorry, Cesare, but I knew you had a nervous breakdown because of work...Citarella told me that. And I never said anything to you because I didn't want you to get even more worried...You know, I actually felt guilty for giving you such a big project and then disappearing...

Cesare shook his head without saying a word.

—Okay. So tell me, what happened then? This hairdresser gets herself a boyfriend and you lose it, right?

—Yes, Ivo, that's it.

—But why?

—What do you mean, why? Because she hadn't told me anything about any boyfriend, and I didn't think it possible that she'd need one. That she, my Historic Baby Doll, would need another man...I always thought I was enough for her. She had me, for fuck's sake...Why did she go and find herself someone else? So, I went mad. I thought I was finished, understand? Washed up at forty-three. I blamed it on the fact I'm losing my hair...

—But where?You aren't losing it.

—Yeah, I am, Ivo...If you look closely at my temples...

—I can't see anything...So then what happened?

—What happened then is that...Well, we saw each other less and less, and so I even took her on holiday.

—On holiday?

—Yeah, to France. But it didn't work out and we broke up for good...But even though I feel a bit better now, I'm still not perfectly okay.The way the nervous breakdown came on, it could always come back.

—No, it won't come back.

—But I really miss her, Ivo...I really do. Every day...You can't imagine how much.

—You miss screwing her.

—Yes, of course, but it's not just that...I don't know, Ivo...Suddenly I don't understand anything about my life anymore. Nobody knows this, of course, apart from Citarella...But then there are other problems. Things aren't good at home, either...with Arianna. She doesn't suspect anything, of course, but some days I just can't bear to have her near me, Ivo. I just can't. And it's not her fault, poor thing...Ah, she said to say hi. Even my tennis is down the sink...

Ivo had already heard a few rumors: after many months without playing because of his tennis elbow, Cesare had started again a few months ago, but he was losing to everyone. Not just to those in the Third Category, who were now wiping the floor with him, but also to many of the unranked players he had easily beaten just a year ago. He played in the evening, inside the air domes, almost in secret, against kids, and lost every time. At the top table, Ivo had heard that the shrunken man who had taken to the court for those matches looked absolutely nothing like the Beast: he was always late, unshaven, out of breath, thin. He had even started to look a lot like his father. Once he had even walked onto the court wearing a *pink* Lacoste shirt.

—Ivo, it's ridiculous, believe me. I've never played this badly in my entire life. I'd lose to a kid from the tennis school, to my son even. My forehand always ends up inside the service line, as limp as a monk's dick. I can't control my backhand anymore: one hits the net, the next the sky. I serve at least one double fault in every game, and I'm hitting two second balls. I'm always late on the ball, I get tired at once and sweat like a waiter. I'm a mess, Ivo, a mess. I've decided to quit, maybe forever.

Cesare didn't have the heart to tell Ivo he'd also lost to his doubles partner, just the evening before, 6–2, 6–2. He had been beaten by Dante Zucchi, the never-ranked architect with a forehand as soft as lard who had consistently lost every singles game in the Coppa Italia. Nor could he tell him of the supreme disgrace: the set he had lost that very morning against Marmagli, the least talented club member of all, the dried-up lawyer who, upon seeing his umpteenth weak backhand roll into the alley, fell to his knees in the middle of the court like Bjorn Borg and burst into tears of joy.

—Ivo, it's a total mess, and I've come to ask your advice because I don't know where else to turn...

A pause.

—I was cuckolded by my Historic Baby Doll, he confessed, finding the courage to turn on himself the cruelest of all locker room jokes, the one he had always enjoyed inflicting on every poor soul that crossed his path, and after that confession Cesare suddenly fell quiet, his eyes closed and his head bowed, overwhelmed by the relief of being free of that burden.

Ivo immediately knew the perfect response to give him, but he decided that no, he couldn't. Absolutely not. He couldn't and he shouldn't. It was a stupid, cruel idea. Really too cruel. But then, however, he said it, and immediately regretted it, embarking on a long speech that was both fraternal and paternal, heartfelt and timely, during which he first flogged and then masterfully cured the Beast's madness.

Barrocciai spoke at length of the *infinite absurdities love can drive a man to commit*, even the toughest, most determined, and most shrewd of men, as Vezzosi certainly was. He threw in a few fake memories of his own past infatuations of youth and laughed about them, taunting that young and tenderly enamored Ivo who had never existed.

Then he ordered Cesare to look him *square in the eyes* and asked him if he had ever entertained the idea, even for a moment, of leaving his beautiful, faithful wife and his boy who was showing great promise at both tennis and school; if he had ever thought of abandoning his splendid family, the only true wealth a man can ever have, for such a free young woman.

Ivo held a magisterial silence, leaving time for that terrible adjective to sink into Vezzosi's traumatized soul, then he dug the knife in and repeated: "Free, very free. Perhaps too free."

How could he not think that while she — this hairdresser — was with Cesare, she wouldn't also have other entanglements, other adventures, perhaps even *many* other adventures, none confessed, besides the one with the idiot who was now her boyfriend?

Cesare waited for a while, his eyes wide and his mouth half open, before realizing that Ivo wanted an answer, and so, stunned by that onslaught of lucid common sense, by that heartfelt ode to family that had just been given him by the city's most unrepentant bachelor, he lied and said no: he had never thought of leaving Arianna.

Barrocciai welcomed this announcement with a regal smile and proclaimed that Cesare should *immediately banish all sadness* and start to see this inexperienced guy's arrival on the scene as manna from heaven, because—he leaned over the polished surface of the rosewood desk to get closer to his friend, who did the same thing, and so they found themselves face to face, closer than they had ever been before—*How in hell was he going to put an end to all this, otherwise?* When would he have ever left her, this hairdresser who was incredibly and fortunately never impregnated despite the fact that, in the fire of their passions, they never—that's right, isn't it?—took any precautions?

Cesare looked away, closed his eyes, breathed in until his lungs were filled with air, and exhaled with the power of a narwhal, then reopened his eyes and smiled for the first time since he had set foot in that office. He stood up and held his hand out to Ivo, who stood up and shook it. Ivo said that Cesare was a very lucky man, and he reminded him of the limitless crop of beautiful and available young women who populated *this marvelous Italy of ours*, and who certainly couldn't wait to have some fun with a guy as handsome as the Beast. Cesare hugged him, filled with gratitude, and thanked him for having helped in a way no one had done before.

—Thank you so much. Really, Ivo, thank you. You are a real friend.

He left Barrocciai's office with a light heart, and only when he got in his car did he remember—though only for a moment, before instantaneously batting them away—the surprising words Ivo had begun his speech with: that strange, cutting introduction that, for a few seconds, if truth be told, had upset him. "Believe me, Cesare, in life there is worse, a lot worse, than being cuckolded by a lover."

AT THE BANK

IT WAS OBVIOUS that the bank sitting in the middle of the field, which at that very moment was being furiously leveled by a yellow, inexorable bulldozer had been a farmhouse.

Maria saw it straightaway, and smiled to herself because its peasant origins made it feel less foreign, almost friendly. One aspect she found particularly reassuring was the fact that those thick walls would have made heavy work for any potential thieves. Pasquale, on the other hand, terribly on edge as he was, only noticed when he walked in. He looked around for a few seconds and started to point out to Maria how many of the interior features of the house had been hastily torn out. The atrium of the bank, which was roughly cut in two by the cashiers' desks, had undoubtedly been a large kitchen where the farmworkers would have eaten with their families, he told her, and there was a big fireplace that could still be glimpsed behind the cursory whitewash of the plasterboard that partially covered it.

The Citarellas waited obediently in line at the desk for ten minutes only to be directed to the second floor, and went slowly up those stairs. They were very intimidated by all that silence, which was broken only by the tapping of typewriters and the hushed incorporeal voices deep in telephonic conversation, so full of obscure words they found entirely incomprehensible.

Upon reaching the second floor they found no one there to welcome them. Two employees brushed past several times without giving them so much as a smile, while the Citarellas stood there in the middle of the narrow corridor, waiting for a sign.

It was the first time they had ever entered a bank, because it was the first time they had money to deposit. Maria had never had any, and everything Pasquale had earned up until that point had been immediately spent on maintaining the family, buying the land, building the *baiadera*, expanding it, paying for the Fiat 128, and repaying Vezzosi for the properties Pasquale had bought so that their families could finally leave the rented attics.

When Pasquale pointed out the four offices in front of him and said that they must have been the farmhouse's bedrooms, Maria turned to face him: with his hands in his pockets, his face flushed by the emotion of being in a bank, her husband would have stood there in the middle of that corridor until closing time, without saying a single word. She had to take the initiative, because she was the one who had insisted on depositing their money in the bank rather than keeping it hidden in the kitchen, behind the packets of pasta.

One evening, at dinner, she had even said that, if given to the bank, that money would have earned them interest, meaning it would have grown significantly. Perhaps by even ten percent. The table had fallen silent and her three men had all looked at her — Pasquale and Dino were speechless, Tonino extremely interested — and she had been asked to explain what she meant. She had announced that on TV they had explained that money costs, but it also brings rewards. Both things. Seeing her men blinking in perplexity, Maria had continued.

—If you borrow money from a bank, they charge you interest, but if you take your money to a bank, the bank pays the interest to you. Do you understand, Pasquale?

Upon hearing that he too would be able to earn money without lifting a finger like the gentlemen in the movies—the ones who play tennis in the morning, watch horse races in the afternoon, and spend the evening at the theater—Pasquale had smiled and ended the conversation, saying it seemed impossible to him, but that he would give it some thought. The next morning, goaded by Maria, who could no longer sleep with the thought of all that money hidden in the kitchen, Pasquale said he would ask Vezzosi, but when he saw her shaking her head disappointedly, he seized his courage with both hands and did exactly as she had suggested: he called Barrocciai.

When Ivo explained to him that *of course* money should go straight to the bank, and that Pasquale could actually go to a small branch that had recently opened next to the old factory and say that he had sent him, Pasquale told Maria to call and make an appointment with the bank manager.

So that is how they ended up there, standing in that corridor, dressed in their Sunday best, anxious and silent, alone and ignored, with Pasquale's pockets and Maria's handbag full of banknotes which they wanted to deposit but no one in that bank seemed interested in taking.

When she saw the yellow bulldozer starting to move toward the bank as if it were about to flatten it, then suddenly come to a halt, sink the shovel into the black earth, and uproot a big thicket of briar, Maria moved toward one of the offices, followed closely by Pasquale.

She stopped on the threshold and saw a man in shirt and tie sitting at a small desk perusing a newspaper printed on yellow paper, so she went in and asked to speak with the manager. The man lifted his head in surprise, revealing a face like a setter, and replied that he was the manager.

—Right, good morning, then. Our name is Citarella and we have been sent by Mr. Ivo Barrocciai. We wish to open an account. My husband here needs to deposit four million lire.

—Welcome. Please sit down. I'm Mr. Ciapini.

Upon hearing Ivo's name, the bank manager had stood up with a big smile on his face and moved straight toward Pasquale to shake his hand, while Maria received no more than a nod.

They sat down and began to pull out the banknotes: Maria extracted a bundle from her bag in one go, while Pasquale had to contort himself on the seat to fish them out of various pockets. The bank manager's smile grew steadily wider as he counted them. When he reached three million, he called an employee by surname and ordered him to count them again and *immediately* prepare the paperwork for *Mr. Citarella*'s account. Pasquale, hearing himself referred to as Mr. Citarella, turned violet. It was the first time anyone had called him that in earnest, and not as a joke.

After a few minutes of embarrassed small talk, during which he tried to gain as much information as possible on Pasquale's work and, in particular, his relationship to *that great man, Ivo Barrocciai*, Mr. Ciapini lowered his voice and looked him in the eye: he explained that they could *happily deposit* all of their earnings, even the *unofficial* ones, because, luckily, in Italy, banks maintained full secrecy and he wasn't required to report anything to anyone, *except the magistrates, of course*, but — he smiled, shrugged his shoulders, lit a cigarette — "they're not going to be concerned with respectable people like you and me, Mr. Citarella."

Pasquale nodded seriously and stayed silent. He hadn't understood much of what the bank manager had said, but he knew he didn't like it at all. What was *unofficial* about his work? He was a decent person. He was an honest man. What did the manager mean? And what did *magistrates* have to do with it? Perhaps he was alluding to his being from the South. Was he insinuating he was involved with criminals? He gave a confused look in Maria's direction: he saw her smiling, serene, and felt reassured.

The employee returned with the documents and passed them to the bank manager, who then passed them to Pasquale and pointed out where to sign, tracing a minuscule *x* next to a blank line. Pasquale, who was now irritated, stared at the x, which offended him because it reminded him of how the illiterate sign their names with a cross, so he lifted his eyes from the page and threw the bank manager a look as hard as stone.

—And whose name will this bank account be in?

The bank director asked him for his identity card. He found it and showed it to him.

—The account will naturally be in your name, Mr. Citarella!

Pasquale shook his head.

—No. That won't work. The bank account will have to be in the names of Pasquale and Maria Citarella.

The bank manager's smile froze.

—Mr. Citarella, I'll be honest with you. This is the first time anyone has ever made that request.

Ciapini leaned toward him and, sniggering, glancing swiftly over at Maria, whispered, "Best to keep women away from the money . . ."

Maria saw her husband stiffen. His violetness was gone, along with any emotion or shame.

—I will not be signing anything unless the bank account is also in my wife's name. I will take my money and go home. Or rather, I'll go to another bank.

—No, you see, Mr. Citarella, perhaps it's not . . . Let's be clear, I was saying it for your benefit . . . You could authorize your wife to use it, make her a joint signatory . . . so that she can sign but always and only if you have signed too . . . It's to ensure peace of mind. For safety's sake.

Pasquale shook his head, looking the manager straight in the eye until he once again shouted the employee's surname and instructed him to redo the documents.

Maria didn't say a word. Her heart was beating fast. The moment she had heard her husband proclaim the words "Pasquale and Maria Citarella" into the stale air of that poky office, she was moved, because they hadn't discussed whose name the account would be in, and she had never once thought that Pasquale would have asked for it to be a joint account: he was the head of the family, he had earned the money, she was just a wife and a mother, a housewife ... *Well now, I see I must have done something right for our family over all these years,* she said to herself, and, to avoid crying, she started digging around in her handbag pretending to look for something, blowing her nose every so often, as if overtaken by a sudden cold.

When it was her turn, Maria signed with a beautiful flourish, concentrating hard on signing the second-most important document of her life with the princesslike signature she had perfected at middle school. She didn't notice the tender smile on her husband's face as he watched her, and when he passed her the checkbook the bank manager had given him, she placed it delicately in her bag, with a care that she would have shown a love letter, if Pasquale had ever written her one.

They left the bank arm in arm. During their brief walk to the car she laid her head on his shoulder, and Pasquale held her, telling her it was an important day, that October 31, 1978. One to mark down on the calendar.

THE SUMMER OF '79

AT THE END OF JUNE, when she arrived with Vittorio at the seaside for a vacation that would last until mid-September, Arianna realized she was sick and tired of spending every summer in the same refurbished lemonary they rented every year.

She could not stand anymore the little town she had liked so much when she arrived years ago, with a newborn Vittorio. It now seemed to her a defective imitation of the famous seaside town just a few kilometers away — a five-minute bicycle ride. The sand was coarser and the names of beach establishments more insipid and the pine trees not as tall and the streets narrower; even the inhabitants, even the *tourists* seemed uglier than those of the famous seaside town, where the houses for rent became small villas, the seafront was decorated with palm trees, the beach was one hundred meters long, the sand as fine as silk, and the people, well, *they were on an another level*.

Arianna would take refuge there at any opportunity. She felt comforted just by hearing the accent of the Milanese women who populated and commanded that famous seaside town, and studied them with an obsessive attention to detail: their clothes, bags, shoes, hairstyles, even their sayings. She memorized it all.

She was setting them in her sights, certain that if everything kept on going well, she too would soon be able to move to the famous seaside town, and sunbathe in one of those beach establishments with lofty-sounding names such as Royal and Augustus and Imperiale, and Cesare would take her to dance at that exclusive nightclub that looked like a house, where it was said the Milanese ladies and gentlemen went to play cards from the afternoon until dawn, interrupting the game only for their oysters-and-champagne dinner, and they were used to losing large amounts of money to each other without getting angry because it would all start over again the next day, and the loser would become a winner.

A bored prisoner of the small seaside town, Arianna read all of the books she had brought from home, ventured out on long walks on the beach, never smiling at the comments and shouts of appreciation from lifeguards and tourists, tanned as never before, and became as beautiful as beautiful can be — then she realized it was still the tenth of July.

Vittorio saved her summer. Long gone the times when he would spend his days playing soccer on the shore, now he spent his afternoons at home lying on the sofa, immersed in that blessed *otium* that gives thoughts time to leaven. He interrupted it only to read the three books of *Dune* and undertake lengthy conversations with his mother, who had never seemed as understanding and tolerant and serene and intelligent as when they exchanged opinions on the bright future that awaited him. The rest of the time he spent listening over and over to the first album he had ever bought: *The Stranger* by Billy Joel.

The idyll was interrupted one morning in early August, around nine, when a tarpaulin-covered truck with BAROCCIAI TESSUTI S.P.A. painted on the side stopped in front of the lemonary, and out of it came Moreno Barbugli and Cesare.

They rooted around in the back for a while before producing the fruit of Cesare's guilt, the brand-new blue Vespa 50 Special with black seat that Vittorio had wanted so badly and which his father had suddenly decided to buy for him, dead set on ignoring the protests of Arianna, who had never agreed to discuss the possibility of buying her son a scooter.

—Vittorio! Vittorio! Come here! Cesare was shouting. *Vittorio!*

The Beast was back. A few days earlier, he had decided that the work on site had to be completed once and for all, and when he was given yet another excuse for yet another delay in the electric wiring of the factory, he swore at the top of his voice, got into the Alfetta, and literally dragged the electrician to the site. The next day, the wiring was finished.

He didn't stop shouting until Vittorio came in the garden, still in his pajamas, bleary-eyed and half asleep, and when he saw his son's eyes light up upon seeing the Vespa, Cesare hugged him and told him that was his gift. Then he started shouting for Arianna, who had seen everything and was furious and refused even to come out and say hi.

After a few minutes Cesare shrugged, shook his head, cuffed his mute son, jumped back on the truck, and ordered Barbugli to get going. The truck started up with a tremor, leaving behind it a cloud of thick black smoke that took more than five minutes to disperse.

Vittorio spent a while looking at the Vespa without so much as touching it, knowing that his mother was watching from her bedroom window, behind the shining leaves of the large magnolia.

When he was twelve Vittorio had been told of all the terrible deaths of his peers on a scooter — a real massacre, it seemed — and so he had never driven a Vespa. On the day of his fourteenth birthday, his mother had made him swear to God he would never drive one, and he hadn't broken that promise. But now he *owned* one. Vittorio looked up, saw his mother watching him, held out his arms, smiled, and pointed at the shiny new Vespa, wordlessly asking to be released from his promise. Arianna disappeared from the window.

He got it started with the unnatural equine kick that had to be given to the pedal, and sat there for a long time admiring it, stuttering and immobile on its kickstand—the perfect image of his desire.

Learning to drive it wasn't easy, but after many trials and tribulations, he managed it. Oblivious to the fact that his was undoubtedly the slowest Vespa of all time—its maximum speed, achieved on the waterfront at the very moment a crowd of young cyclists in training overtook him screaming cruel and offensive nicknames, was painfully below forty kilometers per hour—Vittorio was on it from morning until night, and used any excuse to drive it along the infinite waterfront that ran for hundreds of kilometers to Monte Carlo, kissed by the eternal sunshine of that gentle August.

He was so happy for that new, immense freedom that even Arianna had to smile when she saw him leaving home in his white Lacoste shirt and blue Bermudas, revving the gears until he reached his final snail-like speed, followed by a cloud of light-blue smoke. One day Vittorio even managed to persuade her to go for a quick spin along the seafront with him, and Cesare was very surprised and pleased by the pristine Audrey Hepburnian class with which Arianna sat sidesaddle, graciously holding the waist of their son, and did not think or realize that, even at thirty-eight kilometers per hour, they were moving away from him.

But the greatest fun they had in that summer of '79 was going to the cinema together, almost every evening. After a day on the beach and a quick dinner, Arianna and Vittorio threw pastel-colored sweaters over their shoulders and walked through the pittosporum-lined, narrow streets of the small, not famous little seaside town to the open-air cinema that was right at the center of the town's minuscule square. Arianna and Vittorio saw so many films together, from the end of June to mid-September, and what films!

The program was a brilliant *helzapoppin'* of genres and inspirations, decided upon unilaterally by Valeriano, a surly, local cinephile who also worked as ticket collector and projectionist, and who intersected his elitist tastes with the episodic availability of the films, taking pleasure in showing movies old and new, good or bad, famous or unknown, without any apparent order or hierarchy. No film stayed for more than one evening, and there was just one screening, at nine sharp.

So, in that summer of '79, mother and son saw *Grease, 2001: A Space Odyssey, Fantozzi, The Cat o'Nine Tails, Tommy, Jaws, Amici miei, Heaven Can Wait, Capricorn One* (Arianna had trouble keeping Vittorio quiet during that movie, as he had started to complain loudly and wanted to leave, indignant that anyone could doubt Armstrong and Aldrin's moon landing), *Animal House,* and then *Barry Lyndon, Close Encounters of the Third Kind, Saturday Night Fever, Four Flies on Grey Velvet, Halloween, The Warriors,* and *West Side Story,* and *Love Story,* and *The Deer Hunter,* and *Zabriskie Point.*

They also saw the surfer film *Big Wednesday,* with which Vittorio fell in love and which he convinced his only friend Fede to go and see too, and Fede took along his sister Rebecca and his friend Marty, and they all fell for it and decided to go and see it again whenever it was being shown at a cinema they could reach on their Vespas.

So they started to follow the peregrinations of that single copy of *Big Wednesday,* learning not only each scene and every line by heart, but even all the celluloid's imperfections, the scratches, the image jumps, the crackles, the boom of the volume saturation during the final scene of the great ocean swell.

They picked at their dinners while their mothers protested, then met up in the square and set off, and because the copy changed location every evening and at times it was being shown in the cinemas of even smaller towns perched high above the steep roads of the world's smallest mountain chain, they even had to wrap up, as it was much cooler up there.

The only thing that mattered was arriving on time to see the waves slowly lapping the beach in the light of dawn, which permeated the opening scene, and hear the tale of the hot wind that blew down the canyons and was called Santa Ana, and be instantly absorbed once more in that sad and jubilant story of time lost in an unreachable Californian arcadia where time was counted in waves.

Once the film was finished, Vittorio and Fede and Marty and Rebecca returned to their Vespas without saying a word and started to slowly make their way home consumed by longing and melancholy and even nostalgia for days which were not that far away from them, and for characters who were young and blond and happy at the beginning of the story, but ended up old and lonely and failed — Matt and Jack and Leroy, the heroes who ruled that poor and splendid California that turned its back on the rest of the world to fix its gaze on the ocean, waiting for the big swell that one day *will sweep away everything in its path.*

Only when the movie was transferred to Liguria did the band of Vespa filmgoers break up, leaving the four of them to watch the pathetic waves, barely a few centimeters high, that arrived on the shore of the small seaside town, and Vittorio and Arianna began going to the cinema together again and had the good fortune to be there for the final show, the only one with a double bill: *Superman* and a short film by a French director they had never heard of.

After the Man of Steel had saved California and Lois Lane by flying around the planet faster than the speed of light, the screen abruptly turned white, then black, and a road began to unravel beneath a movie camera that had been fixed on the bumper of a Gran Turismo car which set off at dawn down the Champs-Élysées at blazing speed, toward the Arc de Triomphe.

The motor rumbled at full throttle and it was like sitting inside that speeding car that never stopped, not even for red lights, while it shot past other cars that seemed to be immobile. As it arrived at the Arc de Triomphe, the tires screeched madly and away it sped at full throttle toward the Place de la Concorde in a flurry of red lights that were totally ignored without the car ever slowing down, and after crossing the deserted square, the Gran Turismo launched itself down toward the Seine and then turned into the Place du Louvre, heading up toward the Opéra, and it never slowed, never, not even for an instant, and then it went down narrow streets and on and on and on it ran on the pavé, brushing past ladies with poodles, passersby, pigeons, garbage trucks, until it stopped before a stairway that looked over the whole of Paris, and a blond girl in a light dress emerged and the driver ran clumsily to embrace her, and then the image froze and a title appeared:

C'ÉTAIT UN RENDEZ-VOUS
FILMÉ PAR CLAUDE LELOUCH

When the screen turned black, the few remaining spectators — Vittorio and Arianna, and a couple from Milan in their forties — demanded loudly to watch the film again, so Valeriano ran it again and again until one in the morning, when he went to the stage and told the last remaining spectator that he would only show it once more, and that was all, so Vittorio chose just to listen to that brief yet prodigious film: he closed his eyes and relished the furious twelve-cylinder song of what was undoubtedly a Ferrari.

DESTINY DOES NOT EXIST

LONG LINES OF FLATBED AFTER FLATBED loaded with stacked rolls of fabric were crammed into every corner of the factory, and next to them dozens and dozens of upright rolls stood like battalions of robust little soldiers. This is what Ivo Barrocciai saw as he walked down the steel staircase that led from the offices to the warehouse. He heard the screeching of the forklift truck on linoleum, but couldn't see it. He could hear Carmine's voice instructing the workers, but couldn't see him or them. All he could see was a sea of black or navy blue pieces of Prisca, the soft duvetyn which was so reminiscent of cashmere in its finesse and sheen it was hard to believe that not even a trace of that miraculous fiber could be found in it.

Ivo stepped onto the linoleum and was forced to slalom between the upright rolls, taking great care not to touch them, and smiled when Carmine Schiavo—head of the warehouse, originally from Ariano and a friend of Citarella's, the first man employed by Ivo—appeared and shouted: "Hey, Ivo, either you stop selling rolls or you take us to a bigger warehouse. Look, I had to stand them all up, so they take up less space..."

Barrocciai smiled with relief. The telephone call from Carmine had worried him. So abruptly had he been summoned to the warehouse that he was afraid of one of those last-minute technical problems: a consignment of pieces that were too heavy or too light or the wrong color.

Being called just to see the warehouse filled to the rafters, however, did not worry him at all. He actually found it comforting. All those rolls had been sold. Carmine just had to ship them to the clients, in order to make room for more. It was a logistical problem and, as such, didn't interest him. He decided to call his father: Ardengo had to see the full warehouse!

— Come on, Ivo, seriously, what are we supposed to do? We've got another hundred pieces coming in and nowhere to put them. And it's raining outside. You tell me what I'm supposed to do...

— How about sending them to the clients?

—They're going tomorrow, but the shippers are saying they won't be able to pick up again today.

—What do you mean they can't pick up today? Why not?

— Ivo, they've already picked up a thousand pieces from us today. They say they have to work with other clients too...

— Carmine, call them again. They have to come.

—They've just left. They filled two trucks. One guy sprained his wrist. They're coming back tomorrow.

—Who broke his wrist? One of our guys or one of theirs?

— One of theirs. It's not broken, it's sprained.

—You're a doctor now, are you?

— Ivo, let's not get off the point... No jokes now, please. What about the new factory? The pharaonic thing? When will it be ready? Because we don't know what to do anymore here...

While Barrocciai was shrugging it off, trying to think of a smart answer, an invisible forklift truck bumped softly, very softly, barely touching it, into a flatbed full of pieces that was leaning against the wall, and the smaller flatbed that had been placed on top of it started to pitch, first to the side, then forward.

Someone shouted "Watch out!" as the small flatbed slipped down and the pieces that were on it slid off, striking their upright sisters, which came crashing down as if tired of standing on their feet, one after the other and all at once, in every possible direction, like gigantic dominoes, and Ivo and Carmine had to move quickly out the way because each roll of Prisca weighed twenty-five kilos. They managed to take refuge in the old cubicle, and from there they watched the rolls tumbling over throughout the warehouse with a series of thuds that somehow fused together into a single, colossal, grandiose thud. Then an immense silence fell.

— Hey, guys, is anyone hurt?

A chorus of no's, then a trembling voice.

— Ivo, I'm so sorry. It was me.

— Are you all sure?

A chorus of yeses.

— Sure. My God, what a wipeout!

— Good God! squeaked a female voice from the top of the stairs: it was Gabriella, surrounded by the ladies from the sales and accounts departments, some with their hands on their heads, some with their hands over their mouths, some crossing their hands over their chests, some just staring open-mouthed at the sight.

Finding himself imprisoned inside the cubicle by his own pieces right after having been threatened by the fruits of his labor, Ivo Barrocciai first felt embarrassed, then furious.

— *Vezzosiiiiiii!* he screamed. And then *Citarellaaaaaaaaa!*

Hearing him shout like that, everyone stopped still because no one of them had ever heard Ivo raise his voice. Then he shouted again.

— Can someone get us out of here? I've got two motherfuckin' engineers to deal with, for Christ's sake!

It was the first time he lost his cool in the factory, and that infuriated him even more. It was his fault, there could be no doubt about it, and this certainty fanned even more the flames of his fury, and Ivo erupted in an uninterrupted stream of profanities that every so often resulted in colorful and powerful expletives that sent the ladies rushing straight back to their offices and the workers running to help him with long, awkward steps, taking great care not to step on the fallen pieces now lying on the pavement like giant Shanghai sticks.

Ivo had been terrified to see all those rolls falling toward him as if in a revolt, but most of all he was furious to discover himself a superficial, negligent, distracted, careless slob. All he had thought about was selling, not the good of the company or those working in it. Dazzled by all those orders and the thousands of pieces, he hadn't realized that there was a safety issue at the factory, a huge one, and probably had been for months. It meant nothing that none of the workers had been hurt and that in the blink of an eye all of the 352 fallen rolls were back on their feet, or that Carmine kept on apologizing while the young driver of the forklift truck was crying with relief in a corner.

This should never have happened, Ivo kept on saying. Not in his factory. He went back up the steel staircase asking himself if that wasn't dangerous, too. He sat at the desk, took a sip from the glass of water a shaking Gabriella had brought him, asked to be left alone, and cursed some more, extensively, under his breath, with anger and passion, until he grew ashamed of himself and stopped.

He called Cesare at his office, hoping not to find him, but he did find him, and he started to shout. He told him he had almost died because of him, and he could not wait anymore and that he wanted to be in the new factory by tomorrow morning, and then he screamed that he wanted to know immediately why the factory wasn't ready by September 1979 when he'd bought the land on Christmas Eve 1973, bloody hell, and thank God he did call

Andrea Vecchio, otherwise there would still be radicchio grow-ing in that motherfucking field, and then he swore at the top of his lungs.

When he stopped to take a breath, Cesare tried to mollify him, but Ivo wouldn't have any of it.

—I don't want to hear a single word, Cesare. It's a miracle that me and the guys in the warehouse are still alive. I want you here in fifteen minutes!

And he hung up. When Cesare finally arrived, having first stopped by the building site to pick up an extremely agitated Citarella, Ivo's anger had subsided. His disappointment, how-ever, had not. Trying to keep his voice as low and calm as possi-ble, he asked the reasons for that *unacceptable and shameful* delay, and Cesare replied that if it only stopped raining, they would finish all the building work within a few days, perhaps even tomorrow.

Ivo answered by shaking his head over and over for a full min-ute, without saying a single word, once again furious because he had lost his patience when the wait was over, as children do, and then he found himself wishing that it wasn't true, so that he could go on moaning about the delay and beat the desk with his fists and scream and shout about all of his sacrosanct rights.

He somehow managed to control himself, gave Vezzosi the coldest glare he could manage, and told him he *bitterly* regretted having ever trusted him with such an important job. He certainly wouldn't have done it today. He told him he was thinking of get-ting rid of the lot of them and handing the work over to a real company, instead of a makeshift gang like them.

All Citarella could think about — his face red as an Irishman in the cold, his blood pounding at his temples — was when Tonino, just a few days ago, at dinnertime, had asked him if that factory they had been building for years was like a cathedral, because at school they had just learned about cathedrals, that it took a lot of people and a lot of time to build them, and Pasquale had answered yes, and said he was so proud of being one of those men building factories, which were the modern cathedrals.

Ivo asked Cesare to show him the contract, because for some reason he couldn't find it, and his accountant didn't have a copy of it, either. He told him he wanted to check if a penalty was due in case of rescission, and if so, how much, because he would happily pay an honest sum just to be free of them once and for all.

Cesare looked at him with the eyes of the Beast, then said he couldn't find the contract because there was no contract. It didn't exist. Had he forgotten? They had never signed anything. They were friends. They had shaken hands. That was their contract.

Ivo lowered his eyes and remembered, and then he grew emotional at recalling the days spent in the cramped cubicle, daydreaming with Cesare about how they would build the most beautiful factory in Italy, but then his anger returned at the thought of the pitiful fate of those dreams, and he grew angrier still because, if Vezzosi was telling him the truth, he had just been informed that despite all the disputes and the problems and the nervous breakdowns and the delays and the incompetence and the ineptitude, the factory was pretty much *ready*. Just as he had hoped and dreamed. Of course, all he was being given now were just the walls and some of the machinery, and with an entirely unacceptable delay, but did he really want to send them away now that they had almost finished? And how long had it been since he had gone to see his building site? *What's going on now, Ivo? Don't you want it anymore? Really?*

He closed his eyes and tried to regroup, but the memory of the rolls that seemed to chase him as they fell by the dozen was still too vivid, and so he hissed that the fact there was no contract was a sign they were imbeciles, and he was even more of an imbecile because it wasn't possible to build a factory worth two billion lire and just shake hands on it, just hoping it would all be fine, and then he finally fell silent, his fury finally purged, and immediately regretted having called Cesare and Citarella imbeciles, as he saw them sitting in front of him, rooted to the spot by the fear of being fired.

It was eight o' clock in the evening of a cold day of September and there was no sound in the office but the muffled beating of an incessant rain. Then Citarella cleared his throat and spoke.

—What makes me an imbecile, Ivo? Is it because I trusted you? I trust you and I always will...

Upon hearing those words, something inside Barrocciai melted, and all that was left of his rage drained off and vanished, and his innate cheerfulness started once again to run freely through his veins. He didn't want to be angry anymore, but he had to keep his position, so he nodded gravely and told them they could go. He would see them on site the next morning at eight o'clock sharp, to see exactly where they were up to—and if either of them had lied to him, he wouldn't just be firing them and all the other workers on the spot, but he would also have to close the woolen mill and send home *every single one of the fifty people who work there*, because it had become dangerous to work there.

—I want to know the exact day it'll all be ready. Understood?

PIRANHAS IN THE AQUARIUM

THE NEXT MORNING Ivo arrived on site at midday. He had checked with Gabriella: he hadn't been there for a year and one month, and he wasn't ready for the sight, which left him literally openmouthed.

When he began his inspection, flanked by Cesare and followed by an anxious Citarella, Ivo had to make an effort not to smile as he looked into the immensity of the cement basin that would soon become the Olympic swimming pool, or as he measured with giant steps the cavernous immensity of the twin sheds that would house the weaving and the spinning mills, or as he inspected the small adjacent rooms that would house the warpage and darning, or as he greatly appreciated the dimensions and the light of the technical, administrative, and sales offices.

But when he stepped foot in his immense office, only slightly smaller than a tennis court, Ivo became as excited as a schoolboy and finally allowed himself to smile because, even in the midst of all that dust, his dream had come back to life once again, and he was really building the most beautiful factory in the whole of Italy.

Reassured, Cesare began to ask questions and Ivo merrily answered all of them, and Pasquale was entranced at seeing those two men giving shape to the future, forcing it to become the one they wanted, creating reality out of a dream. So, he thought, it was possible to change your future instead of waiting for your destiny. Maybe destiny didn't even exist. Maybe only the future exists.

—Now though, Cesare, let's not get lost in all this bullshit, there's still a lot of work to do!

—Don't worry, Ivo, I'll organize it all…No, Ivo, come on…Please don't look at me like that…No, don't laugh…I had a moment of weakness, it's true, but that's all in the past.

Citarella, listening intently, didn't notice Ivo's quick wink.

—And Cesare, tell me…If I've understood correctly, everything still needs to be painted. We're talking about ten thousand square meters…It's a huge job.

—Yes, and actually, Ivo, it's a big problem. You just can't find people who can do it properly anymore.

—I know, I know…We're going to have to get someone in who is really good at painting, not one of those amateurs who are always hanging about around us…Have you thought of anyone?

—Yes, Ivo. There is one guy who's very good. His name is Cicisbei. I'll call him right away.

It was only then that Pasquale, entirely devoid of any sense of humor, exhausted by the sleepless night he had spent watching Maria sleep soundly, innocent and oblivious to the tragedy that was threatening to send them all back to Ariano Irpino to twiddle their thumbs for all eternity, managed a weak murmur of protest.

—Pardon? Ivo, Cesare, excuse me, who's this Cicisbei guy? I'm sorry, but…I mean, painting is…I paint, don't I? Because I'm good, I'm not an amateur.

Ivo hugged him and rubbed his knuckles hard into his head, shouting, "Come here, come here!" and Cesare leaned in to squeeze Citarella's balls, and in the confusion they all fell to the floor in the dust and rolled about laughing.

Then Ivo invited them all to lunch at the city's finest restaurant, the one with piranhas in the aquarium, regardless of what they were wearing, "because no one should ever be ashamed of what they wear to work, and they should be proud of it, for fuck's sake!"

He took Citarella by the arm, sat him in the Pagoda, and set off at top speed with the roof down, Barry White blaring from the speakers. Moreno Barbugli, Franchino di Oste, and Claudione all got in the Alfetta with Cesare, Claudino followed them on his Piaggio Ciao. They shared two trays of spaghetti allo scoglio and an enormous fritto di lisca, all washed down with bottles of Vernaccia di San Gimignano, which at one point seemed to take on the effect of strobe lighting, given the speed at which they were arriving full and ice cold, and leaving empty and still ice cold.

It was almost four o'clock when they left, a hot September sun was shining on the city, and Ivo gave everyone the rest of the day off.

BEAUTIFUL

THE FIRST TIME VITTORIO SAW HER was at the end of his first day of high school, and she took his breath away. He froze, dropped his schoolbag, and murmured to himself.

—You are so beautiful…

Who knows what her name was, what kind of music she liked, who had shown her how to dress like that! She was wearing Camperos boots which were admirably greased with seal fat to achieve the perfect shade of brown, Levi's 501s so expertly faded as to reveal the white warp lines in the still-bright indigo of the denim, a lambswool sweater with Greek frets on the collar that peeped out from under the shearling coat, a dark-blue woolen beanie hat, and a nylon canvas Invicta backpack with white-and-pink stripes, and she was hugging a friend, laughing loudly and seeming perfectly happy.

For a moment it seemed that her gaze had come to rest on him, and Vittorio swallowed hard. It wasn't possible. Why should she look at him? He was wearing his old loden overcoat buttoned up wrong, flannel trousers, black penny loafers, a white shirt, and a brown lambswool cardigan; his curls were messy and sweaty after his run to get out of the school before anyone else.

He looked at himself: a boy who had suddenly grown up, still dressed by his mommy.

He stared at that girl as she walked away arm in arm with her friend, and didn't take his eyes off her until she turned the corner and disappeared, taking with her all the beauty of the world. To regain his composure, Vittorio had to stumble into a bar, sink a Fanta, change a thousand-lire note for ten hundred-lire coins, and take refuge in the small room in the back to play Space Invaders.

He walked home in a daze, paying no attention to the buses that roared past him, and when he arrived home, he was surprised to find his father sitting at the table, waiting for him.

Cesare Vezzosi was in an excellent mood. He was joking with Arianna and pinching her bottom every time she came near him. Vittorio's first thought was that they must have made love that night and now they wanted to somehow remember it, celebrate it, making allusions that may have seemed subtle to them but were to him painfully clear and very, very embarrassing.

He had no interest whatsoever in that part of their lives, and wanted to know nothing about it. He would have preferred to have nineteenth-century parents, old and serious and asexual, but more than anything he wished to have an ugly and insignificant mother, so he wouldn't always have to pretend not to hear when his school friends whispered that Vittorio's mom was *seriously, seriously hot* on those rare occasions in which Arianna went to pick him up from school.

He couldn't have known, or even suspected, that Cesare and Arianna had *just* made love, and on the very table where he was about to be served his lunch, their passion reaching its height the very moment Vittorio had rung the doorbell because he still hadn't been entrusted with the house keys.

It had happened all of a sudden, when Cesare had for once returned home in a good mood and was enflamed at the sight of his wife walking toward him and apologizing profusely because the lunch wasn't ready, wrapped in an overly tight apron that outlined her toned, slim figure, her hair scraped back in the Amazonian ponytail he had always liked so much, her cheeks still red with the worry of being late with tortellini.

He kissed and touched her all over, and she, who was not expecting it, melted like an ice cream and they ended up on the kitchen table, screwing intensely, *going at it hard*, like lovers, wrapped in a concentrated silence that was broken only by their moans, gripped by a fierce desire for one another they hadn't felt in such a long time.

When they sat around the table and Cesare started to suck noisily at his broth, Vittorio couldn't bring himself not to say anything, as he usually did, and so he very respectfully asked his father to please stop that incredibly ill-mannered way of eating.

Cesare stared at him. If he hadn't made love just a few minutes earlier, and with such results, he would have been furious to hear himself admonished in his own house by a boy just out of short trousers. But serene as he was, he decided to smile and proclaim himself very proud of being made the way he was: with all of his virtues — he looked at Arianna, who turned red and immediately lowered her gaze — and all of his defects, and he turned to face Vittorio, who was taken aback by the look his father gave him, and waited in vain for even the briefest smile to appear on his face.

After the last gurgling spoonful cleared away the last tortellino along with the last drop of broth — to mock Vittorio's plea, he had indulged in a veritable Brandenburg concerto for broth and spoon, featuring gurgles, gargling, exultant swallowing, followed by the slapping of the tongue against the palate, and, by way of conclusion, a warm, satisfied, cetacean vent — Cesare rested his spoon on the table and announced that the moment had arrived for his only male son to learn two or three important things about life. Arianna froze, watching him with her mouth open, terrified he wanted to talk about sex.

—The first thing you need to know, dear Vittorio, is that the world does not live in peace. America and Russia are in the middle of the Cold War, as they call it, which isn't really war but isn't peace either, because they are actually spying on one another and have nuclear missiles pointed at their cities.

— No, Cesare, I'm sorry but they aren't *their* cities. Otherwise the boy won't understand. Explain that Russia has them pointed at American cities, and America at the cities in Russia...

Her husband's eyes darkened, and Arianna turned to go back in the kitchen, a smile on her lips, unable to resist the temptation.

— I was saying, Vittorio, that we are living through a break in history. To put it in tennis terms, these years are nothing more than a change of sides while we wait for World War II to start up again, or perhaps even World War III. Except this time it'll be an atomic war, and *we will all die*. Those Russian shits, you've got to know this, have *hundreds* of missiles with nuclear warheads pointed at our beautiful Western cities filled with art and history and culture, and all that bastard of a Russian premier has to do is press a button to set them off and destroy everything, killing millions of us and canceling all of our culture and traditions.

Arianna called out from the kitchen.

— Cesare, tell him about the Americans, too...

A disgusted grimace spread over Vezzosi's face, and for a moment he looked like a wolf — Mánagarmr, Vittorio thought, the terrible wolf from *Edda*, which he had just finished reading: the monster that eats the dead and who, on the day of Ragnarok, will devour the Moon.

—Arianna, please, you concentrate on the washing up, I'm talking to our son. Always remember this, Vittorio, even if we aren't Americans, we Italians will always be allies of the Americans, and thank God we are, because Americans also have hundreds of missiles pointed at Russian cities, which are all cold, miserable, and really ugly...

—Moscow isn't ugly at all, Vittorio, don't listen to him, and neither is St. Petersburg. They are wonderful cities! When you finally start reading Tolstoy, instead of all that science fiction, you'll discover that too!

—But what has that got to do with anything? What's the matter with Tolstoy? What are you saying, Arianna? What's the matter with you? You know absolutely nothing! They were beautiful at the time of the tsars, those cities, yes, but now they are shitholes! The Communists have destroyed the lot! They burned the churches and the cathedrals and built barracks on the ruins! And St. Petersburg doesn't even exist anymore: they call it Stalingrad, or Leningrad, I don't know. Something *grad*. But Arianna, please, I'm telling you for the last time, don't interrupt me. If you interrupt me again, I'm leaving.

—Okay, I'm sorry.

—Your mother is a bit of a Communist, Vittorio.

—Not even slightly, Vittorio. Don't listen to him.

—Well, as I was saying, the Americans are pointing their missiles too... Of course, what else are they supposed to do? Just sit there and get blown to bits by the reds? The president can fire them at any moment, but the Americans would never do it first, remember that. Because we're the good guys, understand?

—We also live in a democracy, while in Russia there is a dictatorship! That needs to be said too!

Cesare stood up.

—I've been interrupted again, and I'm off. I said it and I'm doing it. Vittorio, remember, you must always be on America's side! And remember that in life, the West is always better than the East, and the North is always better than the South!

—But Dad, that depends on where you are, doesn't it?

—No! The West ends in California! Then there is the Pacific and the international date line, and then China, and with China the East starts again. California is the limit of the civilized world! And now, goodbye to you all!

—Oh, come on, Cesare, said Arianna, looking in from the kitchen, with a wet apron and a bowl in her hand, a half smile painted onto her soft mouth. Please, stay a bit longer: go on, finish your speech...

—I said I would go, Arianna, and I will.

—Dad, wait. Please. I knew about the Cold War, and I've actually just been reading a science fiction short story that deals with it. Can I tell you about it?

—Of course, said Arianna. She sat at the dinner table, lit a cigarette, and said to her husband, "Come on, stay a bit longer. I'll clear up later, okay?"

Cesare sat down again and watched her inhale and blow the smoke out gracefully. He had never smoked in his life, and he couldn't bear smoke, but he had always liked seeing his wife with a cigarette in her hand, and never had a problem with her smoking in the house. He had never told her, but he found the simple, perfect gesture with which she smoked highly arousing, and admirably free from the usual vulgarity and inelegance displayed by smokers. Arianna never sucked in her cheeks as she inhaled, or puffed them out in that ridiculous fashion as if there was so much smoke inside them as to exert a pressure. She had never given in to one of those demonic exhalations of smoke through the nose, or while she spoke, and he never saw her with the cigarette in her mouth and her eyes half shut like a poker player, because when Arianna smoked, she never did anything else. She just sat and serenely dedicated herself to the consumption of nicotine and the simultaneous chewing of peppermint gum to rid her breath of the smell of tobacco. She softly blew the smoke away, always toward the ceiling and far from anyone sitting near her, and never allowed it to stagnate around her mouth. She always put the cigarette out well before it was finished, just past halfway, to avoid looking like a woman desperate to take another drag; and when she put it out in the ashtray, always with the same single, rapid gesture, the cigarette butt immediately stopped smoking.

—It's the story of an American soldier...Well, first you need to know that at the beginning of the story, the Russians have destroyed New York and Boston and Washington and Los Angeles in a nuclear attack, and no one in the US government or army has survived...The president is dead, the vice president is dead, the head of the armed forces is dead...All of them, dead. The only military man to survive is an old general, who must be accompanied to a top secret base in the mountains from which he can fire hundreds of nuclear missiles at the Soviet Union, and there is just one soldier escorting him, okay?

Arianna nodded.

—On their journey through the mountains by Jeep, the soldier starts to think that he is not sure about what he should do, okay? That is, should he take revenge for his country and the millions of dead by sending the same death upon his enemy, or —

—Of course, damn it. It's called retaliation.

—Or give at least one-half of the world the chance to survive...

—The first one for sure...

—Cesare, let him finish.

—A soldier can only choose the first option, Arianna.

—I don't remember you ever being a soldier, Cesare. You didn't even do the military service.

—What's that got to do with it, Arianna? I had to start to work, I couldn't waste time in the military...But I am of course someone who has great respect for the American army, Arianna. That is pretty obvious...

—Wait, Dad. The soldier isn't actually just a soldier, but a man who thinks freely, and he asks himself if he is capable of being responsible for the deaths of so many millions of people...He who has never hurt anyone in his entire life...

—What? Why? He's not the one pressing the button.

—But Dad, he is involved, because he is the only one who knows the way to the base in the mountains. If he doesn't escort the general to the base, nothing happens, you see? If, instead, he takes him there, the general will obliterate half of Russia and kill millions of people.

— Hey, a soldier is a soldier. He's got orders.

— Come on, Cesare, let him finish.

—Yeah, go on, go on...I really want to see where this is going.

—Well, in the story, when they arrive at the secret bunker, just as the old general is about to press the button, the soldier decides to shoot and kill him and let millions of Russians live.

— He's a traitor.

— But he saves millions of people, Dad.

— He betrays his nation and his people.

—Yes, but he saves the rest of the world.

—That means nothing! He's a coward, a vile coward.

— But Vittorio, that way the soldier has become a murderer anyway...

Arianna put out the cigarette she had smoked too fast, without enjoying it, filling the living room with the unnecessary smoke of her graceful exhalations.

—Yes, Mom, but he decides to live with just one murder on his conscience, rather than millions.

— Noooo! He has betrayed all of his own people, all of those who died! He's also a deserter. I don't like your story at all, Vittorio. What, are you going to become a Communist, too? In the meantime I'm going back to work hard for private property. Arianna, can I get a coffee or should I go to the bar?

—Wait, I'll make it now, she said.

— No, now it's too late. Bye, Vittorio. Say hi to Karl Marx.

He then turned to Arianna.

— Bye, sex bomb.

And he left, leaving them staring at their feet, both bright red.

The next morning, as soon as the bell rang for break, Vittorio set off down the long corridor that led to a dozen classrooms, in search of the beautiful girl. She wasn't in the corridor, or in

Section F. The friend she had hugged so eagerly the day before was there, but she was not.

Stunned by that totally unexpected absence, Vittorio vainly looked into all the first-year classrooms. She wasn't there, either. Infinitely disappointed, he told himself she might be unwell, and he imagined her with a mild cold or a blister.

The next morning she wasn't at school, either. And not even on Wednesday, Thursday, or Friday. Vittorio fell into the darkest of moods. All those absences at the beginning of the year! It was impossible! Had she fallen ill the first day of school? But she hadn't seemed the slightest bit unwell! She was so beautiful...

He began to think that she might have changed schools, or maybe her family had been forced to move all of a sudden to follow her father — whom Vittorio imagined thin and severe, tall, with spiky hair, a banker or someone in the military who had been abruptly transferred to another city, so they had to quickly pack all their suitcases and jump in the car at dawn, headed for the unknown.

He spent an interminable Friday afternoon shut up in his room listening to *Jesus Christ Superstar*, terribly worrying his mother because of his decision to hear over and over at full volume all thirty-nine lashes that Pilate ordered Jesus to suffer.

On Saturday morning, Vittorio decided that if the beautiful girl was still absent, he would go and talk to her friend, the girl who was hugged that morning and was in Section F, whose name — he found out — was Cinzia. He would say hello to her, introduce himself, get to know her, and then, using some ploy, would ask who her friend was and why she didn't come to school anymore.

At break time, however, as he was walking the long corridor toward Section F, Vittorio realized he didn't even have the courage to talk to Cinzia. He walked past her twice, completely ignoring her, and she did the same.

On his way home he told himself he really was an idiot who would never get anywhere in life. This for sure. But it made no sense at all to keep on looking for a girl who had disappeared without a trace. Perhaps she was from the future, he joked, and had teleported to another space and time. Maybe she wasn't even a terrestrial. He sighed, decided she would be the first of his unlucky loves, and forgot her.

ASHURBANIPAL

IT WAS THE MORNING OF THE EPIPHANY, January 6, 1980, when Ivo called Arianna from New York to tell her he had met the Marquis Emilio Pucci and had greeted him with a bow and called him Maestro, he who in his entire life had never bowed to anyone.

Pucci, the great Florentine whom Ivo respected more than any other stylist, that genius of taste who in the 1950s, right after the war, had invented women's ski suits made of stretch wool gabardine and dyed them in bright colors, before going on to revive and ennoble scarves, shirts, blouses, evening dresses, sundresses, swimsuits, skirts, handkerchiefs, jackets, and trousers and shorts—everything a woman could wear—with the most colorful, rich, and elegant prints that the world had ever seen: totally abstract, brand-new, and yet born of an ancient and profound, quintessentially Italian tradition, each drawn by him, always inspired by the intoxicating beauty of whatever the Maestro saw around himself—the jewels in the crown of Italy: Cortina and Florence and Capri and Taormina and Syracuse.

Ivo told Arianna he had been to Studio 54, an *absolutely crazy* nightclub where a very important client had insisted on taking him, and he had met Andy Warhol and Salvador Dalí, who were the client's friends, and *everyone, Arianna, everyone except me, of course, was taking every possible drug, you should have seen it!*

Now that the new factory was pretty much finished, he added, he wanted to buy himself a very large house, *a mansion*, to refurbish and redecorate completely. He wanted it on the hills over Florence, with a huge Italian-style garden of centennial oaks and cypresses and pines and mimosas, a greenhouse with tropical palms and ferns and delft tiles on the walls, an immense fountain, and a tennis court. He told her that the idea of the mansion had come to him at the Metropolitan Museum of Art, where he had spent the entire Sunday alone, devastated as ever by the jet lag.

As he roamed those silent halls, he had seen a bas-relief with a cuneiform inscription — *Assyrian*, he specified — which read: "I built thereon [a palace...] for the enduring leisure life of my lordship Ashurbanipal II," and he had been enchanted by the description of that immense palace built almost nine hundred years before Christ in the lost ancient city of Nineveh, which must serve for *the purification of the King, the adoration of the Gods, and the ritual protection from Demons*. It was enormous and elegant, surrounded and protected by sacred plants such as boxwood, mulberry, cedar, cypress, pistachio, tamarind, and poplar.

And then, once he had finished giving her all that unsolicited information in the total silence of his fortieth-floor room overlooking Central Park, his gaze fixed on the sinuous back of the *client*, a sleeping Haitian beauty whose name he had momentarily forgotten, Ivo fell silent and stayed that way for a while, listening to the barely audible noises Arianna made while smoking.

A little more than a year had passed since that morning, and its memory had become weak and distant, held in suspended animation by a regret that never forgets or disappoints. Even his telephonic courtship had become nothing more than a simulacrum: every time he called her, he felt like a commander of one of those World War II destroyers which, hoping to sink enemy submarines, blindly released depth charges in the abysses, never knowing whether they had hit their targets but continuing to drop them anyway, day after day.

He never knew how much she liked it when he called her from abroad and his tales became films projected onto the ceilings of the bedroom in which she always lay during those calls, bored and tired, free only to imagine herself happy elsewhere.

He told her about London and New York and Amsterdam and Frankfurt and Munich. He told her of the crazy German highways that he would drive on at 220 kilometers per hour to get to the factories that some of his powerful clients had built in the middle of nowhere in the Bavarian countryside, among the cows and the crows, simply because they were born in those places and didn't want to leave, just like him, and he would always manage to drop her into every call, telling her how fantastic it would be if she were with him, next to him, and explained all the wonderful things they would do together and described all the fantastic places they would visit.

For her, with her, he would have even made an effort to suppress his hatred for the French and France, and he would have gladly brought Arianna to Paris to eat foie gras and escargots and lobster and Malossol caviar, and drink champagne and the sublime mineral white wines from Burgundy, and then he would take her to the Ritz, to a room with a view onto Place Vendôme. He told her of the fun they would have ordering those monumental breakfasts to their room—all kinds of pastries, fried eggs, pâté, wild salmon, every kind of cheese, strawberries with cream and champagne—all of which they would only pick at because both of them, in the morning, preferred just an espresso and a plain croissant.

Once—just once, and she immediately regretted it, though Ivo basked for a while in that small victory—Arianna allowed the words "in another life" to slip from her mouth. She said that she would love to go away with him *in another life*, because she had never left Italy, and then added that, *always in another life,* she wouldn't even mind taking part in the longest and most boring of his work meetings: she'd be happy just to sit to one side, listening or reading a book, and wouldn't have bothered anyone.

Ivo went to the window and looked at the whole of New York City sprawling in front of him. He felt like a fool. Arianna continued answering his phone calls, yes, but why shouldn't she? All she was required to do was lift the receiver once every ten days. Why should she interrupt the worn-out decadence of a passion only to risk setting it aflame once more?

She was simply waiting for his desire to grow weak and die, until the day in which all that would remain of those moments together in the Pagoda under the storm would be a barely perceptible widening of smiles every time they greeted one another on the street or at the tennis club Christmas party.

Only with time, after suffering the cruel decay of their bodies and souls, would they understand whether it had been an irrelevant folly or the last, splendid, precious moment when their lives could have still changed course.

No, Ivo decided. It was over. Best say it now, from New York. Leave her—if "leave" was the right verb, then, for an affair that had never really started. He closed his eyes and told her that this was his last call, and that he would never call her again.

Arianna was silent for a while, just breathing into the receiver, then she spoke.

—No, please don't stop. Not yet. Call me again a few more times. Then you can stop.

WHOSOEVER UNCEASINGLY
STRIVES UPWARD

ONE COLD MORNING in mid-March, as he was returning home from school and fantasizing about being given a motocross bike, Vittorio saw her.

A long, transparent ruler poked out of her rucksack full of books, and she was walking some fifty meters in front of him, trudging but at a good pace, dressed exactly as she had been the day he had seen her: the shearling coat, the Camperos, the perfectly faded 501s. His heart skipped a beat, and he decided that he would follow her home without being seen, at any cost. If she got on a bus, he would have steeled his nerves and jumped on that bus, too.

The girl cut a perfect diagonal across a square, turned a corner, and stopped in front of a large door. Vittorio managed to hide himself behind the wall of a medieval palazzo just in time, and when he dared to stick his head out like the cartoon coyote, he saw her vainly rummaging in her bag for a while, then she raised her eyes to the sky, huffed, rang the doorbell, and drew close to the intercom.

—Mom, it's me.

A buzz, a loud metal click. The door opened and she walked in. Vittorio rejoiced silently, shutting his eyes and squeezing his fists. He waited a good minute, then walked up to the doorbell. There was just one name card, but it was blank. The door number was 40 and the sign attached to the wall nearby proclaimed VIA ALBERTO FRILLI.

He returned home full of a wild hope that he vainly struggled to contain. During lunch he spoke without pausing for breath, and informed his parents that Harlan Ellison was undoubtedly the finest writer of all time. And not just of science fiction. Seeing their eyes glaze over, he ran to his room and returned with an enormous book that was more than one thousand pages long. He placed it on the kitchen table and read:

"Repent, Harlequin!" Said the Ticktock Man
I Have No Mouth, and I Must Scream
The Beast That Shouted Love at the Heart of the World
The Deathbird
Adrift Just Off the Islets of Langerhans: Latitude $38° 54'$ N, Longitude $77° 00' 13''$ W

Then he gave the smile of a madman, asked where the phone book was, took it under his arm, kissed his mother on the forehead, said goodbye to his father with an unprecedented slap on the back, shouted, "Ave Cesare, moriturus te salutat," and went to lock himself in his room.

He had decided to find the phone number of the family that lived at number 40 in via Frilli, and the only way was to check in the phone book the address of everyone who had a phone number, starting with the surnames beginning with A. He sat on his bed and set off at a brisk pace, thinking he would be finished before dinnertime, but when his father growled for him to come to the table, Vittorio had only got to CAVICCHI Andrea, without finding anyone who lived in via Frilli. After dinner, a terrible headache came over him and he fell fast asleep.

The next morning at school he decided not to force himself through the ordeal of walking the length of the corridor at break time just to see Cinzia and not find the courage to greet her, so he stayed in class, confident in his new method and his good fortune.

After lunch, he started again from CIABATTI Teresa. When he arrived at FARINA Sergio, he had a shock: this man lived in via Alberto Frilli, at number 12. He jumped to his feet and celebrated that small victory. Comforted, he quickly ran through the *F*'s and the *G*'s, the few *H*'s — a German textile firm and the hotels — and halfway through the *I*'s, he was called to dinner.

He hadn't found any other residents of via Frilli, and his eyes were so tired from the effort of reading the microscopic characters in which the addresses were written, that he decided not to continue.

The next morning at break time he met Cinzia halfway down the corridor and she smiled at him and greeted him with a timid "Ciao," to which he responded with a stilted smile. It was a good omen, he said to himself. Once at home, he announced he would *lunch frugally*, put *The Wall* by Pink Floyd on the record player, and immediately resumed his search through the phone book.

At *L*, he found two residents of via Frilli, first LEOTTI Antonio at number 18, then LONGO Carlo at number 38. By the time he got to MARZOCCHI Edoardo, it was dinnertime, after which he decided to go on and arrived at PAZZAGLIA Alessandro, having found just one other resident of via Frilli: PATRIZI ZIBETTI Marco, at number 2.

At eleven o'clock, his father entered his room and ordered him to *turn the music off and go straight to bed, now!* Vittorio obeyed willingly, exhausted both by the task and from having listened to Pink Floyd all day. Before falling asleep, he asked himself whether he had undertaken an impossible task. What if her family didn't have a telephone? And even if they did, and he found the number, would he call? Really? Would he find the courage? And even if he did find it and he did call, what if she didn't answer? What if her mother or, God forbid, *her father* answered? What should he say? "Could I please speak to your daughter, sir?" And what if she had a sister, and the mother or father said something like, "Yes, sure, which one would you like to speak to?" What would he say? The beautiful one with the sheepskin coat and the Camperos? He didn't even know her name...

The next day at school Cinzia said hello to him again, and he reciprocated promptly. For a moment he thought about the possibility of stopping his stride and starting a conversation and finding the right moment to ask her in the most indirect manner about her friend, but then he decided it was too much, and gave up.

On his way home, Vittorio decided to pass by the girl's house, and walked the whole of via Alberto Frilli as if it were his domain. He marched in the middle of the road, pointing to the house numbers and pronouncing under his breath the names of the people who lived there. When he arrived at her door, he drew close to it, stroked it, and went home.

He ate his lunch absentmindedly, providing only monosyllabic answers to his mother's concerned questions, as she had just returned from a meeting with his teachers and had been told that her son was barely following class anymore. Vittorio sloped to his room, sat cross-legged on his bed, put on Pink Floyd, and got going. By dinnertime he had got to *T*, and the only numbers of via Frilli he hadn't found were numbers 30 and 40.

Though he ably defended himself from the skirmish instigated by the bored, empty questions his father had been urged to make by Arianna, Vittorio felt lost. He only had eight pages of the phone book left, and was now certain that the girl's address had somehow escaped him. He hadn't seen it, he had somehow missed it among the thousands of names he had searched through in those fevered days, and now he didn't know what to do if he reached the end and didn't find the number. Should he start back at *A*, or should he just ask Cinzia, who for some incomprehensible reason continued to greet and smile at him?

Vittorio lifted his eyes from the plate, announced he felt unwell, got up from the table, and went to his room, followed by his parents' stunned gazes. He lay down on his bed, picked up the phone book, and decided there would be no music during this final push. Perhaps it was the music that had distracted him. He quickly finished the *T*'s and the brief *U*'s. At the *V*'s, he found the resident of number 30, via Frilli: VAIANI David.

He had now found the number of all of the residents of via Frilli! All of them but her, and the phone book was nearly finished. There were three columns of *V*'s left, and a page and a half of *Z*'s. Vittorio left the room, went to his mother, who was watching television on her own in the living room, and told her that, from tomorrow, he wanted to start dressing differently: no more flannel trousers, no more penny loafers, no more lambswool sweaters. He wanted to wear jeans every day and fade them himself, he said. He wanted to buy Camperos and denim shirts with mother-of-pearl buttons and lumberjack shirts and a Levi's jeans jacket with fleece lining and a whole load of other really cool things he liked and never told her about. It was important, he said.

Arianna stared at him, taken aback by that sudden announcement, perturbed by her son's unheard-of ultimatum-like tone, offended by his attack on her sartorial choices.

— Yes, of course, whatever you like.

Vittorio smiled, hugged her, and added that he would no longer be cutting his hair, too, and went back to his room. He lay down on the bed, picked up the phone book, and started to read through the names in the comfort of an unburdened soul. And there, right at the end, he found it: ZUCCHI Dante, 40 v. A. Frilli . . . 3 40 05.

He didn't feel as thrilled as he had expected. It still meant nothing. He had to call her right away, even if was a bit late, or he never would. If he started to think about it, he would find a dozen reasons to postpone the call, and then it would become too difficult. It was now or never. So he got up, tiptoed to his parents' room, sat on the bed, and dialed the number.

His heart was beating like a drum, and he closed his eyes while the connection was established. A light click, the ringing tone, and a young female voice answered. Vittorio introduced himself and excused himself for the impertinence—using exactly that word, "impertinence"—then said that he absolutely had to talk to her because she was the most beautiful girl he had ever seen in his life. When he heard her laugh, he told her how he had come to find her—the story of the phone book and Pink Floyd—and confessed that, despite all his research, he still didn't know her name.

When she said she was called Milena, he answered that it was a truly beautiful name, and then he told her many other things, and the phone call went very well indeed.

MONTE CARLO

WHEN IVO INVITED ARIANNA to Monte Carlo to see the finals of the international tennis tournament, she laughed and said that he was truly, truly mad, but couldn't help imagining just how beautiful Monte Carlo had to be in early spring, with the perfumed breeze that slips over the calm sea, the cool champagne, the oysters, the Hôtel de Paris, and all the other marvels that Ivo had just finished describing to her.

In the short pause that followed, he added that without her it wouldn't just rain but hail, the breeze would become an Arctic wind, the oysters would be smell of gasoline, and the champagne would be flat and tepid.

Please come, he said, and she answered, No, thank you, but Ivo noticed that she had enjoyed the call. So he called straight back asking to speak to her husband, who upon being invited to go to the country club in the Pagoda to see Borg playing against Guillermo Vilas accepted immediately, filled with excitement, and couldn't stop telling him how *sensational* that tournament had been up to that point.

—All I'll say, Ivo, is that the world's top players were there. Not only Borg and Vilas. There were Lendl, Clerc, and Gerulaitis, and all of them, think about it, lost to Borg without winning so much as a set, and then there was old Orantes, and Gildemeister, Victor Pecci, Connors, who lost to an unknown French player, Panatta, Bertolucci, Barazzutti. Even McEnroe! All of them!

Ivo arrived to pick him up at eight o'clock the following morning. It was Easter Sunday. Arianna came to the window to wave them off, and couldn't help smiling when she saw Ivo, with Cesare already in the car, getting out of it with the excuse of removing a single pine needle from the windshield, turning toward her, putting one hand on his heart and pretending to faint.

When he got back in the car and found Cesare sitting there, Ivo realized that he wouldn't enjoy himself at all, and decided to bring Citarella along.

—Citarella in Monte Carlo? They won't let him in, for sure ... Where's he going to sit?

—Well, I've got a spare ticket because Andrea Vecchio told me at the last minute he couldn't make it. We'll put him on the backseat. It'll be a bit uncomfortable, but he'll fit. Come on, let's go. Where does he live?

When Ivo Barrocciai arrived in the Green Zone, he was filled with excitement. He had never been there, and immediately loved it.

—You see, Cesare? You see what these people have done? They built themselves an entire neighborhood without asking anyone's permission. And they were right! Who should they ask, the pope? Aren't they the people? And who does the land belong to, anyway? It's theirs, they bought it with their hard work! And why shouldn't they build a house on their own land if that's what they want? Can't you see, Cesare, that these people are making their dreams come true? Can't you see that this is the real Italian dream? They left everything behind: their towns, their houses, the land, their families, their traditions ... Cesare, these people have made a *biblical exodus* to escape poverty, do you understand that? In the hope of a better life! Isn't that fantastic?

Vezzosi nodded doggedly while Barrocciai slipped through the middle of the Green Zone in his Pagoda at walking pace, with the roof down, and he smiled and greeted everyone. And how he enjoyed himself pointing out to Cesare the boys who whizzed in front of them on their bikes and played soccer in the middle of the street; the men in their work clothes who, despite the fact it was Easter morning, were climbing into their Piaggio Apes overflowing with tools and trundling away; the couples in their Sunday best making their way slowly toward the church; the women shouting from balconies emblazoned with drying sheets!

—Look, Cesare! Look at life! The wonderful, amazing adventure that is life! These people are heroes, all of them! Without them, Italy would be nothing! They wake up in the morning and work all day and go home only when it's dark, just in time to dine with their families and watch television and fall asleep, and the next morning they set off again, and so it goes for years and years, and they live the happiest of lives without even realizing it, without even worrying for a second about happiness, because all that counts for them is their duty, for fuck's sake, and the future! Can you see them? For them there is no past and no present! Only the future! They have nothing, but instead of despairing they find joy in every small victory! And they never moan and never cry ... Look at them! While they save themselves and their families from poverty, they're building the future of a whole country! My God, if I wasn't who I am, I would want to be one of them!

As they arrived at Citarella's house, Ivo climbed out of the Pagoda and rang the doorbell. A boy quickly came to the window and went straight back in, then a robust, not totally unattractive, not particularly tall woman appeared on the balcony and looked out at them.

—Good morning, Mr. Barrocciai! I'll get Pasquale for you right away!

—Good morning, dear Mrs. Citarella. Have we already met?

—With that car, you couldn't be anyone but Mr. Barrocciai! Pasquale talks about you all the time. Good morning, Mr. Vezzosi, how are you? Pasquale! Pasquale! He's just getting dressed for Mass...Would you like to come in for a coffee?

—Thank you, madam, but I'll have to take you up on that some other time. We have come to get your husband. Today he'll have to miss Mass. We're going to Monte Carlo!

—To Monte Carlo? Really? Pasquale! Put on your best clothes, you're going to Monte Carlo! Put on your white shirt!

Pasquale came running down the stairs just two minutes later, buttoning a white shirt, and didn't ask why they were going to Monte Carlo, nor did he once mention the extreme discomfort of having to contort himself to fit on the rear jump seat of the Pagoda. He thanked Ivo profusely, and spoke only when asked a question.

There was traffic on the highway, and when they got to the border at Ventimiglia there was an awkward moment at passport control when it transpired that Citarella didn't have — actually had never had — a passport, and hadn't said so earlier because he thought that Monte Carlo was in Italy. The policeman brought his head close to the car window, looked at Citarella, shook his head, and said that without a passport he couldn't cross the border.

Pasquale whispered to Ivo to let him out for a moment. He walked up to the policeman and began to talk to him in a totally incomprehensible dialect, gesticulating wildly. The policeman responded by gesticulating even more. After a while, they shook hands, and Pasquale returned to the car.

—We can go, Ivo. There's no problem. He's a *paisà*, from Bovino...

They arrived at the country club around one and took their courtside seats. When a pale sun emerged from the clouds, Ivo and Cesare put on their black Wayfarers and Pasquale slipped on a glamorous, totally unexpected pair of mirror-lens Ray-Bans, and they watched the merciless psychological destruction of

Vilas by Björn Borg, 6–1, 6–0, 6–2, and Citarella couldn't stop sniggering at the sight of all those rich people turning their heads *like windshield wipers* to follow every shot.

Immediately after witnessing that disappointing mismatch, however, they had the good fortune of watching one of the best doubles matches of all time, in which Adriano Panatta and Paolo Bertolucci surprisingly bested Vitas Gerulaitis and John McEnroe, 6–2, 5–7, 6–4.

During their journey home, Ivo wanted to stop for dinner in the famous seaside town encircled by the smallest mountain range in the world, and while they ate their penne agli scampi and drank Gavi di Gavi, he launched into an excited, confused speech.

Ivo said that Panatta and Bertolucci's victory over two champions like Gerulaitis and McEnroe had been a real marvel, because it went *well beyond tennis*. It gave him great hope for the future and was a huge inspiration for his work. That triumph over the world's top players had *enlightened him* — his exact words — and had shown what a *perfect Italian victory* is: one achieved with talent, class, style, spontaneity, elegance, and a profound knowledge of the game.

— It's no coincidence they won in Monte Carlo, boys, because this is really our house and it doesn't belong to the French at all…On that slow red clay, between the pines and the palms, beneath the soft spring Mediterranean sun, refreshed by the breeze that, if you smell it properly, you can tell has traveled over the sea from here…I'm sure that in Forest Hills or in Boston or in Cincinnati, Panatta and Bertolucci would never have won against two beasts like Gerulaitis and McEnroe…They wouldn't have even gone to play in America in the summer, with that ridiculous humidity, to wear out their knees and ankles on that gray earth which is harder than cement…Not when they could stay here and enjoy the sunsets and the sea bass and the Gavi di Gavi. Speaking of which…

He got the waiter's attention by holding the bottle upside down and smiling, to get him to bring them another.

—What was I saying? Yes, because Panatta and Berto-lucci are *fundamentally, even genetically different* from the other greats like Hewitt–McMillan, Newcombe–Roche, Smith–Lutz, Gottfried–Ramirez, McEnroe–Fleming…And this is exactly where their greatness and their absolute Italianness lies…Those two aren't just professionals, they're artists! The best amateurs in the world…Lazy, brilliant, indolent, free…Yes, they're free and couldn't be freer, and incapable of devoting their lives to just one thing, not even to the sport they globally excel in. They may win a little less than the others, yes, but on certain days it is impossible to beat Panatta and Bertolucci, and do you know why? Because winning in Monte Carlo or at the Foro Italico in Rome *means so much more to them* than winning in Cincinnati, and so they give their very best, but you can't give your best every day, you know? And so when they win like they did today, they are no longer just tennis players, they become something more…They come to embody absolute class and, therefore, the very best of Italy. The spirit of the time, even. Yes, the spirit of the Italian time, that is…I don't know if you're following me, guys. I don't think so, both of you have blank faces…But it's all crystal clear to me, obvious even…

He poured himself an ice-cold glass of Gavi di Gavi and drank it in one go, right to the last drop.

—Here, today, there is a great lesson to be learned, and the lesson is that this is Italy's time in the world, and we have to do everything we believe in, and in our own way, because everything is going to be fine! A good star is shining over us, understand? It's impossible to get it wrong! Life is now! Today!

Ivo fell silent and stayed quiet for a whole minute, breathing in deeply with his eyes closed, then he announced that his dream would be to live just like that. His entire life.

—With this wonderful abandonment, he went on. After a full day of work in my new factory, if God willing I'm ever able to get in there…

He raised his glass.

—With my friends...

And he pointed at them.

— In incredible places like this...

He stretched out his arms to indicate the magnificent water-front and the seemingly infinite beach and the pure beauty of the smallest mountain range in the world, whose marble shone brightly in the light of the full moon, and remained for a full minute in that position of Christ the Redeemer.

—And with the women that I like, he added, this time without managing to look at anyone.

Then he instructed the waiters to bring another bottle of Gavi di Gavi and three lobsters alla catalana.

CINZIA'S PARTY

AFTER ALL THE HARD WORK to find Milena and the many brilliant phone calls that had followed that first one, at Cinzia's party Vittorio found himself completely tongue-tied. It took him half an hour just to go and introduce himself, and then, once he was standing in front of her, all he managed to do was say "Hi, I'm Vittorio," smile like an idiot, and hold out his hand as if she were a friend of his mother's or a teacher.

When Milena shook it, her friends started giggling and he felt terribly embarrassed and moved away without a word, and could not find the courage to go back to her again, even though Milena hadn't laughed at all when he had held out his hand, and even if that hand-shaking thing had seemed a bit strange, she thought it was a somewhat old-style, respectful gesture, and had actually liked it.

It was Cinzia's fifteenth birthday party, and after the cake and the happy birthday sung in chorus, someone turned out the lights, turned on the Technics amplifier, and started playing slow songs, one after the other, over and over: "A mano a mano" and "Storie" by Riccardo Cocciante, "I giardini di marzo" and "E penso a te" and "Il mio canto libero" by Battisti, "I Can't Tell You

217

Why" by the Eagles, "Moonflower" by Santana, "If You Leave Me Now" by Chicago, and "Stay" by Jackson Browne, and the boys and the girls—all the same age, all at the first dance party of their brand-new lives—started to dance slow.

Following an ancient ritual, a boy had to get up from the line of chairs he was sitting on, walk the five meters that separated him from the chosen girl, and ask her to dance. If and when the girl accepted, the newly formed couple moved toward what had become (with the table full of snacks and Coca-Cola now moved against a wall) the dance floor and started to sway back and forth, experiencing for the first time both the charm of those songs and the absolute novelty of the closeness between bodies, which was, however, still relative, because the girls held out their arms and rested their hands on the shoulders of the boys, who in turn rested their hands on the girls' waists, thus establishing a distance that, by the end of the song, had almost always been somewhat reduced.

Milena was in high demand—second only to Beatrice, who had a reputation for being easy—but she only agreed to dance with two boys, who were kept rigorously at arm's length, and never for more than one song at a time. Every so often, Vittorio thought she was throwing furtive glances in his direction, but he couldn't be sure.

He had developed a complicated procedure for looking at her: as he didn't want her to notice him doing so, he pretended to look out of the window, where he could see her reflection in the glass as she spoke with her friends and giggled and kindly declined the offers to dance from the boys who approached her. Every so often, however, damn it, it really looked like she was looking at him all alone, with his back turned to the party, pretending to stare at the sky like a convict.

He was embarrassed. Once again. For all sorts of reasons. Because he had held out his hand to her as an old uncle would do. Because he could not find the courage to speak to her. Because he was watching her reflection in the window instead than talking to her, though in the glass she was truly, truly beautiful. Because he was showing himself to be completely different from that brilliant boy who had found her number in the phone book and then called so many times to tell her all kinds of brilliant and funny and highly personal things.

Only when the sky started to turn yellow did Vittorio notice the sunset. His gaze changed focus: it left her reflection and turned to the sky in flames. He realized that it was, in a way, his first sunset, as in his whole life he had never looked at one for more than a few seconds, and he found that he couldn't bear both its indescribable, superhuman beauty and the fact that the world put on such a magnificent show every evening for anyone to watch, and nobody cared. It seemed a terrible waste, exactly like his boyhood, and then he thought that if the sun was setting, the party would soon be over.

If something did not happen, he would have failed their first meeting and she would think he was an idiot and would end up sooner or later catching the eye of another boy, somebody older and bolder, maybe with a car, and they would have ended up like Brenda and Eddie, the protagonists of "Scenes from an Italian Restaurant," that song by Billy Joel he loved so much: "*the popular steadies, And the king and the queen of the prom, Riding around with the car top down, And the radio on,*" who decided to marry, but then "*started to fight when the money got tight, And they just didn't count on the tears,*" and then "*got a divorce as a matter of course,*" and nobody heard from them anymore.

Vittorio thought of all the hours spent listening to Jackson Browne and the Eagles and Chicago, learning their songs by heart so that he could translate them for her, if she had asked. He remembered all the times he had tried on his clothes in front of the full-length mirror in his parents' room, finally deciding on a blue lambswool sweater, blue jeans that were not Levi's 501s, and a pair of old Superga tennis shoes he had personally washed three times in a row to eliminate any trace of clay.

The doorbell rang. The first mother had arrived to pick up her son or daughter. It could even be his, or Milena's. Everything could already be over.

No, he told himself. He withdrew from the window, went over to the record player, waited a few seconds for the song to finish—it was "Moonflower," by Santana—removed the disc from the turntable, extracted the album's other disc, put it on the turntable, and placed the needle at the beginning of the pause before the last song of side 2. Then, without stopping, without thinking, Vittorio went over to Milena, who saw him approach and immediately lost interest in her friends' conversation. Just as Santana's guitar started up the magic of "Europa," he spoke to her.

—Do you want to dance?

She got up and followed him to the center of the floor, and didn't straighten out her arms as she had with the other two boys, and didn't rest her hands on his shoulders, but wrapped them around his neck, and they began to dance.

—Thank goodness you finally came over, she whispered to him, and he blushed and smiled. Then, while he was thinking of something dazzling to tell her, Milena said it was a wonderful song he had put on, because she had seen him suddenly turn from the window and go and fiddle about with the stereo. So he told her everything about Carlos Santana and "Europa," and then he said that he dedicated it to her. That it was hers. If she wanted it, of course. She said nothing, and when the song ended, someone put it on again and again, and they kept on dancing to "Europa" until they decided to sit down, and they were very close, their shoulders touching, right next to Beatrice who was kissing Ricky Mariotti, and a little farther over was his friend Fede Carpini, who was kissing another girl.

At first they were embarrassed, then they started to laugh, and Vittorio thought that, in that evening blessed by the gods, he could dare to do something else he had never done before. With great caution, his heart beating wildly, he slowly slid his arm behind Milena's back and then moved it down until it touched her lightly, and when she felt that very slow and very shy and very clumsy embrace, she drew closer to him, very close, and spoke softly.

—Listen, I've never kissed anyone before.

—Me neither.

Their awkward smiles dissolved into laughter, and Milena moved her mouth closer to Vittorio's and their lips touched, and then she opened her mouth very slightly and so did he, and they stayed like that for a few seconds, sharing breath, until he very gently pushed his tongue into her mouth as he had been told he was supposed to do, until it touched her lips, and when Milena's tongue touched his. It immediately seemed to him a very unpleasant thing, this kissing with tongues, something that was absolutely impossible to like, but he stayed there and so did she, and they kept on kissing and kissing until Cinzia's mother called out for her, and Milena said, "I have to go."

—What a shame, though...What a terrible shame...

—So, I guess you and I are together, now.

—Yes.

They looked at one another and smiled. Milena gave him a quick kiss on the cheek, ran to hug her mother—a slim and elegant woman who looked absolutely nothing like her—and left with her, arm in arm.

THE BEAST IS BACK

UPON HIS RETURN FROM MONTE CARLO, Cesare's mood improved considerably. It seemed that Ivo's lucky star had started to shine on him too. All of a sudden he slept like a baby and had no trouble getting up in the morning, fresh as a daisy. He arrived on site before Citarella. He enjoyed the signs of the onset of a spring that promised to be exceptional, and even started to take care of the way he dressed, and resolved to return as soon as possible to the unkempt carpe diem that had always governed his life and that, in his opinion, had never betrayed him.

One evening he came home early and sat in the living room, still full of energy. Arianna was out, Vittorio was locked in his room. He sprung from the armchair, left the house, went to the record shop, and bought an old album by Barry White, *Can't Get Enough*. He went home, placed it on the turntable, and as "You're the First, the Last, My Everything" started to play, Cesare Vezzosi felt himself once again filled with the feral energy he had been born with. He began to sing along, there in his living room, totally indifferent to horribly mangling every line, clicking his fingers in time and even performing the deep sighs and scratchy moans of Barry the Master, and then he began to actually dance to that joyful, orgasmic celebration of women and love and sex and the good life, and danced and sang right to the end of the song because he was still alive — yes — and healthy, and he could still do anything he wanted with his life.

After a dinner he spent inundating with unusual compliments the routine meal his wife had put on the table, Cesare called Arianna to the bedroom under the pretense of going over the bank statements together, and he screwed her passionately, telling her over and over just how amazingly beautiful she was.

The next morning he woke in an excellent mood, looked in the bathroom mirror, and decided that the bad times were finally over, and for good. There was no need to fear anything; the work would be finished in no time. There was no problem, as Ivo said. Unconcerned that it was half past six, he shouted into the silence of the sleeping house: "Go, Cesare, Go!" and banged his hand down on the bathroom sink, waking Arianna and Vittorio with a jolt.

That day, he returned to the tennis club. He hadn't been there since the morning of his obscene defeat at the hands of Marmagli, a year earlier. His friends at the top table welcomed him back like the prodigal son, rising to their feet and giving him a seemingly never-ending round of applause. They shooed away the last admitted member and immediately reinstated the Beast at the head of the table, and no one sat down until Cesare had shouted his battle cry, "The same ones always win!" and, to Zucchi's classic question — "Cesare, have you been playing?" — he had answered with his usual phrase, which that day was finally true: "No, today I got laid!"

Cesare Vezzosi ordered spaghetti al pomodoro with a single basil leaf, and then announced that his tennis elbow had finally gone, so, perhaps, who knows, he might even be able to start playing tennis again. But first he wanted to ask his friends. Was it a good idea? On hearing these words, Dante Zucchi got to his feet and hugged him silently, causing a new round of thunderous, interminable applause from all those sitting at the top table, who were once again on their feet.

At his first training session — against the wall at seven o'clock in the morning of a gloomy day, in total secrecy — Cesare found that his forehand was like a bullet, and his backhand seemed capable of slicing those yellow Pirelli balls in two. He was out of breath in ten minutes and had to restring his racket because the gut was a little loose, but the first day was encouraging.

He spent a whole week playing against the wall and then, on a Monday, Cesare crushed Marmagli, 6–0, 6–0, in a challenge that the skinny lawyer had referred to as a *rematch*, but was in effect a massacre, in which he failed to reach a score of 30 in any of the twelve games they played in less than half an hour.

Then it was the turn of everyone else who had benefited from his collapse, starting with Zucchi, who was so happy to lose 6–1, 6–1, that he immediately began to dream about re-forming their doubles team and competing at the Tuscan championships.

The next day a meeting was held in the sauna, and Loris Ciardi and Lapo Focosi, legendary veterans and former European champions, officially asked Cesare to re-form the Coppa Italia team with Zucchi.

Ciardi conceded that the season had already begun and the Zucchi–Marmagli team had started very badly, losing in Borgo a Buggiano and Scandicci. He added, sniggering: "These fools, Cesare, insisted on playing their doubles Australian style!"

Focosi explained that maybe it wasn't too late: if Cesare and Zucchi started out winning, there was still a hope they could make it to the Tuscan finals.

It was then Marmagli's turn to speak; he begged Cesare to immediately take his place on the team. He bowed down to a great talent, he said, and asked only if he could be the nonplaying captain of the team, "Like Nicola Pietrangeli in the Davis Cup," he said, pretending not to see the mocking smiles of the two veterans.

Zucchi, only half joking, got down on his knees in front of Cesare and clasped his hands together.

Cesare nodded gravely, looked at those four naked, sweating, expectant men, and proclaimed, "Dear friends, the Beast is back!"

From that day on Cesare started to find comfort and encouragement in every little thing that happened to him. Each day without a registered letter or a visit by the finance police made him stronger and more trusting, so he decided to concentrate on tennis, bringing Zucchi back up to an acceptable level and leading him to a historic comeback that saw them beat the teams of Pieve a Nievole, Capannori, Montecatini, Lucca, Pistoia, and Arezzo, and took them to the final of the Tuscan championships, which they won in the tiebreaker of the play-off against Match Ball Firenze thanks to a definitive, triumphant, futurist smash from Vezzosi which created a dent in the soft red clay of the adversary's court and bounced so high that it went over the back net and ended up in the muddy Arno, which ran slowly alongside the court.

Meanwhile, at the building site, the works were miraculously and simultaneously completed, the factory passed all its tests, and the first loom began to weave, immediately followed by another twenty-nine and, a few weeks later, by Ardengo's two old but very efficient spinning machines, which immediately began to tease and card and spin. Ivo was moved almost to tears when—on return from Cape Town where he had spent a week selling flannel in the mornings and spending the rest of the day cavorting along that wild coast in his rented BMW convertible, caressed by the ocean winds and the long, bleach-blond hair of the Afrikaner interpreter he had nearly brought back to Italy with him—he found the first reel of yarn produced by the new factory lying on his rosewood desk.

Cesare realized that if he really wanted to reach the finals in Bari that September, he had to start training seriously. His Tuscan rivals walked on court already defeated, terrified by his reputation, but playing on a national level would be a different matter. He had to rediscover his metronomic rhythm, add at least twenty centimeters of depth to his shots, improve his side movements, and refine his physical fitness. In short, he had to train as he had never trained before.

He told Arianna and Vittorio that between the building site and the training he wouldn't see them much — "Even less?" she asked with a sarcasm that passed him by — and embarked on a tour de force which, at the end of July, brought him and Zucchi face to face with the fearsome Lo Turco–Perroni pair of the Taormina Sporting Club, whom they defeated in a third-set double tiebreaker to win their place in the national finals.

July flowed into a silken August, and as the air started to grow fresher and the factories of their pulsating city resumed roaring like lions, Cesare left for Bari in a joyful caravan of blue Alfettas, all alone because Arianna and Vittorio had decided to spend the last days of their holiday in the seaside town curled up under the smallest mountain range in the world, citing both the ridiculously long journey and the absolute necessity not to neglect holiday homework.

As soon as he arrived, the Beast realized that he would have to face up to the terrible challenge of beating, in just one weekend, both his adversaries and the ghost of the memory of the Historic Baby Doll, who for some incomprehensible reason had reappeared in his thoughts and whose memory, one night, had goaded him so much that the next morning, just before taking to the court, he had locked himself in the office of the director of the championship and called the beauty salon — he had never managed to forget that crude sequence of odd numbers — just to hear her voice once again. He felt both disappointed and relieved when the phone was answered by a rude male voice which explained that the salon was now under a new management, and that he knew nothing about the previous owner other than that she had got married and gone to live in Florence.

Flanked by ghosts, armed only with his loyal Dunlop Maxply, Cesare Vezzosi, known as the Beast, shone like a supernova and won all of his matches, single and double, without ever losing a set, governed by a unique competitive ecstasy that allowed him to beat teams from Milan, Rome, and Naples almost by himself, leading the architect Dante Zucchi to a national victory and bringing him to tears as Paolo Bertolucci hung the gold medal around his neck.

The Beast became the Unranked Champion of Italy, and no one asked him why, at match point, just before hitting the miraculous ace that ended game, set, match, and tournament, he had suddenly stopped bouncing the white Pirelli ball on the clay and had let it drop to rub his right hand on his left arm, as if in an awkward caress. And no one, during the party that followed, remembered to ask him whom in the crowd he was looking for when, in the moment of triumph, he had slowly stared at every person in the stands, his eyes wet with what everyone assumed was emotion or sweat.

MADDALENA OR MILENA

VITTORIO ADORED HER. He dreamed of her all day and all night. They spent their afternoons in his room, on his bed, kissing and listening to music and telling each other about their precious lives, embracing for hours. But if Milena seemed perfectly happy with the status quo, Vittorio couldn't stop thinking how things hadn't really moved on since the passionate kisses they had first exchanged at Cinzia's party last spring.

While his father found it very amusing that Vittorio's first girlfriend was the daughter of his doubles partner, and at the dinner table he would encourage his son *to fuck Zucchi's daughter*, causing both Vittorio and Arianna to turn red and get angry, his mother didn't like at all *that girl* who had taken it upon herself to buy Vittorio jeans as if she had always dressed him badly, and really hated that Milena spent almost all her afternoons at their house and never said a single word to her apart from a hushed, hurried "good evening" when she was entering and leaving Vittorio's bedroom, so Arianna started to refer to her, half joking, as *that girl, I can never remember if she's called Maddalena or Milena, who has been coming to see you every day for six months now and clearly never has any homework to do.*

After a long, empty summer during which they hadn't really seen each other because of their families' divergent holiday plans, in September Vittorio decided to take the initiative, and one day, as they kissed, he touched her breasts. She didn't seem surprised or angry, didn't say anything, didn't pull back. She did, however, show a mute yet decisive resistance to the liberal advance of those uncertain hands: each centimeter would be a triumph. And she would be the one to authorize it.

It was the beginning of a slow, laborious, yet constant progression. Almost immediately Vittorio managed to win the right to touch them over her sweater, but it was well into October before he managed to touch them *under* the sweater. By November he was allowed to place his hand on top of her T-shirt, and then—it was Christmas, Christmas Eve 1980, after Mass—*under* her T-shirt, and never in his life had he ever received such a wonderful gift as being able to hold her nipple between his fingers and feel it stand and grow hard in just a few seconds.

It was only after mid-January that he finally conquered the right to *see* those small, freckled, ivory breasts of hers and touch them freely, with his whole hand, every time they kissed.

And then, in the harshest of winters, Milena began to bloom, and became more beautiful each day. A light seemed to burn inside her, and she lit up the world each time she smiled. Her movements, once clumsy, were now animated by a new grace. Her hair, thicker and doubled in volume, took on a warm copper tone, and each time he touched it, Vittorio had the impression he could hear the silvery sound of harps.

Although Milena was only sixteen and dressed like a tomboy, with the shearling jacket and the sailor's cap, and her idea of a perfect Saturday evening still consisted of watching the same videocassettes of *Rocky* and *Rambo* and *The Blues Brothers* over and over while eating French fries with ketchup and mayonnaise and drinking Coke straight from the bottle with him and Cinzia, it was hard not to notice that her mouth, breasts, legs, and gravity-defying ass were no longer mere body parts of a young girl, but a woman's tools of seduction—involuntary, of course, entirely involuntary, given that Milena had never once wanted to seduce anyone.

Her parents' reaction to this transformation had been to boast to anyone who would listen about their daughter's undeniable newfound beauty, and if her father was a bit more constrained out of fear of the scorching jibes of the Beast, her mother started to buy fashion magazines to compare her to famous models, and insisted that in a few years Milena would certainly be joining their ranks: all it took was the *opportunity to be seen by the right people.*

Rather than being glad of all the attention that was suddenly coming her way, Milena suffered. She didn't like that kind of popularity at all, and was living in a state of permanent embarrassment because she didn't know how to react to being noticed wherever she went, and couldn't bear those horrible catcalls in the street, especially when they came from men her father's age.

Most of all she hated the fact that she was becoming a sort of prey. She wasn't ready for the sudden immersion into vulgarity provoked by her becoming *seriously hot pussy,* as she was told increasingly often. She didn't want to be hot pussy. She didn't even want to be beautiful. She didn't care about all that. She just wanted to be left alone.

Vittorio couldn't believe his luck, and did nothing but silently watch as his girlfriend bloomed. By listening to her worries and holding her in his arms for hours while listening to Billy Joel, he embodied the polar opposite of the savage world that was starting to close in around her. In the kaleidoscope of Milena's new world he had to remain the half-mad, romantic boy who read books no one else read and listened to music no one else listened to and understood her as no one else did.

MOTEL AGIP

IT IS THE FIRST SUNDAY OF MARCH, half past two in the afternoon, and Cesare has just announced that the three of them will soon be leaving for the seaside: he needs to visit the building site of a villa and talk with a few people. Arianna tells him they can't. They had agreed to go to Florence, has he forgotten? He had promised her a walk on via Tornabuoni and a dinner at Buca dell'Orafo with Giorgio and Stefania.

He stares at her and seems to remember, then he nods and says they'll have to change their plans. He wants to go to the seaside. Actually, he *has to* go to the seaside. He has an appointment, and doesn't want to go alone.

Arianna says she doesn't want to go to the seaside, because in the winter it really is too sad, and no one is there.

Cesare groans and raises his eyes to the ceiling. Vittorio says he can't go either, because he has homework to do and then Milena is coming over.

Cesare sees them united against him and gets angry. He begins to shout, the veins of his neck suddenly bulging, and orders that they are all going to the seaside, damn it, and right away. Arianna protests that it's not possible, they had a prior engagement, and you can't just call it off like that, at the last minute. It's rude.

Cesare gets even angrier, he beats his fist on the table and shouts that he is the head of the family and he is the one who makes decisions, and if he says they are going to the seaside, they are going to the seaside. And then he starts swearing. Arianna says nothing, nor does Vittorio. Cesare snarls that it is his house, and they are just guests. They should never forget that. His guests.

On other occasions—because he had already said once or twice that his wife and son were guests in his house—Arianna had always swallowed her rage and let it slide, but this time she gets to her feet, looks her husband in the eyes, tells him he really is a shit, grabs her trench coat, and leaves the house, slamming the door.

In the elevator she laughs to herself, proud to have finally made her voice heard. She gets in the Fiat 500 and sets off suddenly, with a long, involuntary screech of the tires that fills the empty street and reaches the third-floor apartment where Cesare and Vittorio stand in silence, staring into the void.

Arianna drives around aimlessly for ten minutes or so, allowing her anger to pass. Then she sees a telephone booth, stops, and calls Ivo at the only number she has, the one for his office.

It's a Sunday and there is no way Ivo will ever be there, but she tries anyway, so that when he calls her again—*if*, that is, he calls her again, because more than a month has passed since his last call—she will be able to tell him, and herself, that she had at least tried, at least once.

Arianna almost jumps when, after just three rings, he answers directly—not the porter, not the receptionist: him, Ivo. He spouts a curt "Who is it?" but softens immediately upon hearing her voice, and when Arianna asks him whether they might get a coffee, he accepts immediately, hangs up, and declares over the sampling meeting he had called on a Sunday afternoon because the next morning he would be leaving for America, and that he had just initiated. He accompanies the astonished technicians out of the office with a flurry of awkward excuses and promises to call them *from Manhattan*, then he swiftly closes the factory, gets in the Pagoda, and meets Arianna at the bar of the Firenze Nord service station, where she had proposed they meet in order to get as far away from the town as possible without actually going to another one.

They greet without embracing, not even air-kissing. They just smile and sit at a table with a blue tablecloth and make small talk, drink their coffee, and when Arianna puts out the Marlboro she had lit, Ivo suggests they might stay a little longer. She asks where, he smiles and points to the Motel Agip, and when Arianna turns to look at that white giant with 150 rooms, she thinks that she is still very angry at Cesare and doesn't want to go home, and the idea of ending up with Ivo in that perfectly clean hotel frequented mostly by traveling salesmen doesn't seem in any way squalid or degrading to her. It's not beautiful or romantic by any stretch of the imagination, but it has the great virtue of being right in front of them, comfortable and clandestine, just a hundred meters from her white Fiat 500 and his light-blue Pagoda, so Arianna smiles and says, "Why not?"

They walk into the hotel arm in arm, wearing dark glasses, laughing at their secrecy and joking about being incognito. Ivo consigns five thousand lire into the hands of the porter and asks him if he is a curious man. The porter pockets them rapaciously and assures Ivo he is not.

They get into the elevator and Arianna's eyes sparkle, and Ivo kisses her as soon as the doors close. Their top-floor room is bright and spacious, and they kiss again without even locking the door or shutting the curtains, then in the light of the dying day they slip onto the bed, still fully dressed, and she is moved to tears when she realizes how much Ivo desires her: the childlike enthusiasm with which he greets the sight of her marmoreal naked form as he slowly undresses her, the sighs of pure admiration when he can finally look at her pussy up close, the delicacy and thoughtful slowness with which he kisses all her body.

Then, after they have made love, Arianna starts to talk relentlessly as if freed from a vow of silence, and says that she is very happy that this has finally happened, and it's all because of him, because he was tenacious and never discouraged by all the times she had told him no, sometimes even rudely, and when Ivo says that she has never been rude, she stops him and says that yes, of course she was rude, many times, and also distant, hard, cruel, yes, unjustly cruel for a long time, months and months, and then she tells him how sorry she is about it, and how glad that he had perfectly understood that every time she said no, she did not mean never, and that he just needed to be patient and keep trying without ever feeling insulted or forgotten or let down, because sometimes that's all you have to do with women.

And Ivo doesn't have the heart to tell her that tenacity has nothing to do with it, that he just wanted her and had never stopped wanting her, every day; that he had never decided to court her respectfully and wisely — he had simply had to learn to accept being kept at a distance, if that was what she wanted; that he had never used a particular strategy or set of tactics to seduce her, because he knows no strategy at all.

Ivo doesn't tell her that each time he had called her in all those months, he had just given in to a need, and doesn't tell her that every telephone call was like a knife's blade being plunged into his pride, pushing him to forget about her.

He doesn't tell her that every time he heard her voice monosyllabically answer the phone, he told himself that he had to be a complete fool to keep on calling her, and that some days his disappointment was so strong that he decided he wouldn't call her anymore, but those days never amounted to more than a week before the need to hear her voice once more — even if she was tired or in a bad mood — started up stronger than before. He doesn't tell her that after almost two years he had given up on her, and resigned himself to searching for fragments of her in the women he met on his travels around the world.

He just kisses her mouth soft as angora, and they hold one another and stay like that, listening to each other breathe, whispering sweet nothings in that warm bed in an unfamiliar room, and watch through the window as the sunset sets Florence aflame.

When Arianna slips the keys into the door and enters home, Cesare and Vittorio are standing in the entrance hall, waiting for her. Cesare apologizes, and says he did not go to the seaside. He also called Giorgio and told him he did not feel well. She said she went to see a movie in Florence, *Kramer vs. Kramer*, and understood an awful lot of things. Vittorio smiles and goes back to his homework. Cesare shrugs and goes back to the living room to watch the second half of the soccer match, leaving Arianna standing there, next to the door, still wearing her trench coat.

When she asks if fillet and salad are okay for dinner, she gets no response.

A GREAT,
INEXPLICABLE SHOW

IT WAS THE DAY OF THE ASCENSION, a splendid Sunday in May, and the Citarella family were quietly walking home after Mass when Dino asked if they could visit Barrocciai's factory.

Pasquale turned to look at Maria, surprised and pleased. He had never taken the boys to the site, nor even Maria, because he had never thought it would be of any interest to them. He didn't know, and certainly couldn't have imagined, that they had already asked their mother several times and she — uncertain whether Pasquale would like the idea — had always answered that it was not the time yet, and they would have to be patient.

So when they arrived home, they got into the Fiat 128 and set off. Pasquale didn't stop talking for a second, inundating them with anecdotes about the construction and all of the strange requests made by Barrocciai, who sometimes seemed completely mad but was actually *an intelligent man and a very good person indeed*, because in all those years, not one payment had been late, not even by one day, not for a single person, not even when there were monumental fuckups, and *God knows there were a few of those! There were dozens of them!*

He turned down the great straight road that was now via Nicola Tempestini and pointed to the impressive white facade of the factory. Dino said it looked like a ship's sail, Tonino said it looked like the page of a book and that he would like to write on it with a gigantic fountain pen.

Pasquale explained how they had finally managed to get it so white: at first Ivo had wanted it finished with brickwork, but when he saw it, he said it looked *too English*, so he ordered the brickwork to be painted white; then, when he saw it white, he said it wasn't white enough, and pulled from his pocket a strip of bright white cloth and said that color was called *optic white*, and he wanted the factory's facade that exact color—as bright as that, as splendid as that.

—Boys, you don't know how long it took me driving all over Tuscany with that rag in my hand...

They got out of the 128 and Pasquale pointed to the row of cypress trees. They come from Bolgheri, he said, a very special place, and he explained the difference between male cypresses, like those—"straight as a rod, with branches that grow upward"—and the female cypresses, "which are all bushy and wild, with branches going all over the place."

As the boys stared in admiration at the iron fence that ran the length of the factory's perimeter, Pasquale told them that at the beginning, Barrocciai said he wanted to have the whole fence built in wrought iron by a Florentine artisan, but then Vezzosi managed to persuade him to buy it by the meter from a metalworker in Northern Italy because the Florentine artisan would have cost him a fortune, and Ivo, rather than thanking him for saving him money, got angry and said that he hadn't got this far to save money, and left the office, slamming the door.

When Maria asked him if the terra-cotta flower boxes that could be seen just beyond the fence ran all around the factory,

Pasquale started laughing and said yes, and they even had their own automatic watering system: "I think it's electronically controlled," and then he told them how Ivo had fixated on the idea of planting strange plants with names he had never heard of, like cedar, pistachio, and tamarind, and the gardener didn't know what to do because they were all exotic trees and couldn't grow in a flower box.

— Do they also work Sundays, Pasquale? I can hear a noise...

— Since the day they opened, they only stop on Sunday afternoons, Maria. Ivo has got so much work! Good God, he has it coming out of his ears! And not just him! There is work for everyone, more than you could imagine...

Maria closed her eyes to try and distinguish each individual sound within that muffled, Schönbergian cacophony that emanated from the half-opened doors of the factories around Ivo's. It wasn't easy: it would have been hard work even for a textile technician to isolate the single instruments playing in that great concerto, because the metronomic crushing beat of the looms mixed with the whirring and clicking and clacking and dragging of chains from the spinning mill, and the whirring hiss of the twisters fused with the vibrations of the warpage, and all of these sounds fused with the compact, continuous growl of the finishing machines.

Maria asked herself where all that fervor came from — that activity, that irresistible desire to get up early and go to work even on Sunday which pervaded every square meter of their city and a large part of Italy, pushing so many to believe themselves capable of succeeding as entrepreneurs. Even her brothers, who had arrived from Panni to work as laborers, had set up their own business — a yarn-twisting factory. They who just a few years ago didn't even know what a twisted yarn was, now were taking photos in front of their tiny rented shed next to a highly polished brass plaque on which they had inscribed RITORCITURA MONTECASTRO & C.

Wasn't it a miracle that anyone could try his hand at opening a business? When had it ever happened before, in Italy, that you could disregard your destiny and choose to pull yourself out of poverty with your own hard work, freely, without having to ask for permission or handouts from anyone else? Isn't freedom itself a miracle? Is there a logical explanation to the sudden, simultaneous flourishing of so many poor people's most unbridled material dreams and ambitions? And what is it? How was it possible that from one day to the next, you suddenly felt authorized to have hope for the future?

Maria could not answer these questions, yet she could not believe it was simply a matter of being available to sacrifice and willing to work all day every day to the point of exhaustion. How could that be enough? How could they, all of them — Pasquale, her brothers Michele and Nicola, Vezzosi, even Ivo Barrocciai — be so suddenly and extremely good at working and making money?

There had to be another reason, but no matter how hard she tried, she just couldn't find it, and so, amused by the sight of such a great, inexplicable show, Maria told herself that it must all be due to some kind of benign spirit that had capriciously decided to settle over their city and its people, bringing with it a load of work and good fortune, and redemption, and pride, and that flickering of faith in the future that she could see shining in the eyes of all the men and women living in the Green Zone.

But then she was struck by another thought. If it was all due to luck, then there was no guarantee that, one day, that invisible spirit wouldn't mysteriously leave as capriciously as it had arrived and fly off to light up other cities, other nations, other people, taking away all the work and the good fortune and the hope. How would they live without it?

For a moment, Maria tried to imagine that same landscape wrapped in silence and desolation: the factory doors rusted and shut, the parking lots strewn with litter instead of the newly washed cars of owners and workers, the empty streets infested with potholes filled with putrid water. She was horrified, and had to move closer to her husband and hold him tightly until that vision disappeared.

No, it's not possible, she told herself. The world cannot change so much for the worse that the work of men like Pasquale wouldn't receive any recompense, that the sacrifice of the poor wouldn't be rewarded! It would be as if the world and all of its beauty had been created by chance, rather than by our Lord God! It would be the end of everything!

The boys asked about the ten-meter-wide asphalt path that ran around the factory: was it a racetrack? Pasquale answered that no, it was an *avenue* — or at least that's what Ivo called it — for the trucks to deliver the bales of wool to the spinning mills, and Tonino said that if only trucks drove down there, then what was the reason for all those tire marks? Because trucks don't leave tire marks...

Pasquale started laughing, then lowered his voice and told them that Barrocciai had bought himself a Ferrari, but that it was a secret: he kept it hidden in the warehouse under a tarpaulin, and only took it out on Sunday afternoons. Sometimes, at dawn, he drove it fast all around the factory, and Carmine would clock his time.

The boys begged in chorus to be allowed to see it, and Pasquale told them that there were still lots of other things to see at the factory, but they kept on insisting until he promised to show it to them. He opened the gate and they went in, and Pasquale showed the entire factory to his family. He showed them the offices and the production areas, and he enjoyed seeing his sons doubled over in mock fear upon hearing the thundering of the looms, or absorbed by the labyrinthine beauty of the bundle of threads in the warps. He showed them the caverns of the warehouses filled with bales of noil and all kinds of wool, even the one made from rags, which Barrocciai religiously referred to as *recycled*. He told them to smell the wool and put their hands inside the bales, as Ivo had taught him to do, and admired their faces, including that of Maria, as they lit up upon feeling the heavenly softness of angora and the roughness of alpaca, the silky smoothness of mohair and the miracle that is cashmere.

He pointed at the tarpaulin-covered Ferrari, and the boys ran over to it as Pasquale shouted to them not to touch anything — for the love of God! He lifted the tarpaulin with a flourish like an illusionist, and voilà, there shone that marvelous automobile, red like fire, and everyone's hearts skipped a beat, even Pasquale's. As the boys walked around it with their mouths open, whispering "308 GTS," he explained that once he had heard the sound of the engine, and it was *like a cross between thunder and a lion's roar.* Tonino said that he wanted to work hard in life and earn lots of money and buy himself a Ferrari and drive around the Green Zone with his father next to him, leaving tire marks just like Barrocciai.

Then Pasquale covered the Ferrari and they left the warehouse, and as soon as they were in the forecourt, Dino hugged him, and Tonino did the same, and said how that factory really was a cathedral, and Dino added that he wanted to work there too, first as a manual worker and then as a designer. Maria watched them in silence, full of unspeakable admiration and pride for this husband who had had such an important part in that titanic enterprise.

All of a sudden she understood all of Pasquale's bad moods and headaches and stomachaches and cramps and sleepless nights, and wanted to apologize for not asking to see the site sooner, but then she decided to keep quiet so as not to ruin the moment, and fought hard to hold back the tears that were already gathering in her eyes, crybaby that she was.

Pasquale apologized for the fact that not all the walls were painted, and he explained how he had fallen behind with his work because he had to check that everyone else was doing theirs properly. He said that he was very sorry about this because he didn't want them to think he was work-shy.

When he saw Maria and the boys start laughing, he joined in, but he really meant what he had just said, because he didn't like seeing the factory with its walls half-gray, half-white — not at all — and he added that he would start painting them outside of work hours, because there was so much to paint and he didn't want them to bring in assistants, or worse, another painter, that damned Cicisbei who wanted to take his work.

In fact, he proclaimed, he would start that very afternoon, and when the boys protested that they couldn't even spend a Sunday with their father, Pasquale cut them off and decreed it was his duty and that there would be no discussion.

But Maria looked at him tentatively, and when he saw those long faces in the only sad moment of an otherwise perfect morning, Pasquale decided that he couldn't take them home yet, so he told them he had another surprise.

He escorted them back into the offices, got them into the elevator, and told them to close their eyes. Then he led them by the hand to the swimming pool, which stood immense and shimmering and empty.

Pasquale couldn't help but smile, dazzled by the force of that vision: the night wind had blown away the clouds that had been floating over the city for days, revealing an empty, impossibly tall sky which was of the same color as the tiles in the pool, and beyond the pool there was the bright carpet of dozens and dozens of little factories that had now invaded the plane, reaching as far as the eye could see, brusquely interrupted by hills that were so far away as to be whitened by the distance, and beyond those hills lay Pisa *la bellissima*, and then the Mediterranean.

Pasquale told them they could open their eyes.

HIS FIRST THING

VITTORIO RETURNED TO THE SEASIDE at the end of his second August without Milena, who had been unfairly sequestered to Calabria by her parents for a holiday filled with study because she had failed Italian and Latin due to all the time she had wasted — so they said — with him.

His father had sent him to a college near Wimbledon for a fifteen-day English course, but Vittorio had ended up sleeping during the morning lessons, spending the afternoons writing and rewriting passionate letters to Milena, and consuming his evenings and nights in the company of an enthusiastic group of his peers from all over Italy, so he hadn't learned or spoken English that much.

It had been a wonderful holiday, though. He had fallen in love with London, and traveled the length and breadth of the city on the Underground and the double-decker buses, always alone, free and undisturbed. He had played tennis on grass, touched the sacred lawn of Centre Court at Wimbledon, slept in the same room with a girl, seen punks, eaten porridge, escaped death twice at pedestrian crossings because of evil cars incomprehensibly coming straight at him from the right. On the train to

Victoria Station he had been awestruck to discover that the huge power station with four chimneys that graced the cover of Pink Floyd's *Animals* did exist, but he couldn't see the flying pig.

One Saturday afternoon he got off the Underground at Covent Garden and found himself in the midst of a crowd of teenagers more or less his age, and they were laughing and shouting for some reason, and he was infinitely moved by the idea that he too could join that ferment. He had bought himself a tartan scarf, a pair of Nikes, a Union Jack T-shirt, and a pile of albums, trying to familiarize himself with Genesis and Van der Graaf and instead discovering King Crimson—"*Confusion will be my epitaph*," he kept repeating like a raving lunatic as he walked the halls of that small college invaded by Italians. And on his last night, which everybody decided to spend outside, in the park of the college, under a gigantic oak tree, he almost received a definitive lesson in sex education from an eighteen-year-old Milanese who was infatuated with him.

Once he returned to Italy, he realized with horror that his mother had thrown away the 501s Milena had given him with the excuse they were *all worn out* after the uninterrupted wear he had subjected them to over the winter. He didn't tell her that she had ruined everything, nor he did he confess how long it had taken him to get them into that very desirable state. He said nothing, and decided to buy a new pair, immediately, on his own. That would teach his mother a lesson.

So, in a glowing afternoon, Vittorio arrived in front of the only jeans shop in the small town embraced by the smallest mountain range of the world, leaned on its kickstand the new Vespa PX 125 his father had just given him, and turned off the motor.

He hated the idea of having to go in, greet the shop assistants, submit himself to their stares and questions, explain that he wanted a pair of 501s and nothing else without giving off vibes that he might be open to trying on another style from Levi's or another brand like Lee or Wrangler or even an Italian brand, negotiate the issue of size without entering into a discussion on the percentage of shrinkage after the first wash, and disregard any attempt to question his desired length because Vittorio believed jeans should rest precisely on his malleolus.

But he had to do it, all of it, so he took a deep breath, steeled his nerves, and went into the shop. He was immediately taken aback by the unexpected double ring of the bell above the door, which covered for a few seconds the beginning of "Bette Davis Eyes," the languid song by Kim Carnes that he adored and had already heard a thousand times that summer.

He looked around: stacked all over were dozens and dozens of piles of jeans of every brand, model, and color, and he was certain that he would never be able to find the 501s on his own. He could recognize them at first sight when he saw them worn by his friends, but distinguishing them in the midst of dozens of other similar jeans, all piled up together with their labels covered, was quite a different matter.

So he had to wait for an old shop assistant — even older than his mother — to make her way slowly toward him, her red lips half open in a smile. She was wearing 501s, too. She greeted him with a slow, satisfied "Hi," and stopped half a meter from him, so close that he could smell on her breath the mint-flavored chewing gum she was chewing to cover the smell of the cigarette she had just smoked. Vittorio made his request, specifying both waist and length, and she searched briefly in a pile and handed a pair to him — they were right there, in front of his eyes — with another prolonged smile.

Here they were, finally, his Levi's 501s, with their button fly and their white stitching and the red label on the pocket with the word "Levi's" written in white. Dark blue. Hard as cardboard. Made with the cotton that grows in the fields of Georgia and Alabama, dyed with indigo. Vittorio smiled, and the shop assistant led him to a changing room, lightly brushing his arm as she opened the curtain. She closed it, but it left a gap as fabric curtains always do, and Vittorio saw her throw him a furtive glance.

She was not old at all, the shop assistant. At thirty-seven—which made her two years younger than Arianna—she had just entered that magical age in which certain women become absolutely irresistible to anyone with eyes to see. Her name was Marianna, she had just come out of a disastrous marriage and was thinking that if there weren't other clients in the shop, or the manager, she would have screwed that kid on the spot, right there in the changing room, while the hoarse voice of Kim Carnes promised *all the better just to please you*.

Vittorio, however, was just a boy, and did not understand the potential of that glance. He pulled on the jeans as fast as he could, to minimize the time he spent half naked and visible through that gap in the curtain. They fitted him perfectly. He had guessed exactly the right waist and length, and so he didn't even have to leave the changing room to be examined by those ravenous eyes that would have finally been able—legitimately, dutifully—to come to rest on his body. He put his shorts and espadrilles back on and left the changing room with his 501s in hand, announcing that they were fine, thank you.

She gave him another slow smile, said "Come with me," and sauntered toward the till. Vittorio followed her, handed her four ten-thousand-lire notes, asked for a discount as he had been told to do, and received it. The till opened with the ring of a bell, and Vittorio found himself with a two-thousand-lire note in his hand, featuring Galileo contemplating the stars. With studious attention, the shop assistant placed the jeans in a plastic bag bearing the shop's name and handed it to him with another smile and a final, languid *ciao*.

Vittorio left the shop triumphant. He had done it. He had managed it all without a single problem. He had even been given a discount! Then he remembered something very important and went back into the shop, catching Marianna talking to a colleague.

—Where were you? There was just a gorgeous young guy in here, with long curls!

Vittorio pretended not to have heard, and asked for a felt-tip marker. The shop assistant's fingers brushed against his own as she handed it to him, her nails painted a bright red. He lay the jeans on the cashier's desk and, in front of her, wrote his name inside them, next to the pocket. In uppercase letters: VITTORIO. He had sworn to himself that he would sign his first pair of jeans.

—What a lovely name, Marianna chirped as he said goodbye with a brief, sunny seventeen-year-old smile, thus unknowingly, involuntarily, and fruitlessly completing the list of all the things he had to do to be liked by her.

A few minutes later, as he was driving his Vespa on the waterfront, Vittorio found himself thinking about having sex with that shop assistant: he couldn't help noticing the uniform tan on her cleavage, and wondered if she was *one of those women who sunbathed topless*. He imagined going back to that shop, being taken by the hand, led to that same changing room, undressed, and passionately fucked. His dick immediately stood up, painfully contorted between the shorts and the seat of the Vespa, and he had to stop the scooter in order to regain control of the situation inside his Bermudas, but he soon realized it had already gone well beyond any immediate solution and was entirely impossible to mask, so Vittorio set off slowly, smiling, with his young dick pointed toward the zenith of the sky.

His life was dominated by sex. With the help of third-rate skin flicks shown on late-night television and the punctual, exhaustive consultation of the pages of *Playboy*, his masturbatory pantheon had grown exponentially. During the long winter months in which he had secretly accumulated the forty thousand lire he had just spent on the 501s, Vittorio had seriously considered the possibility of spending part of that money on a blow job, which he had always heard described as the path to terrestrial beatitude. But he soon found out his incapacity for that dishonorable transaction: he would have never been able to overcome his embarrassment and approach a prostitute, agree on a price, and go off into a field or a bedroom.

Instead, a related yet more refined idea had grown in his mind during that season of fervid wanks. He toyed with the foolish idea of offering the money to one of his female schoolmates, or to that friend of his mother's who was always paying him compliments, or to some stranger who for some reason he always imagined he would meet on a train, in exchange for a blow job. But he had never found the courage to take that first step, and so the idea had vanished miserably while the problem remained before him, urgent and unresolved, and continued to torment him to such an extent that, after a thousand false starts, trembling and babbling like a madman, one evening he decided he had to find the courage to overcome the unspeakable nature of the act and talk about it with Milena—not about paying for it, good God no, but about the possibility that she might one day be the one to perform that task.

It was the day before she left for Calabria, the only one her parents had allowed them to spend together all summer. She had gone to meet him at the beach and they had swum together in the sea, embracing and caressing under the water, and then they had shut themselves in the shower room to kiss as they had never kissed before, and when he dared to touch her tender pussy, she showed no resistance, and so Vittorio slipped in the tip of his trembling finger and she closed her eyes and bit her bottom lip hard and held his wrist tight and moved it just as she wanted, and after a while she gave first a hiccup, then a brief moan, and reached orgasm. She started laughing out of sheer joy and emotion, and her eyes sparkled as she moved to touch his penis, which had grown so erect that it protruded from Vittorio's swim trunks, and she started to rub it clumsily until he kissed her hard and he came, too, and his legs gave way, leaving him almost to fall to his knees while giving off the brief wild-boar-like grunt that—when they left the shower with their eyes lowered, wrapped in the towels belonging to Arianna, who was tanning herself in blissful ignorance—earned them scandalized looks from the three matrons in flower-print suits who had been waiting to take a shower for the last ten minutes.

That evening, while they were in Vittorio's small bedroom in the lemonary and were kissing endlessly and listening over and over to "Romeo and Juliet" by Dire Straits and repeating with Mark Knopfler, "*I love you like the stars above, I'll love you till I die*," Vittorio summoned up all of his courage and asked her in a tiny voice what she thought of the idea of maybe giving him—not now, of course, some other time—a blow job.

Bathed in the pinkish light of an astounding sunset, just a few minutes after having sworn him eternal love, Milena wasn't expecting that question and replied dryly that *if they had to do something more*, then she would prefer to make love with him. And so, while Dante Zucchi, parked in the street outside, started to honk to speed up the proceedings, Vittorio and Milena agreed to lose their virginity to one another at an unspecified moment in the future, but certainly within a year of that evening, before the end of next summer.

When Vittorio finally arrived on the beach, the jubilation of sunset was so intoxicating that even he had to notice it. His dick still erect, the bag carrying the jeans held tightly in his hands, all he could see around him were three far-off lifeguards combing the fine sand and two old men walking in silence with their hands behind their backs like two big, pensive storks intent on traveling along the beach all the way to France, and then to Spain.

The sea sparkled. No one paid him any attention. In a heart-beat he took off his espadrilles, removed his shirt and Bermudas and underpants and put on his new jeans despite the complication of his still half-erect penis, realizing instantly how his body could be at the same time hard, soft, and delicate.

Vittorio stood in front of the sea for a few seconds, wearing only his 501s, then he waded in. It wasn't cold at all. As he walked, the sea filtered in between him and the rough cotton of his jeans, which instantly wrapped around him. His new skin.

He wondered whether he would leave the water with blue legs. Maybe only then the 501s would be truly his, staining him, changing him. Tomorrow he would lay them out in the sun and they would become hard again, rock hard, only slightly faded. From that moment on, he would wear them every day. They would take all of his wounds, and would rip when he fell off his Vespa, and would be stained by blood and sweat and tears and all the other fluids jeans are always stained with. And they would finally be his.

Vittorio stayed there, with the sea up to his waist and his dick finally bending downward as if it had been admonished. He just stayed there, motionless, until the sun plunged into the sea.

BLUE

—PASQUALE! PASQUALE! PASQUALE!

—Hey! What is it?

—Come up here!

—What's wrong?

—Holy Mary, I said get up here!

—Is there a problem, Barbugli?

—Nooo! Get up here! What are you doing in that courtyard?

—What's wrong? I've got to paint a last coat on one of these walls!

—Come up here one moment, for the love of God!

—Tell me what for, Barbugli!

—Nooo, I can't. You need to see for yourself.

—Okay, I'm coming.

—Look.

— ...

—Can you see?

—Good God...

—It's just finished filling.

— ...

— ...

—It's so beautiful...That's not a swimming pool, it's a lake...

251

—Look at all that blue...

— ...

— ...

—It's enormous...

—God knows how many liters of water it takes to fill it.

—Three million.

—Really?

—Vezzosi told me.

—Holy Mary, three million liters!

—I'm not sure I could swim from one end to the other...

—I think I could swim the width.

—Me too.

—Are you a good swimmer, Pasquale?

—I go a bit like a dog, but I don't drown. What about you?

—I swim like a lifeguard, with my head out. I learned to do it in Viareggio when I was a kid.

— ...

—Pasquale, why do you think Ivo had this swimming pool built?

—I don't know. I asked him once, but he didn't answer...

—I'm sure he wants to send a message...

—To who?

—I don't know. But he wants to say something to someone. I'm sure of it.

—Hmm...

—Pasquale, shall we dive?

—Absolutely not.

—Come on, why not?

—Nonono!

—We're not going to ruin it...

—Nonono! It's not ours.

—Just one dive...

—Do you know how long Ivo has been waiting for this pool? Years. He will be the first to swim in it. I'm going to call him now, to tell him it's ready.

—But it's eight in the evening, he'll be at dinner…

—Where is the reel with the telephone cable, Barbugli? Because there must be a phone up here somewhere…

—It's under that sheet.

—I'll call him now…Hello? Ivo?

—Pasquale, good evening.

—Ivo, listen, the swimming pool has been filled.

—Ah. Good. What's it like?

—Ivo, it's incredible. It's so beautiful…And it's enormous. It's like a lake…

—Good, good…

—Tell him it's all blue.

—Barbugli, who's standing next to me, said to tell you it's all blue.

—Excellent! Take a swim, guys!

—No, Ivo. Thank you, but no.

—What do you mean, no? Why not?

—No, Ivo, we would never do such a thing!

—Come on…Dive in, boys! I can't come because I've got to take some clients out for dinner, otherwise I'd join you…

—But Ivo, you've been waiting such a long time…

—Pasquale, you and Moreno go for a swim, and tell me what the water's like…

—No, Ivo, it doesn't feel right…I can't…

—Just listen to this guy…Go on, Pasquale, dive in…

—And we're all sweaty…

—Pasquale, come on…Listen, now I need to get off the phone. I have to go to Florence to pick up three Americans from the Baglioni Hotel. You guys take a swim, and tomorrow morning you'll tell me what it's like.

—Are you sure?

—Absolutely.

—Okay, thank you.

—Ciao, Pasquale.

—Bye Ivo, have a good evening.

—What did he say? Hey, Citarella, what did he say?

—He said to take a swim.

—I knew it! That's just like Ivo. Come on! Let's dive in!

—But I'm really not sure…

—He told you to, come on…

— …

—Come on!

—We need to be quick though, Barbugli, because I have to get home for dinner…

—And I don't? Come on. I'm ready!

—How, naked?

—Of course! Let's go! I'm jumping in!

—This guy's crazy!…Hey, Barbugli, what's it like?

—Cold, is what it's like. Holy Mary of the highest skies of Finland, it's so cold! Get in!

—Okay, I'm coming in…

—Glacial Jesus! You need to swim, otherwise you freeze…

—Oh, *mamma mia*, it's freezing! *Mamma mia*, it's so cold!

—Let's see if we can warm ourselves up by swimming to the other side.

—Shall we see who makes it first?

—Ready, set, go!

Saturday, 7 August 1982

PERIWINKLE

A BLACK ALFETTA with its headlights on shoots into the fore-court of Barrocciai Tessuti, barely missing Ivo, who stands right in its center, under the midday sun, watching a single swollen cloud drift slowly across the sky. The car stops with a furious slam of the brakes and out steps Sergio Vari, who walks slowly toward Ivo while the opening notes of "Like a Rolling Stone" pour from the open door and roll across the forecourt.

— He didn't approve it, Vari says.

—That's not possible, says Ivo.

"*Once upon a time you dressed so fine,*" sings Bob Dylan.

— He didn't approve it.

— It's the fifth fucking time . . . It was perfect . . .

— Come on, Ivo, you're color-blind . . .

—What's that got to do with anything? The technicians told me it was perfect.

— He might approve it tomorrow.

—Tomorrow? What do you mean, tomorrow? Is he going to approve it or not?

— He'll approve it tomorrow. I'd put money on it.

— So why tomorrow and not today?

—I'm not going to tell you.

"*Now you don't talk so loud, now you don't seem so proud...*"

—And why's that?

—Because you'll get angry and you'll call him and tell him to fuck off.

—No, I'd never do that...

—Yes you would...Listen to this bit, Ivo, it's beautiful...

"*How does it feel, how does it feel, to be without a home, like a complete unknown, like a rolling stone . . .*"

—What is he saying?

—Who, Sergio? The client?

—No, Bob Dylan. What exactly is he saying in this bit?

—Can't you understand it?

—You know I don't speak English.

—Ah, that's right...What did the client say, then?

—He said that he hasn't approved it because yesterday in Milan it was overcast, and he only approves colors when he can see them in the sunlight.

Ivo wonders if this is the right moment to point out the matter of the shoe—because when Sergio got out of the car, he had just one shoe on: a dark-blue suede moccasin, soft, with tassels, with his other foot wrapped in a woolen sock—to that thirty-nine-year-old Bolognese with intense blue eyes and jet-black hair down to his shoulders, a snake charmer extraordinaire and a dyed-in-the-wool Communist from the day he was born in the basement of his house during an American air raid, dressed in a perfectly creased linen shirt, dark jeans, a Navajo belt complete with coins and a mother-of-pearl buckle bought many years ago in Venice Beach, who interrupted his education right after middle school because of an irresistible fascination with soccer, and had lived his youth in the splendor that was Bologna in the sixties, managing promising, shambolic rock groups made up of his peers and then setting off on a yearlong holiday of meditation spent contemplating the sunsets of Goa, where he sensed that the times they were a-changin' and decided to come back to Bologna and get a job in fashion, immediately becoming the best textiles agent in the whole of Italy, and certainly the only one who could translate into the rigid language of producers the brilliant if confused ideas of the *new designers*—that gang of enthusiastic, insecure, mostly Italian but also Japanese, American, and even British young stylists he accompanied to Barrocciai Textiles to show off the collection and meet Ivo and spend an afternoon in the swimming pool because, apart from a few rare exceptions, these kids had no technical knowledge whatsoever.

They talked mainly about colors, and couldn't pronounce the names of the weaves. They asked for things that were technically impossible. They stroked the reverse of the fabrics as if it were their cat, without realizing they were not touching the finished side. They mixed up the fibers and the finishes, and called every wool fabric that weighed more than three hundred grams *cloth*. But they learned everything instantly and were ready to take everything in with their quick eyes, and were continually taking mental notes, and though they did not know what fabrics to use, they knew perfectly well which clothes they wanted to make, and you could sense that they had a bright, bright future ahead.

As they praised the beauty of the factory and stared at the swimming pool with their mouths open wide, eventually buying just a few meters of the very best fabrics, these young designers told their own story of how all over Italy and Europe and America millions of enthusiastic and newly proud people were now buying *the new*—new jackets and new skirts and new shirts and new tops and new sweaters and new shoes and new scarves and new trousers and new overcoats and new dresses and new suits and new foulards, garments that did not replace something that was already in their wardrobe and had been worn out, but pieces that had to be completely different in cut, design, pattern, shape, and color.

It was up to these young men and women to represent the new in a world that was clamoring to discover that, in Italy, a courageous, totally contemporary fashion was exploding, inspiring itself and even finding its roots in the ancient, artisanal know-how that had been the driving force of the Renaissance itself. It was no less than the zeitgeist that propelled the sales of these young people, with Brunelleschi and Michelangelo and Leonardo da Vinci doing their marketing for them.

Sergio Vari had been the first to understand this, and had instinctively developed an unrivaled sales vocabulary which the young designers adored listening to, hypnotized by his soft Bolognese accent and the hypnotic, psalmodic singsong that was artfully punctuated by deep pauses and then suddenly violated by memories of concerts he had been to fourteen years ago, while the distracted world had other things to contend with — "A hundred of us went to see the Jimi Hendrix Experience, in May '68, and then I went to see him backstage ... He was wearing bordeaux velvet trousers and an incredibly tight Indian jacket ... He was as thin as a rake, seriously tall, with a gorgeous broad next to him, and he asked me if I enjoyed the show."

He excelled in a masterly use of melodious and carnal adjectives to describe the textiles' qualities, as if the choice of the right fabric and the right color for a jacket or a coat was a Timothy Learyesque adventure in fashion, the new and perhaps last unexplored territory for Western culture which he, and only he, could lead those amazed young designers into, helping them to avoid the many perils of taking the wrong path or getting lost on *bad trips*. He was basically their guru.

It was of little or no importance that Sergio didn't possess even the slightest grasp of English or the most elementary technical rudiments: he had always refused to learn either, convinced that in order to sell fabrics in the sentimental way he did, there was no need for those things, and if he ever required a translation or some technical advice, Ivo was there.

If Barrocciai initially balked at dealing with the illogical requests and minuscule orders proffered by this wave of young designers, he quickly realized that he couldn't ignore the new, and patiently dedicated a considerable part of his time and energy to satisfying the fixations of these young men and women who were on the cusp of becoming billionaires but still continued to ignore the difference between flannel and velour, or alpaca and angora.

—Sergio, you must be joking...

—No, Ivo. I'm not. You wait, if it's sunny tomorrow in Milan, he'll approve it.

—Sergio, you are not normal, you know...And neither is your client...

—Why, are you normal, Ivo? And, in any case, it's *your* client! I don't make textiles. I sell them.

It had all started a month earlier, when Vari had turned up at the factory carrying the photograph of a beautiful, brown-haired girl with eyes the color of dark chocolate. She was wearing an indefinably colored overcoat as she walked down an elegant street in the center of London, perhaps New Bond Street.

She was lit by a pale sun as she looked at either a man, the future, or the void of existence itself. It looked like a frame from a film by Antonioni, and for a minute Ivo struggled to lift his gaze from that photo. He wondered who she was, what her name was, where was she at that exact moment—and immediately fantasized about seeing her walking down the hall of the Dorchester toward him, smiling, wearing that coat, her cheeks flushed with the cold of Christmas, happy to be meeting him for a dinner date.

After that day at the Motel Agip, Barrocciai had stopped looking for Arianna in every beautiful woman he saw, and resolved instead to admire how she took refuge in the carefree and guiltless, almost bold infidelity which she seemed to enjoy so much because it was born out of freedom and desire, not from need. Exhilarated by being suddenly able to desire and immediately obtain, she freely decided—often whimsically—if and when and how to see him. Arianna would call and Ivo would rush to organize every detail of their infrequent yet heartfelt, happy, and forcefully brief meetings in the very finest hotel rooms within an hour's drive from their town—no more Motel Agip.

Each time they met it was the rediscovery of a newfound freedom, a luxury and a gift for both of them. They laughed and agreed on everything, and always said they loved one another—of course they did!—but they couldn't run away together because she was already married with a son she adored, and Ivo was married to his business. So the months went by smoothly, and they never once asked themselves what they were doing, because they knew very well that a quarrel—just one banal quarrel—could be enough to extinguish the fragile affair they had decided to let burn as bright as a comet, hoping that its trajectory across the empty sky of their lives would last as long as possible.

Spellbound by that photograph, Ivo started to wonder if it was in some way possible to meet that girl with the lost gaze who walked through New Bond Street with that marvelous overcoat whose color defied description, and only came to his senses when Sergio Vari announced that the color was called periwinkle, and the client wanted it in Cabora, but before placing the order he wanted to approve the color from a sample.

Cabora was one of the most beautiful fabrics in their collection: a wool-angora-cashmere-nylon mix that weighed 520 grams per linear meter and was sold to the best coat makers in Europe, who were enthusiastic about that unique composition which invoked both the otherworldly, vaginal softness of angora and the desire to protect oneself from the cold by wrapping up in the softest and most impalpable of fibers.

Of course, Cabora wasn't easy to make. The wool, angora, cashmere, and nylon had to be spun and twisted together in a very delicate thread that could only be used in the weft of the fabric, and though Cabora had to shine with the heavenly luster of angora to please the German ladies it was mostly destined to, the buyers also needed it to be resistant to creasing, ripping, and the friction caused by use. So the minute it came off the loom Cabora had to be finished with the greatest care, using a procedure as long as a *via crucis*, in which anything could go wrong. You could dye Cabora a special color, even a very light color, even a pastel, like that periwinkle, but it was a nightmare. Anything could stain it, even air.

Ivo, still lost in the contemplation of those dark-chocolate eyes, had asked dreamily what periwinkle was, and Sergio Vari had immediately taken on the role of teacher, and announced that periwinkle is the color of the charming flower of a humble plant that was used in the Middle Ages for love potions: "It's a fantastic tone of sky blue and violet and gray, Ivo, one of the most graceful colors on the face of the earth."

Ivo had looked at Sergio, smiled, and the order had been accepted. Now, two months later, with all the white pieces ready to be dyed in periwinkle, five sample colors had been rejected by the customer.

— Come on, Sergio. Let's go see the technicians. You can explain to them that this genius didn't approve the color because it was cloudy in Milan.

Ivo and Sergio Vari cross the forecourt and enter the office of the head technician, who is completely uninterested in the vibrant summer afternoon illuminating the world beyond his windows, and is unraveling a handful of wool to ascertain the length, quality, and cleanliness of the fiber, flanked by two younger assistants.

— Germano, Sergio has something to tell you.

The head technician, a robust and patient man who was as awkward and distracted in life as he was precise and accurate in his work, throws Vari a terrified glance, fearing him like the plague since the day Ivo introduced him as *the greatest textile seller in Italy today, perhaps in Europe*, and the Bolognese immediately and maliciously announced that there were four whites in the next summer collection — "Germano, we will have *optic, candid, dirty, and jonquil white"*—and three blacks, the first of which would be "the color of the deepest darkness"; the second would have "a reddish flare that will be reminiscent of a great fire at night, like Troy burning"; and the third wasn't exactly a black, but the "absolute blue of a moonless night."

When, two months ago, Ivo had shown him the pastel color from the photograph and said that a client wanted it in Cabora, Germano had rolled his eyes and answered that it was impossible: reproducing a color from a photograph was a fool's game, and he had never heard of anyone asking or doing it.

—That color is made up of at least four or five other colors, Ivo, and mixing the pigments will be hell and you will end up wasting a lot of time and throwing away a lot of pieces, and I'm not here to damage pieces, not even if you ask me to.

Then he had looked Sergio Vari straight in the eye and proclaimed that he will have to tell a client no at least once in his life. Then he had asked who the client was, and Ivo had told him.

He was the most important of them all. *Numero uno.* The first and the best. The one who had started everything. The artist whom Ivo had been unable to persuade to work with him until Sergio Vari had arrived. The poet who had declared that his suppliers, just by virtue of being chosen by him, were the best in the world. And the absolute idol of Germano's jovial, rotund wife, who had only been able to afford a single white shirt and a pair of shoes by that designer—and only recently, after the raise Ivo had given her husband without him requesting it.

Germano had blushed, said "Ah!" and then he repeated it—"Ah!"—and then he murmured about how, perhaps, for that client and only for him, it might be possible to try and make Cabora in periwinkle.

—So, guys, listen up, Vari announces, I went to see the client yesterday evening. He said he can't approve the periwinkle because it's cloudy in Milan, but as soon as the sun comes out, he says he'll look at it again and will give us an answer.

Germano nods, smiles, throws a knowing glance in the direction of his two assistants, shrugs, and shouts, "Cheer up Barrocciai! You need patience with artists!"

Then he calmly puts his head back down and continues to untangle the wool, but there is no sarcasm or derision in his smile, nor is there any anger, and Ivo wonders if this is how the *botteghe d'arte* of fifteenth-century Florence worked, leaving the artist free to make any request, even the most illogical, while the shop boys stood mute and admiring before the genius, who was beyond judgment and had to be forgiven every weakness.

There is a long silence, then Ivo turns to Vari.

—And now would you mind telling me why you're wearing just one shoe?

A FUTURE THAT WOULD
NEVER END

WHEN MORENO BARBUGLI WENT TO TELL HIM he had to stop working immediately and consider himself on vacation — Barrocciai's orders — Pasquale Citarella was about to finish painting the back wall of the huge raw materials warehouse, oblivious to the fact that the wall was destined to be permanently hidden from view by columns and columns of wool bales. He protested and asked to finish the job, but Barbugli wouldn't be moved.

—This deed has so been willed where One can do Whatever He wills, O Citarella!

As they made their way along the narrow corridor between the rows of jute bales that contained every textile fiber known to man, Pasquale realized he was very tired as his muscles autonomously began to release the tension, in anticipation of the needed rest that would follow.

Given the vast dimensions of the warehouse and the fact it was so well insulated, it had its own microclimate, so when he walked out into the open, he felt as if he had walked into a wall of hot air, and after a few steps he stopped and closed his eyes to enjoy the great heat that was pouring down from the sky onto his chest and his shoulders. It was the same sun that was warming Maria, who had gone to the seaside with Dino and Tonino for the four weeks of August, waiting for Pasquale, who had missed the first but was about to enjoy the remaining three.

He couldn't wait to take her out for a stroll and watch the sea with her on a bench, at sunset, surrounded by children and dogs and tourists, and hear her breathe quietly, that exceptional woman he had had the fortune to marry, and then go with her to get an ice cream and make fun of her *barbaric* (a term coined by that rascal, Tonino) tastes, which always led her to choose chocolate and lemon together. And go to the cinema with her and ask her to explain the plots of the films that lately eluded him more than ever. And lie in the sun next to her for those few minutes she could manage before escaping to the shade, smiling happily, to finish the crossword. And buy her something useless despite her resistance, because she wanted all their money to be put in the bank and never thrown away.

Maria, Maria, Maria. No one else existed for Pasquale!

He loved Dino and Tonino more than life itself, of course, but they were still boys: when they turn eighteen, he will teach them a few things, but until then, it was best that Maria dealt with them and their problems.

All he was asking for himself was to be able to sleep until ten o'clock without anyone knocking at the door. Then he would put on a fresh short-sleeved white shirt and a pair of Bermuda shorts, go to the bar for his croissant and cappuccino, and smoke a cigarette in sacred peace while walking slowly to the beach, sandals on his feet and Ray-Bans protecting his blue eyes.

Pasquale wanted this and nothing more. He certainly wasn't asking for more rest, because a healthy man like him didn't need any rest. And rest from what, work? He already missed his work, and couldn't wait to be back in the warehouse, in September, to paint the back wall he had to leave unfinished!

He opened his eyes and looked up. Two slow clouds were roaming around the sky, as if lost. He smiled. Everything was going well, and couldn't be any better. And it would continue to go well next month, and next year, and the year after that. Forever.

It was a future that would never end.

NO PROTECTION

MILENA RETURNS FROM LONDON, where her parents sent her for a month to learn English, and calls Vittorio as soon as she gets home. She must talk to him, right away. When he says, "Tell me everything, baby," she takes a long pause. It's not something she can say over the phone. She will get on the afternoon bus to the seaside town that curls up at the foot of the smallest mountain chain in the world.

Vittorio is waiting for her sitting on his Vespa in the little square where the buses arrive, tanned and blessed by the gods, his hair still wet from the shower, dying to see her again, and when Milena finally gets off the bus, she looks somewhat different — thinner, pale, almost pained — but it's just a second, then he is overwhelmed by joy and they embrace and kiss briefly and start to walk along the famous small seaside town hand in hand, talking about nothing.

She buys Lancaster sun cream with no protection to get at least a little tanned before summer ends, because *she is really too white*, and tells him about London and how she really liked the English people, *most of all because in the twentieth century they still insist on having a queen.*

They get back to the square, now filled with adolescents sitting on Vespas, and Vittorio says that he might buy her some hot focaccia, and Milena says yes, of course, but she wants to come too, and takes off her shoes and starts walking barefoot toward the baker's.

There is some kind of collective *Oh!* and all the boys and girls immediately turn to watch her walking barefoot. Then Milena stops, turns to him, and says, "Come on, take your shoes off too," and Vittorio is very embarrassed because now all those boys and girls are looking at him, and he is certainly not going to walk barefoot to the baker's, and so he shakes his head, but she stands there in the middle of the square in her blue T-shirt with OXFORD printed on it, and says again, Come on, Vittorio, try it. So he smiles and takes off his Stan Smiths and rests his right foot on the ground and feels the heat of the asphalt and its grainy texture and starts laughing, then he puts the other foot on the ground and starts walking toward her. She takes him by the hand and they go together barefoot to buy the focaccia, and even though they have to *be extremely careful not to step on something unmentionable that could have unimaginable consequences*, as he warns under his breath, they experience that rare and precious sensation of doing together something they had never done before.

After nibbling at the focaccia, they get on the Vespa and set off toward her house so slowly that the waterfront seems to stretch out to infinity. When Vittorio realizes she is not holding him as she usually does, he lets go of the handlebars and takes Milena's cold hands and squeezes them to his chest, so she can hug him and rest her head on his shoulders and smell his hair.

When they arrive, Milena asks him to come in, even if it's nearly dinnertime: her parents aren't home yet. The house is dark and Milena opens all the windows, then sits on the sofa in the living room and stares at Vittorio, who was expecting some kind of intimacy and is surprised to see her sitting there in silence. So he waits a few seconds before sitting down on the sofa, uninvited, half a meter away from her, thus establishing a distance that is entirely new to them.

Then Milena says she has to tell him something very important, something she has to say now, before her parents arrive home, but she doesn't know how because it really is *something enormous and terrible*, and she suddenly starts crying and can't stop, and Vittorio moves closer and holds her, but she is distant and cold and shaken by sobs, and then he says, "What is it, Milena? What's wrong? Tell me," and she suddenly pulls away from the embrace and looks him in the eyes and tells him they can no longer be together because she broke her promise, and while she was in London, she was with a guy—that is, she went to bed with him, last night—and now she feels so bad, so horribly, disgustingly bad, and she's been thinking about it all day, if she should tell him or not, and she had almost decided not to tell him but then she could never have looked him in the face again, and so she decided to tell him, but now she can't look him in the face anyway, and lowers her gaze and cries and the tears fall on her thighs and her knees and Vittorio can only think of one single thing, and the one single thing is that he doesn't want to lose her, regardless of what she has done, and he is about to tell her this, that he doesn't want to lose her regardless of what she has done, when she looks at him and takes his hands and says that at this point they can't be together as they were before, it was *far too big* a thing, what has happened, and he could never forgive her, right?

And Vittorio looks back at her and is about to respond that yes, of course he forgives her, he'll suffer like a dog but he'll forgive her, of course he will, naturally, and his heart starts beating wildly and he opens his mouth to say it, that one single thing which will settle the whole problem, but then *he sees her*, Milena, and he understands that it is all useless. That it's over.

Because it's no longer Milena, the girl, who is looking at him from the sofa. It's a woman who is waiting for his reaction and seems to expect to be scolded, insulted, probably even slapped, repudiated—but then, finally, liberated.

It's over and it's been over for a long time, since the day Milena decided in her heart that she could be capable of doing what she did. And it is over because she decided that it was already over, and even if it wasn't a real decision, even if she just made a silly mistake, if she strayed as you may do when you are eighteen, well, it's happened, and nothing can be as it was before.

This is what she thinks, and Vittorio's opinion is irrelevant: he has never made love to anyone, so he cannot know how empty and guilty you can feel if the first time you do it, you are betraying someone.

It's over, and it doesn't matter that Vittorio doesn't want to know anything about what she has done in London because truth is a hard and cutting thing, and cruel, and partial, and useless, and damaging, only one little step above a lie, and whoever always searches for it is nothing but a fool.

It's *over*, and all he can do now is gather together every drop of pride and courage and heart, and go. Immediately. But he can't. He just can't. He has to say something, and he has to hear something from her.

—So we are breaking up.

She looks at her feet, then him, then back at her feet.

—Yes, she answers in a tiny voice.

One, two, three heartbeats.

—We're not even going to the concert tonight?

She shakes her head and Vittorio feels like he is about to faint. Everything seems to become confused and lose importance. He notes that the soles of Milena's feet are thick with dirt, and his must be too.

Vittorio stands up and sways for a moment. She stands up, but doesn't move toward him. He looks at her as if to imprint her image onto his mind, but then he thinks that he doesn't want to remember her like that, not with those lost eyes swollen from crying, so he turns to leave, but he doesn't remember anymore where the door is, in that house where he has been so many times before, and his disoriented gaze ends up in the direction of her room, and when he sees all of her shoes lined up in order of height, all the way to the Camperos boots he had bought her in Rome and greased with seal fat, the ones he always had to help her pull on because they were so tight, Vittorio must divert his gaze and turn toward the window, which shows a sky burning with orange.

Then he finally sees the door and opens it and leaves, takes those ten steps over the gravel to cross the garden, opens the gate, goes out into the street, and puts the key in the Vespa's steering lock. When he turns, she is there next to him as beautiful as ever, and Vittorio's heart breaks—he can even hear the small sound inside—and he wonders if he can embrace her, if he can kiss her now that—good God, how is this possible—*they are no longer together*, and just the thought of it makes him sway and his eyes cloud over and he is about to cry, too, but he somehow manages to resist, poor thing, he manages to open the steering lock and sit on the Vespa, and tries to turn it on by pushing the pedal, but the first attempt doesn't work, so he pulls the choke and tries again, but it still doesn't work, and he is assailed by the unbearable thought of having to start the Vespa with a push, and he prays to God that he is at least spared that, and he desperately kicks the pedal again and the Vespa finally sputters to life, and while he keeps it running and a cloud of white smoke forms around them, Vittorio turns to her.

—Goodbye then, Milena, take care of yourself—and then, out of breath—I wish you all the best, because you deserve the best the world has to offer. And please remember that I never lied.

He tries to smile and keeps on looking at her in the desperate hope that she might stop him and ask him not to leave, that she might tell him she has changed her mind, or even *that it was just a joke*. He would accept anything because he doesn't want them to break up, and he doesn't care about what she did in London, really, he hasn't thought about it for a second. He *doesn't want them to break up*, that's it. And he wants to shout it out loud, but he can't even bring himself to whisper it.

Milena draws close to him and kisses him on the mouth and hugs him tight, and while in their tight embrace he whispers in her ear, "I will always love you," and she starts crying again and runs down the gravel path and into the house, slamming the door behind her.

It takes him a few seconds to realize he has to leave now, and so he leaves, or rather his Vespa leaves of its own accord and moves very slowly through the labyrinth of narrow streets with the names of poets, strewn with pine needles. As he brushes past the many small, newly built villas Vittorio wonders if he is now achieving an escape velocity from her; if from that moment on he will be irredeemably distancing himself from Milena, meter after meter, like the astronauts that leave their spacecraft and travel forever through infinite space, stone dead, because that is exactly how he feels, stone dead, and when he finds the way out of the pine grove and ends up on the waterfront, he has to face a sunset so red it seems to be bleeding, and as he ignores every traffic light it's a miracle, a true miracle, that he arrives home safely, without being run over by one of the many cars that speed by toward the nightclub that seems a house, where in a few hours Gloria Gaynor will appear to sing.

THE NUMBER OF THE BEAST

CESARE DIDN'T WANT TO GO to the concert.

He moaned for weeks about how he couldn't be bothered about celebrating Barrocciai for the umpteenth time, and agreed to the invitation only at Arianna's insistence.

He was now a successful man. After his victory at the Italian championships and the more or less simultaneous completion of the pharaonic work, Cesare Vezzosi was the talk of the town. He had already received some offers to build other factories, and his old employer had asked to meet him to discuss the future, because he had just bought out his old business partner and needed someone like Cesare: *someone who sees things through, someone who can solve problems.*

Miraculously, all of the ineptitude, disregard, negligence, and incompetence he had shown over the years it took to build the pharaonic work had melted in the building's imposing beauty, and Cesare had become the man who solves problems.

Success had assailed him all of a sudden, and in the last few months he had bought a white Mercedes 200D with a cream-colored leather interior, two made-to-measure suits—one pinstriped—ten tailor-made shirts, a camel hair overcoat, and the wild-mink fur for Arianna, who had been happy about it, of course, but not nearly as happy as when he told her that instead of staying at the lemonary that summer they would be renting the large house with the magnolia tree.

After his great victory, tennis was not that interesting anymore. He knew he would never again make it to the national finals.

He had found himself a new lover, and she wasn't half bad — a shop assistant, slim, brown hair, always upbeat — but in bed the difference between her and the Historic Baby Doll was immense.

So Cesare arrives at the seaside at the end of the afternoon, bored and bad-tempered. He parks his Mercedes on the gravel driveway in front of the house and, instead of going to the beach to meet Arianna, he sits in the garden in the shade of the magnolia and drinks a glass of iced tea.

When she arrives on her bicycle, it's already half past seven. She was late from the beach because she had been waiting all day for him, she says, then greets him with a quick kiss on the forehead before running upstairs to dress up for the concert.

Cesare looks at her and nods. He doesn't say a word. He finishes his tea, stands up, follows her up the stairs, lies down on the bed, folds his arms behind his head, and watches his wife illuminated by an orange sunset as she silently prepares to go out. As soon as she's ready, he asks her for a blow job.

Arianna had dressed calmly and decisively, pulling on a close-fitting, sleeveless, aquamarine dress that ends just above the knee and highlights that slim silhouette that even Father Time could not attack. She had pulled on one shoe, then the other: the Ferragamo pumps Cesare had bought for her in Florence one Saturday afternoon a few months earlier. She had applied a light layer of makeup in two minutes flat, moving smoothly from foundation to mascara to lipstick, with a brand-new decisiveness and speed of movement.

Her taut and radiant skin, her tan just a shade lighter than the deep bronze of previous years, her hair almost blond and cut in a shorter, more elegant style she had chosen during the winter and which had permanently replaced the old, familiar cut she had had since high school, the definitive rejection of Strass earrings in favor of coral and the adoption of a thread of pearls had transformed Arianna into a serene and elegant woman finally at peace with herself and her life.

She hadn't asked if the aquamarine dress looked good on her, when just a few months ago she would have asked him a thousand times, desperately anxious to please, and the simple rise of Cesare's right eyebrow was enough to send her back to the wardrobe. It was obvious she already knew she looked great.

Arianna hadn't moaned even once that they were going to be late, whereas their preparations had always been a litany of pleas and exhortations for Cesare to hurry. She hadn't looked at him once, not even in the mirror in which she kept admiring herself, and Cesare felt he had become a spectator, an invisible voyeur who had been selected to observe an unknown beauty getting ready for a night out: a secure and liberated woman who depended on no one and belonged to no one, immersed in that soft and irresistible beauty that radiates from many women the moment they reach forty; a superb, distant, almost haughty woman who, if he were to meet her in the street, would have caused him to turn his head and follow her with his gaze. Another woman.

This is what the Beast had thought, and it had turned him on, and he had asked her to give him a blow job. For that matter, as he often told his friends at the top table, a blow job right before going out was *one of his classics*. She always protested—"No, we can't, we're late, I've just got dressed and done my hair. Why do you have to do that? Come on, Cesare, I'll do it when we get back"—but always gave in, warning him to be careful not to come on her hair or her dress.

Arianna looks at him in the mirror.

—No. I've just had a coffee.

Cesare starts laughing and repeats his request, adding a play-ful "please," but she says no again and turns back toward the mirror. It had never happened before, and he had never begged before, so he asks again, in a low voice, even more turned on by her refusal. She answers no once more, but in a less convinced tone, and Cesare insists, increasingly excited at having to beg, and when he sees her closing her eyes for a few long seconds to allow the insubordination to simmer down, already defeated, he starts to undo his trousers.

Arianna sprays a cloud of Shalimar over her neck, stands up, walks toward the bed, and says they have to be quick as she bends over him and takes off his belt.

Over the years, Cesare had often told his friends at the top table that his wife, unlike theirs, didn't know how to give a blow job, but he never added that her lack of interest in the matter, and therefore the scant results of her effort, had always been countered by the magnificent scene of her face lowering itself toward his cock, the sublime dance of the lineaments of her face as she sucked it, and, most of all, the candid, disinterested look that often darted from her eyes to his while she held it in her mouth—the precious gem that made Arianna's blow jobs a remarkable experience, more visual than physical.

Cesare liked it that way. If Arianna had been a carnal woman, he would never have married her. His wife had to be as beautiful as a rose and as faithful as the Virgin Mary. That's what he wanted, and that's what he had found. He had always liked watching her while they were screwing, even more than the action itself: the contamination she had to suffer with that sex that she didn't really like and that, as a result, she wasn't very good at practicing.

That evening, however, the Beast immediately notices that the very technique used by his wife has changed: she no longer uses her right hand to hold his cock, but the left, while with the right she is delicately stroking his balls—something she had never, *never* tried before. She doesn't look him in the eye anymore, but uses her tongue much more and much better, and, at one point, it seems that his wife is trying to become more engaged with the whole procedure, inserting not only the tip of his cock into that fine and graceful mouth, as she had always done, but also much of the shaft.

And then Cesare realizes the most obvious and remarkable difference, which until that moment had eluded him. Just a few seconds after telling him they had to be quick, Arianna had begun a slow, concentrated, passionate, *complete*, entirely new and different and infinitely better blow job than any she had given him during all the years they'd been together, thus revealing that she had changed, and vastly perfected, her technique. And she had not perfected it with him.

When Arianna gives out a light moan, which is also a novelty, Cesare suddenly comes inside her mouth, in a violent orgasm that he tries to prolong as much as possible by holding his breath. And while his wife lets everything slip out of her mouth and onto his flat stomach, the Beast experiences that painful acuity that sometimes follows orgasm. The moment she lifts her eyes to look at him with a timid, surprised smile, her mouth still wet with his semen, Cesare realizes that Arianna has been cheating on him, and immediately remembers Ivo's crude sentence when he had gone to tell him about the Historic Baby Doll, and finally sees that his wife has been cheating on him—with Ivo.

But how? With Ivo? His incredulity mixes with surprise, and together they confuse that painful certainty, and his mind runs wild: for a moment he pictures a muscle-bound lifeguard on top of his wife, and they are laughing, and he lowers the top of her bikini to kiss her breasts, but then that scene immediately vanishes. Impossible. No, it's Ivo, it has to be Ivo. Who else?

He tells himself it is impossible that Arianna had taken a lover on her own initiative: he can't imagine she has either the strength of mind or the imagination or the necessity. She must have given in to the insistence of someone close to her, someone she admires, someone she can't say no to.

And then he thinks that it's not Ivo's fault at all—it's his wife who has become a whore, all he did was make the most of the situation just as any man would have done—but then he stops, enraged, and grinds his teeth in silence, and tells himself that he will beat up Ivo that same night, at his own party, in front of everyone, because you don't do that sort of thing to a friend. You just don't. Never. He won't say a word. As soon as he sees Ivo, he'll walk over to him and beat him until he's lying on the ground, and then he'll kick him in the face and leave him passed out in a pool of blood, and before leaving, he'll spit in his face.

And then his fury deflates and Cesare feels emptier than he has ever felt in his entire life, and as he looks at Arianna's serene face beside his now flaccid cock, he softens and remembers her as a bride, with the white dress and the veil, joyously happy and full of trust and happiness and hope, twenty-two years old, and he wonders how it all could end up so miserably.

Then she gets up from the bed, runs a hand through her hair and tells him, Come on, get ready, we're late.

E LA CHIAMANO ESTATE

AS A WARM NIGHT SLOWLY FALLS on the Tyrrhenian Sea, the soft coastline outlined by the smallest mountain chain in the world is dotted with a long line of headlights. The traffic runs slowly in front of the nightclub which looks like a house and reigns over the waterfront. Each incoming automobile is immediately surrounded by a handful of polite boys in white shirts and blue Bermuda shorts who will assume the task of parking it very, very carefully.

The ladies have the door opened for them while the gentlemen are greeted with deference, and many if not all of the couples who find themselves welcomed so regally get embarrassed and immediately start smartening themselves up: the ladies feel the sudden need to stroke their dresses to smooth out invisible creases and use their reflections in the clean glass of the car windows to check upon hairstyles, while the men make sure that their collars are straight and their shirtsleeves protrude not more than one or two centimeters from their jackets, as they had been taught.

Reassured, they move arm in arm toward the entrance, smiling, their eyes shining with anticipation at the sight of the large illuminated sign that announces to the world that Gloria Gaynor will give a concert here tonight, and that it's sold out.

Tanned faces peer out from the windows of the cars lining up along the waterfront, their curiosity piqued by all that bustle. They all seem to be smiling while sitting in that traffic jam: it feels a bit like being in a movie theater to watch an American comedy, and no one would dream of protesting in any way or, even less, honking, when traffic is completely blocked by the simultaneous parking of three Porsche Carreras and a majestic red Ferrari BB 512, all brand-new with Milan license plates, all arriving at the same time, which end up side by side in full view outside the club after a thousand terrified maneuvers by the boys in Bermuda shorts.

The looks, the comments, even the thoughts of those watching the show from the open car windows are immeasurably different from the looks and the comments and the thoughts that the tattered, desperate characters of Charles Dickens were aiming at the ostentation of the parties of the rich in nineteenth-century London.

Whatever shines in the eyes of those who are staring at the happy few entering the nightclub that seems like a house to attend the concert of Gloria Gaynor is not hate or rage, but merely the light, transparent, sacrosanct, clean, innocent, respectful, creative envy that is the real driving force of the twentieth century and pushes everybody on toward emulation rather than in the direction of the resentful, incessant gnawing that consumes and destroys the soul of those who have not and hold no hope they will ever have.

How can you hate such a young wealth, almost comical for the clumsy and careless way in which it is displayed, when you know it comes from the free and possible exploitation of the ocean of opportunity that reveals itself every day to the eyes of those who wish to see it?

And then, they know each other, *almost all of them*. Many of those who are about to enter the nightclub go over to the car windows and try to persuade those sitting in traffic to park and come and see *Gloria* with them, and those sitting in traffic take great pleasure in these invitations, and say they can't because they aren't dressed appropriately, but they will certainly come next time, and if there will be no Gloria Gaynor, it will be Donna Summer, or Barry White with his Love Unlimited Orchestra...

They are all the same kind of people. They come from the people, and from work, and all they have ever done is live by their wits and their work. They are not in competition with one another: their battle is against fate and fortune and destiny. And they are winning.

Not one of them comes from a rich family, they all started as ordinary workers, right after the war, and the money they have in their pockets comes from manufacturing — the transformation of raw materials into consumer objects, as the dictionaries coldly hold forth, unable to explain how it can actually be a special ability of the heart: a bright, almost magical, entirely Italian comprehension of the way of the world.

They aren't sly, because slyness doesn't get you very far in a world without shortcuts, ruled by simple and tough rules: if they want to earn more all they have to do is invest in their small business in order to make it grow, so they buy or rent larger sheds where they will install new and more efficient machines and hire more people to produce more and more goods, which they will then rush to sell throughout the world, in a glorious and benign and daring cycle that leaves very few resources to pay taxes to a corrupt and distant state, because if they paid taxes — so they say — they could never buy all the machines they have bought or employ all the people they have employed or grow as much they have grown.

And they are not the best; not the fabled victors of an ideal selection process that has finally declared them the most suited to being successful out of millions and millions of people: in the only country in the world in which entrepreneurship is a mass phenomenon, they are, to put it simply, the ones who *tried* and succeeded in a free and open market. Darwin, as far as these people are concerned, can go jump off a bridge.

Ignored or derided by those who would study them, they are individualists to the point of paranoia, and mistrust everything that is public. They see themselves as a plurality of proudly free individuals, and even though they are conformists in their private lives, their real aspiration is to stand out from the masses and be defined, one day, as *unique and inimitable*.

They have read just a few books in their lives, and have never listened to Beethoven or Mozart, and all they know about Lucio Fontana is that he was a lunatic who cut canvas and said it was art. They do not go to the theater and consider movies the perfect instrument to switch off and have fun. They love it when John Wayne shoots Indians, and don't realize they are continually humiliated and insulted by the authors and directors who represent Italy to the world: they barely know their books or films, and have no interest whatsoever in reading or watching them because they have no time for things not immediately useful to them or to their families, and are only marginally aware of having built the foundations of a unique industrial system made of small and very small businesses that was able to create a well-being that, in certain parts of Italy, was so capillary and diffuse that it could be defined as *democratic*.

For many of them this is the first evening out in years, and they are dressing at their best. The men's shirts are white cotton, so duly ironed and starched as to seem brand-new, and there are only a few jackets around, almost all of cool wool: few have dared choosing cotton ones out of fear of seeming crumpled, and only Barrocciai and a lawyer from Florence with a blue Jaguar dared to wear linen. Many trousers have a central crease fixed so hard it looks like a cutting blade, and the fabrics still have that sheen that will be worn away by the nervous pastime of rubbing them with the palm of the hand. The shoes are all very shiny indeed.

Even those who understand nothing about fashion, or the fool who spurns it as useless and vain, cannot help but notice how the fresh, fragrant ladies' dresses rustle and sparkle and shine. They are made of silk, cotton, viscose, linen, or some mix of these fibers, and dyed every possible color and printed with every possible pattern, even laminated, decorated with shoulder pads and designs and even some incongruous slogan, always in English.

Then a beautiful woman dressed in an ethereal periwinkle-colored palazzo pantsuit, with insolent curls bleached by the sun and the sea, undoubtedly Milanese, incredibly alone, quickly advances and haughtily enters the nightclub that looks like a house leaving behind her a sweet trail of Giorgio Beverly Hills perfume, bewitching the souls of the men paralyzed in admiration and thus decreeing the beginning of that sparkling and fiery evening.

Killer looks dart around, while jealousy, ambition, passion, hate, joy, and surprise seize the night. Introductions flourish between those who never had the occasion or the courage to get to know each other, and every shyness vanishes as the air fills and swells with the smell of pine resin, hair spray, and after-sun, and the intoxicating mix of all the *parfums* blends with the scent of baby squids already frying in the kitchens to welcome guests together with a glass of cold Vernaccia, reminding everyone that it is about dinnertime.

Ivo had insisted that his guests shouldn't trickle in one by one, so a small assembly had formed around him, the prime mover, dressed in linen and redolent of Eau Sauvage.

The navy blue suit of Irish linen was an easy choice, but he hesitated long over a shirt. He went through them all, unsure, caressing them on the hangers, before finally choosing the simplest and his favorite, a shirt of natural ecru linen, soft and draping and full of humble knots, dotted by slubs as long as a newborn's finger.

He had bought it ten years before, at a discount, from the stall of a traveling salesman who was desperate to sell it because, in textiles as in life, the fine is often the worst enemy of the refined, and given its magnificent coarseness, no one else wanted that shirt. To Ivo, instead, the ancient intersection of warp and weft in the plain weave highlighted the defective and untamable beauty of linen, which is poor and rich at the same time, light-years away from the shoddy industrial perfection of every other fiber.

How Barrocciai loved linen! Its cool embrace reminded him of that of a woman in love upon whom a minor offense had been inflicted, and he enjoyed so much its ever so brief resistance to contact with the skin, as if the fiber had its own free will and was trying to maintain a minimum of rigidity at least for a moment, refusing to fold instantly around the body and limbs like servile cotton, because cotton dents while linen bows, and creates folds as deep as wounds, splendid and elegant.

Ivo turns to look at his guests: none of them have ever been to the famous nightclub on the waterfront before. Cesare with Arianna; Andrea Vecchio, Citarella, Carmine, and Barbugli with their wives; Sergio Vari, who looks around with wolfish eyes; a growling Brunero, who keeps Rosa under his arm as if terrified someone might grab her and take her away from him; Vittorio, who stares into the void and gives monosyllabic answers to every question shot at him at machine-gun speed by Dino and Tonino, who are immensely excited to be there.

It is time to go in, and Ivo and his guests enter triumphantly, welcomed with deferent greetings from the bouncers and the manager who immediately escorts them to their table, which is positioned regally in the middle of the American bar.

—I'd like Gavi di Gavi for dinner at my table, Ivo tells Cipollini, waiter extraordinaire. There are twenty of us so we'll need twenty bottles in twenty ice buckets, so everyone has his own and there won't be any problems. Let's bring them right away.

—Very well, Barrocciai, Cipollini answered. As always, the most beautiful women are at your table.

Ivo turns to look at Arianna and Rosa, school friends finally reunited, who are sitting next to each other and are attracting the attention of the entire club, radiant and tanned, one blond and one with black hair.

As they both shoot the same smile toward him, Bruno Martino sits at the piano, wishes the audience a good evening, and begins to sing "E la chiamano estate."

THE CONCERT

AFTER THE VOL-AU-VENTS, the seafood salad, the champagne risotto, the steamed sea bass, and the crêpes suzette flambées, the lights are lowered and Gloria Gaynor suddenly appears on the small stage of the club. A compact and enthusiastic round of applause immediately erupts from the audience, stopping only with the unraveling of silvery notes from the piano. Then she starts to sing, in a whisper: *At first I was afraid, I was petrified...*

The venue explodes. Those eight hundred people have been listening to it for nearly three years, summer and winter, singing along to it in their cars and parties and showers, without any fear of getting the words wrong or misunderstanding the meaning of this sad and exultant song of pride they have come to love. Immediately they fall silent and listen to a slow, painful version of "I Will Survive" which, stripped of the rhythm's hammer blows, becomes totally different from the one they were expecting.

It is a blues, a prayer, and it shows how the insufferable sadness of an abandonment can be sublimated and placed, naked and noble, at the center of our poor lives, and then recognized as deeply ours, and accepted, even celebrated and finally conquered, so that we can live with it instead of letting it kill us, and discover a treasure at the bottom of that agony.

A quiet applause similar to that reserved for classical pianists greets the end of "I Will Survive." As another song begins, Vittorio grabs the neck of the newly opened bottle of that champagne with a priest's name and extracts it, dripping, from the bucket. Then he pours himself a full glass. He is enchanted by the way in which the little bubbles rise playfully to the surface, and very surprised by the notes of yeast he can smell: he has never tried anything alcoholic his entire life, not even at birthdays, not even at New Year's. Never. Not even once.

He takes the glass in his hand, raises it to his lips, and decides to drink it all in one go. He laughs at the thought of it, looks around, sees that no one is watching, and upends the glass.

His first impression is the familiar scratch to the throat from the bubbles of carbon dioxide, but right after it comes the rush of alcohol which hits his teetotal brain hard as a punch, and is then followed by a wave of subtle flavors and perfumes, all mixed together—how could bread and fruit and flowers end up in the scent of champagne, and leather, and *the forest?*—that leave in his mouth a sense of polished complexity that he never experienced before. Vittorio decides that if this is champagne, then he likes it a lot, and he will always like it a lot.

There is another great burst of applause. The second song, "Raindrops Keep Fallin' on My Head," is finished. Vittorio applauds and pours himself another glass, which he downs in one gulp. He turns to look at the empty seat next to his own, the one that was reserved for Milena, and pours himself another full glass and slams it back. While another round of applause marks the end of "Feelings," and Gloria Gaynor starts singing "I've Got You Under My Skin," Vittorio pours himself yet another glass and also swigs that one back, and then all the songs begin to sound the same and mix with the applause and he loses track a little bit of everything, and then he has a vision of Milena asleep on a tear-soaked pillow, surrounded by all of her shoes, and he whispers to himself.

—I'll always love you, Milena, even when you'll be old and crippled and mean. And if you're ill, I'll look after you, and if you fall into poverty, I'll give you money, and if you are taken to prison, I'll wait outside the gates with a bouquet of yellow roses. Forever.

He is surprised to find his glass empty. As he fills it once more, he wonders how long it will take him to get drunk, and then he realizes the bottle is empty: it's no use tilting it or standing it on its head, and he cannot wring it out. It's finished. *Poor thing*, he thinks, and out of his mouth comes a huge drunken belch. He laughs to himself, shakes his head, and when his mother turns to look at him, Vittorio nods and reveals to the world his first glorious drunken smile.

Then "Can't Take My Eyes Off of You" begins and immediately fills the dance floor, because upon hearing the words "*I love you baby*" repeated over and over, many members of the audience turn to one another and say that it's true, they do love each other and they have had enough of sitting at a table and sipping champagne and applauding every so often, so the men take off their jackets and undo the top buttons of the shirts and roll up the sleeves and take their women by the hand and start dancing — they who have never even tried to dance *the shake*, and are unable to move in time with the song, instead jumping about as if someone was repeatedly pinching them — in a whirlwind of white shirts, suddenly mottled armpits, flapping flowered dresses, receding hairlines, love handles, gold watches sparkling furiously, pearl necklaces, and beatific smiles and blushing and even a few tears running down the warmed cheeks of those men and women who can finally realize how very precious that moment of total abandon truly is. And when that formidable song draws to a close, they start to applaud and don't stop, and beg an exhausted Gloria Gaynor for an encore, so she starts up another rendition of "Can't Take My Eyes Off of You," this time managing to persuade even the eldest members of the audience to escort their wives to the dance floor because, even if their English isn't perfect by any means, they know what "*I love you baby*" means too, and it really is a remarkable scene, the sight of those poor Italian people who have just discovered wealth letting it all go on the dance floor, and even Gloria Gaynor notices. When the encore is finished, she starts singing "I Will Survive" in the way it is sup- posed to be sung, hard and implacable, strong and mean, as the one final gift to her awkward listeners, who have now taken over the dance floor and look like they want to keep going until dawn. "My dancing machines," that's what she calls them at the end of the song, as they applaud tirelessly and shout, "Bravo! Encore!" And Gloria Gaynor smiles and thanks them and takes a bow, and then she waves and blows a kiss before retiring to her dressing room, exhausted.

The DJ is quick to get the music started up again, but he chooses "Don't You Want Me" by the Human League, and the powerful opening of the song — with its inhuman synthesizers and cold rhythm — throws the dancers off, so they look around and find themselves in the middle of a dance floor, unexpect- edly surrounded by an alien music, and decide to ignore it and confess to each other they have never had so much fun in their whole lives, and greet one another and introduce themselves, and in a great mix of accents from all over Italy they swear to meet up again and go to dinner together, and perhaps out to dance, if Gloria comes back, and then they look at their watches and see it is two a.m. and they smile at the thought of being out so late and decide they must go home, so they slowly move toward their tables, start collecting bags and jackets and cashmere sweaters, and make their way, still smiling, toward the exit, all together, coming up against the simultaneous influx of the hard up, many of them their children and grandchildren who couldn't afford the concert but are now magnanimously permitted to come in and dance to the music played by the DJ, and as the clientele changes and the club empties in order to be filled once more, there are many embraces and smiles and kisses, and as the tales start up of just how fabulous the concert was, it would have taken Umberto Boccioni to capture the scene of the passing of the baton between those who are leaving and those arriving; those who are going home after enjoying themselves for a total of thirty minutes just this once in their entire lives, and those who for the next thirty years will consider having fun a right, a duty almost; those who spent their childhoods taking shelter in ditches and basements from the bombing raids of World War II, and those who have the immense good fortune of being twenty in 1982, in the best Italy ever.

THE REAL BEAST

CESARE WALKS OVER TO IVO and rests his heavy, oversized right arm on his shoulder, and Ivo jumps with surprise. He had been lost in thought, admiring Arianna from the balcony as she danced in the middle of the floor surrounded by youths, just underneath him, together with Rosa, and when he turns to see who is embracing him, he sees the surly smile of Vezzosi. Despite the loud music, he can hear Cesare's voice loud and clear.

—I admire you, you know? I really do.

He pauses.

—As a sportsman, I can't help but admire you. You have managed to do something no one else has. Well done.

—I would never have been able to do it without your help, Ivo answers, and instantly regrets it because he doesn't actually know what Cesare is talking about, whether it is about the evening, the company, the swimming pool, the factory, his enormous success at work, or, God help him — *God help him* — Arianna.

Vezzosi's smile thins into a sneer. In that crowded nightclub, there is no one near them. Ivo starts to feel the weight of the arm wrapped around his shoulder, the alcohol on Cesare's breath, the evaporated scent of his eau de cologne, and immediately remembers the tales of the Beast's many fights: all those head butts he had administered all over Tuscany, the noses irrevocably knocked out of place over nothing...

—Did I ever tell you why they call me the Beast?

Ivo feels the tension growing and stops dead, his heart beating furiously. He shakes his head. Cesare keeps his gaze fixed on Arianna.

—It's a great story, educational even...In little towns, sons take their fathers' nicknames and, if they are worthy, they can keep them. The Beast, the real Beast, was my father, Giuliano. Do you know what he did?

As if aware of the weight of those twin looks, Arianna turns toward them and sees Cesare with an arm around Ivo's shoulders, their heads close, their expressions dark, and immediately begins to worry. She has seen Cesare make that move with his arm before, and they have been drinking, all of them. She throws an anxious smile toward the balcony, but it is left unanswered.

—So, my dad had a friend. A great friend. They were always together. Giuliano was a large man, robust, strong as a bull, a mountain farmer, you know...His friend was small and skinny. They were always together, walking through the fields, hunting hares...Always together, always. Every day. Friends. Real friends. Then one day, war broke out and Giuliano was called up while the other, Paoli, was declared unfit. Dad was sent to Russia, and after a year, nothing more was heard from him. No letters, no telegrams, nothing. His parents, my grandparents, were old, and all they had to live on was the milk from these two old, tired cows they had left, their last two. They used it to make cheese, butter...They ate something, and sold the rest. But the war went on and poverty arrived, the most complete poverty, and still no word from Giuliano. So one day, Paoli goes to my grandparents' house and takes their cows. He takes them away. He makes no secret of it. He tells them. He goes to them and tells them that he is going to take away their cows. He says to the two old people: "*Mors tua, vita mea,*" and leaves them there, to survive on radicchio and vegetables. On charity, too. Then, one day, the war ends and Dad comes home. He isn't the same man. He is thin, pale...But he is alive and he has come home. He goes to his parents to embrace them and he can see they are alive by the skin of their teeth. He asks them where the cows are and what happened, how they have fallen into poverty, and at first they don't want to tell him, because they know he has a bad temper, and because...Listen up, Ivo...*they felt bad for Paoli.* They were devout Christians, you see? Love thine enemy and all that crap...

Arianna is increasingly concerned; she can't take her eyes off them. She tries waving but even if they are both staring down at her, no one responds. Even Rosa turns to watch the balcony.

—In the end, after a lot of insistence, they tell him Paoli has stolen the cows. Dad stands up, goes to Paoli's house, and batters him. Badly. He keeps going at it until Paoli's almost dead. He leaves him there, on the floor, passed out, beaten to a pulp, and then the ambulance comes and Paoli is taken to the hospital and kept there for a month. When he gets home, Paoli is still not in good shape, and goes to the only bar of the town to have a coffee. Dad walks into the bar, sees Paoli, goes over to him, and batters him again. He leaves him on the floor again, a bloody mess, and Paoli is taken back to the hospital. When he comes out for the second time, Paoli locks himself in his house, but after a month he goes out for a walk, early one morning. He meets Dad in the street and Dad beats him up again.

Ivo's eyes begin to dart around, desperately searching for someone: Citarella, Carmine, Barbugli, but he spots them all on the dance floor with their wives. Andrea Vecchio is nowhere to be seen, nor is Cipollini. Brunero is watching them from afar, but it's useless to call over Brunero. Arianna notices Ivo's terrified look, stops dancing, and stands right in the middle of the floor, flushed and frightened and beautiful, surrounded by people dancing happily while her life is about to fall to pieces.

—So the Carabinieri go to Dad and tell him he has to stop, that he has made his point. They tell him they understand, and in fact they hadn't done anything about the three beatings, but that's enough. It has to end there. Dad looks at them and says...Listen up Ivo, this is good...He says, "Dear sirs, that dickhead brought me far too much pain. To me and my parents, who are old. And every time I see him, I'll do it again. You do what you have to. Arrest me, put me in prison, but I will batter him every time I see him..."

Ivo closes his eyes for a moment.

—He was the real Beast, you see? I'm just his son.

Cesare moves away from the balcony railing, and now they are standing one in front of the other. Even the sneer has vanished from Cesare's face, and he slowly stretches out his left arm until he just touches Ivo's shoulder with his fingertips, giving him the perfect reference point for a punch. If it's going to happen, it'll happen now. But a second passes, then another one.

—So, Paoli..., Cesare says, his voice almost a growl, so Paoli left town and never came back again. Never. Understand? Do you like this story, Ivo?

Ivo realizes he must answer.

—Yes, he murmurs, and his gaze leaves Vezzosi's ferocious eyes and moves toward the enormous windows that look over the calm sea and the star-filled skies and stops there.

Cesare looks at Ivo and is astonished to find him at his mercy, mute as a child who has just been told off by his father, immobile, guilty, ready to be beaten, certain to be about to be beaten, and as Cesare admires the scene of his greatest victory—forget the Italian championships—the moment passes, and he loses both the desire and the need to beat Ivo. He has already been beaten. His pride is lying bloody on the floor, and he will remember this moment of utter inferiority for the rest of his life.

—Paoli is still alive, you know. He sells wool now, with his son, who's a thief just like him.

One final mocking smile, and Cesare makes his way down the staircase toward the American bar, a cuckold and a victor, with the same lithe walk he uses to approach the net to shake hands with his defeated adversaries. He won't say anything to Arianna. He's already beaten her too. He has won it all this evening. *Game, set, match, championship.* So why does he feel so empty?

Ivo doesn't move. He just stands there on the balcony, full of shame, relief, disappointment, sarcasm, rage. As his breath and his pulse slow down, his eyes turn from the sky and the sea, and he realizes Arianna is on the other side of the balcony across the ballroom. She is right in front of him, and he thinks he must somehow tell her what has happened, so he points to himself with his right index finger, then points at her, then he makes the sign of the cross. Arianna doesn't understand immediately, as those confused gestures seem like a blessing to her, but then she sees him nod in the direction of the bar, where Cesare is laughing about something with Sergio Vari and Brunero, and so she finally understands.

They are separated by a thirty-meter drop and a large disco glass ball, under which, in the middle of the floor, Vittorio is dancing blind drunk, surrounded by his friends. Arianna brings the index finger of her right hand to her lips, closes her eyes, and blows a kiss to him, then she turns and disappears into the crowd, and Ivo is once again pleased with her, and filled with admiration, and proud of having chosen her and loved her, and if it were up to him, he would never leave her and would always keep her close to him until the day they became old and wrinkled like tortoises.

Ivo realizes he is exhausted. He finds Cipollini and pays the bill of three and a half million lire with a smile on his lips, handing over to the waiter a roll of banknotes tied with elastic that had swollen the pocket of his trousers throughout the evening. He adds an extravagant tip and the cost of a case of twelve bottles of champagne, which he asks to be brought directly to his car.

Heartened by having paid—Barrocciai truly likes to pay, and the more he pays, the more he likes it, because only a truly exorbitant bill can become glorious, memorable, and therefore necessary—he descends the staircase and walks into the American bar and, with arms open wide, intones a booming "Good night, my friends!" to his guests sitting at the table, and quickly leaves the club before they can get up to say goodbye and thank him. Or beat him up.

Barrocciai gives a ten-thousand-lire note to the disheveled kid in Bermuda shorts who brings his Pagoda, asks him to open the canvas top and help Cipollini load the champagne onto the rear jump seat, then he sits in the driver's seat, turns on the headlights, slips a cassette of Sinatra into the stereo, and sets off.

He will go home, but not right away. He will enjoy the slow ride on the empty highway, and when he arrives in his city, he will go and find those factories that are still open, and offer some of that champagne with a priest's name to those who are still working for him on that Saturday night in August: Angelo Camputaro, who is weaving in his vest, a Nazionale cigarette stuck in his mouth, so Ivo would find his new samples ready on his desk when he returns from holiday; the workers at Fidias, who are still dyeing, brushing, trimming, and rolling his fabrics with the same care they would show a child; and all of those guys who are still breaking their backs for him in the dozen or so microscopic third-party businesses his crazily fragmented production chain is made of—the precious, silent heroes to whom he owes each of his hopes and each of his dreams and everything that he owns.

And then he will decide that he doesn't want to go home, but to the factory. He will go up to the swimming pool, strip off, dive into the water naked, and play dead for a while. He will look at the stars as the water gently enters and leaves his ears, making him pleasantly, intermittently deaf. Then he will get out of the water, wrap himself in a large white bathrobe, toast Arianna with his last bottle, and press that special button that makes all of his looms start work in unison so that their infinite beating might be his lullaby, and he will cover himself with his Irish linen sheet and fall asleep in that double beach bed which he had made precisely for these nights — and who knows if he is happy, who knows if he will ever be.

Ivo leaves and doesn't know, cannot know, that Arianna is watching him from the balcony. After that last kiss she had to run into the bathroom so no one would see her cry, but as soon as she had locked herself in, she realized that she wouldn't be able to say goodbye to him because, after what had happened, Ivo would surely want to get away immediately, and so she left the bathroom and ran back up to the balcony but could not find him anywhere in the club, so she looked outside and there he was, leaving alone into the night, in that car.

A dry sorrow erupts in her heart, and she curses her new ability to get used to everything and be bored by everything that has become the only certainty in her life: just a few days before she had started to wonder how she could put an end to the affair with Ivo, and at that thought she had felt dismayed and guilty, and she had desperately tried to drive that thought away, and forced herself to repeat over and over that there was no rush, no rush at all, because things can always change, but inside she knew it was over. The comet had burned out, *and she wasn't enjoying herself anymore.*

So Arianna stays there, in front of the large balcony window, until the lights of the Pagoda turn toward the large pine grove and disappear. She dries her last tear, checks her reflection in the glass for any damage caused by that short-lived cry, and goes back to dance with Rosa as a bright, false smile spreads across her face, foretelling the life that awaits her.

The sky is perfect, so miraculously clear as to seem painted, and the sea is lightly rippled by a breeze coming from Corsica, its blue only slightly more intense than that of the sky, and you should see the smallest mountain range in the world, how it stands out splendid with its marble veins, now and forever protecting the coastline and the town that shines with a thousand tiny lights, tonight, and the brightest are those that bathe the famous dance club that looks like a house, there on the waterfront.

EDOARDO NESI is a writer, filmmaker, politician, and translator. He began his career translating the work of such authors as Bruce Chatwin, Malcolm Lowry, Stephen King, and Quentin Tarantino. He has written twelve books, of which *Story of My People* won the Strega Prize and *L'età dell'oro* won the Bruno Cavallini Prize. He wrote and directed the film *Fughe da fermo*, based on his novel of the same name, and translated David Foster Wallace's *Infinite Jest* into Italian. In 2013 he was elected to the Italian Parliament's Chamber of Deputies.

ALICE KILGARRIFF studied Italian and Spanish at Cardiff University before training as a translator and interpreter. She has worked with Bompiani publishing house, Welsh National Opera (Cardiff), Royal Opera House (London), and many academic institutions. She lives and works in Italy and Wales.

Also by
Edoardo Nesi

STORY OF MY PEOPLE

*Translated from the Italian
by Antony Shugaar*

**Winner of the 2011 Strega Prize,
this blend of essay,
social criticism, and memoir
is a striking portrait
of the effects of globalization
on Italy's declining economy.**

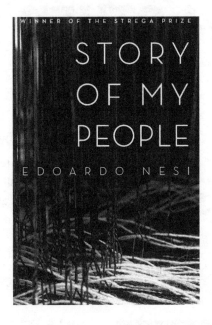

Starting from his family's textile factory in Prato, Tuscany, Edoardo Nesi examines the recent shifts in Italy's manufacturing industry. Only one generation ago, Prato was a thriving industrial center that prided itself on craftsmanship and quality. But during the last decade, cheaply made goods — produced overseas or in Italy by poorly paid immigrants — saturated the market, making it impossible for Italian companies to keep up. In 2004 his family was forced to sell the textile factory. How this could have happened? Nesi asks, and what are the wider repercussions of losing businesses like his family's, especially for Italian culture?

Story of My People is a denunciation of big business, corrupt politicians, the arrogance of economists, and cheap manufacturing. It's a must-read for anyone seeking insight into the financial crisis that's striking Europe today.

"Who would have thought that memoir and polemic could work together so well? A totally absorbing story, and a portrait of modern Italy."
—Sarah Bakewell, author of *How to Live*

"A searing indictment of globalization's failures, and the inability of politicians and pundits to consider its impact on real lives...much of the book is sad, honest, and biting; overall it is an important work." —*Publishers Weekly*

▓ OTHER PRESS

◨ OTHER PRESS

LIVE BAIT by Fabio Genovesi

Told with the tenderness of a Fellini film, the story of a small Italian town where fishing, biking, and rock 'n' roll make the news, until tragedy turns everything upside down.

"If John Irving had an Italian son, he would be named Fabio Genovesi." —*Schnüss, Das Bonner Stadtmagazin*

VILLA TRISTE by Patrick Modiano

One of the most seductive and accessible novels in this Nobel Prize–winning author's oeuvre: a haunting story that captures lost youth, the search for identity, and ultimately, the fleetingness of time.

"The author's lucid prose carries the reader into his hermetic world." —*Publishers Weekly*

CONSTELLATION by Adrien Bosc

A best-selling debut novel based on the true story of the 1949 disappearance of Air France's Lockheed Constellation and its famous passengers.

"A novel of realism propelled by Bosc's energy and unique imagination. The mysterious plane crash of Constellation in 1949 is revived within the pages of this magical novel." —Gay Talese, author of *The Bridge* and *A Writer's Life*